THE
LADIES'
MIDNIGHT
SWIMMING
CLUB

THE
LADIES'
MIDNIGHT
SWIMMING
CLUB

Faith Hogan

An Aria Book

First published in the UK in 2021 by Head of Zeus Ltd
This paperback edition first published in 2022 by Head of Zeus Ltd,
part of Bloomsbury Publishing Plc

9 7 5 3 1 2 4 6 8

A CIP catalogue record for this book is available
from the British Library.

ISBN (PB): 9781800241350
ISBN (E): 9781800241336

Cover design © Leah Jacobs-Gordon

Typeset by Siliconchips Services Ltd UK

Printed and bound in Great Britain by
CPI Group (UK) Ltd, Croydon CR0 4YY

Head of Zeus
5–8 Hardwick Street
London EC1R 4RG

WWW.ARIAFICTION.COM

To Seán, Roisín, Tomás and Cristín,

With love.

Diary of a Sea Swimmer

The cold burns against my skin, numbing it instantly. I wade out, warily knowing that the icy water stabbing against my legs is an inevitable part of this. A bitter blanket weaving about my body welcoming me, a dear friend; I plunge violently in, gasping, salt water teasing my lips. I feel the small jagged stones beneath my feet. And then, I'm in. My arms and legs cut automatically through the water, until the cold has eaten from the outside in and there is nothing to do but surrender to the vastness and in it know that I am somehow suspended safe and all is well. I turn on my back for delicious blissful moments before I must return to the shore and take up my life where I left off before.

From Jo's Journal

Prologue

Mid-May and to Elizabeth, the night felt almost balmy. The cove was just half a mile along the beach. Elizabeth knew she'd come here again, even if she wouldn't have admitted it to herself. When she did, she stood for a few moments. This was where Jo came to swim every single night. Like her window washing every Thursday afternoon, Jo was a woman of routine, albeit to the beat of her own drum. Each evening when all the other women in Ballycove settled down to fall asleep before the television, Jo pulled out an old shopping bag with a threadbare towel and a comb that once belonged to her mother. She walked along this beach until she came to just this spot and then she stripped down to her faded swimsuit and swam energetically for at least ten minutes in the biting waves.

Elizabeth stood for a long while, a little transfixed with the recollections and ghosts that played along in her memory. She had come down here often when they were children, but she hadn't swum for years.

'I thought it was you,' Jo's familiar voice called out from behind her. 'What brings you down here tonight?'

She dropped her bag on the ground.

'Oh, just out for a bit of a ramble,' Elizabeth said easily, regretting now that she'd come here to impose on what was Jo's own form of meditation.

'Maybe you'll join me?' Jo laughed.

'Oh, I don't think so. For one thing, I'm not sure I have your constitution for the cold.' She laughed at this for a moment, and then she remembered as Jo shed layer after layer of clothes that she was nowhere near as strong and robust as Elizabeth had always assumed. Rather, beneath the layers, she had shrunk into a sparrow of a woman with stick-like arms and legs, and not very much more in between.

'You're missing out – that's all I'll say.' And then she was picking her way down towards the waves and Elizabeth was left to think about the fact that she had spent her life sitting on the sidelines. It wasn't where she wanted to finish out the rest of her days.

There was something about today. Something Elizabeth couldn't quite put her finger on, as if it was the start of a new chapter. The water ahead seemed suddenly so inviting. She really wasn't sure that she was in full command of her actions or her senses as she began to throw off her clothes, but soon, she was running with the energy of an excited child, shrieking with an abandon she'd never known before; naked as the day she was born, she ran into the water.

It was exhilarating, a baptism of biting cold that felt as if it might chew her up in no time. It rattled her nerve endings, sending an extravagant swell of emotion through her. It was initiation, as if she was being culled of her old staid life, and suddenly, this unbearable cold became part of her, a wholly new sensation, freeing her from the life she'd lived until now. This was liberating. It was overwhelming. A cascade of emotion welled within her, the salty cold now insulating her from any pain, rather, for the first time, it felt as if all of those fears and secrets could reside as one within her and the biting sea was powerful enough to hold her in equilibrium. Finally she was free.

This moment was her whole life, all rolled up – past, present, future – but mainly, she was here and now and she'd never felt so alive. She dived beneath the water feeling the freedom of it while shocked with the cold, but she filled with immeasurable warmth. It was madness, passionate, wonderful living perfection. She lay on her back, squinting off towards where she knew the horizon sat. She swam out further, far beyond her own depth to where Jo was lying on her back, gazing up at the fading light.

'You did it,' Jo murmured as they treaded the freezing water together.

'It's bloody cold here,' Elizabeth said unnecessarily.

'It is that, but don't you feel alive? I feel the same thing every day I come here. It anchors me in a place that's mine within the vastness.'

'Okay.' Elizabeth wasn't sure what she meant. She just knew that here, in the sable saltiness of the ocean, she felt as if she could do anything – nothing could faze her at this moment.

'I wonder what Eric would say now?' Jo smiled and suddenly they were both laughing their heads off like lunatics. For once, he'd have been completely lost for words. The notion that his respectable wife would be out swimming in the altogether in the moonlight; it might very well have been enough to shock him into sobriety.

The beach was completely empty, apart from a few circling gulls who probably thought they were wholly mad. Elizabeth laughed again; perhaps they were right – maybe she had finally tipped over into a state of happy lunacy, but she didn't care. For the first time in far too long, she felt what it was to be truly blissful.

PART 1

April

I

Elizabeth

It was a week since Eric's funeral – over thirty years of marriage and she thought she knew him inside out, but even now, beyond the grave he had tried to hide the truth from her. Elizabeth had come to Shanganagh Cemetery not to pay her respects on this overcast morning. No, rather she had made the journey because it was time to let Eric know exactly what she thought of him. The night had brought in howling winds, sheet lightning and a cacophony of thunder and rain that she thought might wake the dead. There was no sleeping for Elizabeth, or probably, she figured for anyone else in the village. She had wandered through the house, moving from one gloomy room to the next, waiting for the storm to move off so she might shake off the uneasy feeling of unrest that wouldn't let her close her eyes.

Then, at around four o'clock, she decided to go down and take a look about the surgery. It was strange being down here without Eric. Somehow, his presence had remained here more than anywhere, still dominating everything. Thea Gilchrist – the locum, who'd filled in for the last few months, had been little more than an uncomfortable question mark. Elizabeth moved from the small waiting room, past the shadowy cubbyhole reception desk and into Eric's surgery. She flicked on the light and listened while there was a crackling tickle, as if it was annoyed at being woken at this unearthly hour.

For a moment, she felt a rising note of panic. What if there was a power cut? What if she was left here in the dark, trying to grapple her way back through the narrow corridor and rickety stairs into the main part of the house. The storm seemed to be heightened down here. Of course, it was little more than a converted entrance to the larger outbuildings that ran along the side of the property. Eric had considered it more convenient to roof and fit out this mean little space, while at the side of the house, a long line of stone buildings ran into a huge coach house at the bottom of the garden. Of course, like the house, time had worn them down and they stood slowly crumbling over the years. *Who wants every Tom, Dick and Harry in the back garden?* he had mumbled and so he spent his working life with electric heaters hissing out dry heat and walls that smelled damp no matter how often he insisted that a fresh coat of paint could cure anything.

Elizabeth wasn't sure why she did it, but it seemed as if somewhere she was answering a question; she walked behind Eric's desk and sat in his chair. Any longing to feel his arms around her had long gone between them, if it had ever been there to begin with. It was a strange thing though, sitting here, looking about the room from his perspective; it made her miss him in a way she hadn't felt before. It reminded her of when they had first married and she had admired him, not just because he was handsome, but because he had saved her. There had been something about him, a kind of presence that had as much to do with him being a doctor as it had with any other quality. The whole notion of him holding people's lives in his hands, that within his understanding lay the answers to living and dying, to being well and being ill, to making people in so many ways feel better in themselves.

That was the part that she'd never really been able to articulate, but sitting here, she had a feeling that maybe it was not all as clear-cut as she'd imagined. It was a responsibility – she could almost feel it pressing in on her from all sides. Perhaps it was enough to drive you to drink, even if you hadn't already been predisposed to it.

She sighed deeply. There was no point thinking of these things now. The time had passed where understanding could do very much to change how things would pan out. Then, something small and silver caught her eye. A key? A silver glinting stem poking out from underneath the corner of the half file unit crouched beneath the desk. She bent down, a little gingerly and picked it up. Elizabeth looked at it, for a moment, supposing that it had just dropped from the desk, but then she remembered Thea Gilchrist calling to the house one evening, looking for a key. She had gone away without it. For one thing, Elizabeth hadn't the foggiest about any keys and for another, Eric, with a grumbling menace had told her *that cabinet was no concern of hers*.

Elizabeth picked up the key, slipped it into the cabinet, turned it easily and inhaled deeply as she pulled out the top drawer. Outside a crash of lightning lit up the back garden, so for a moment, it felt as though Eric himself had come back to warn her off. The ominous roll of thunder that followed almost rattled the nerves out of her, but she sat holding open the door for a moment, watching as the garden jerked back into the darkness.

Then, she peered into the open drawer. It was not a deep drawer, rather it was long and the few bits of paper were only to cover over empty bottles that Eric had dumped there to hide from a world he obviously assumed had never guessed his weakness. Elizabeth sighed at the waste of it all. He'd spent forty years drinking himself into a grave that he'd worked so hard to keep others out of. The drawer below that was deeper. It too was a storage space for empty bottles, but there was one file, in itself unusual. Eric was not the sort of man who kept files or indeed records really of any sort, so far as Elizabeth had ever known.

This file was encased in a brown folder with a thick elastic band holding it together. She pulled it out and placed it timidly on the faded and marked blotter that took up most of the desk. With her foot, she mindlessly pushed in the drawer. Another crash of lightning outside lit up the garden eerily at her back. This time, it had less bite to it and although it halted her hands midway on the elastic, it did not make her want to run for the house next door. Elizabeth found herself intrigued by the very fact that Eric would keep a file locked away and hidden. She couldn't help but wonder who he might have been burying it from. Some deep part of her knew – the only person he concealed anything from, really, was Elizabeth.

There was no hiding anything in death, of course. The empty bottles, the gambling debts – she never even knew he'd liked horses. All these years, there was a whole other world that he'd been a part of, placing bets on races from the drunken comfort of the bar counter in Flannelly's pub. The tab had come to two thousand pounds. Old Ned Flannelly had the good grace to look embarrassed when he called to collect the debt. He hadn't wanted to bother her with it. The truth was, Eric would not be dropping into the bar again and so, before he finally shuffled out of life, Ned Flannelly took his chance to collect what he was owed.

It had frightened Elizabeth, to think that they could have that kind of financial debt hanging over them without her even knowing. That same ominous feeling returned to her now. It was easily remedied with Ned Flannelly – all she had to do was walk down to the bank and withdraw from her savings to pay him off. She stopped for a moment before she opened the file before her. What if this file contained more secrets like the one Ned Flannelly had hidden with him for God knows how many years?

Elizabeth was a lot of things, but she braced herself, because she'd never been a coward. She pulled open the file sharply on this thought.

The papers were held in place by a wire grip. She recognised immediately the deeds to the house with a familiar map peeping out from beneath them. The boundary fence in faded blue was a straight line marked out in tired ink. Beneath that were a number of letters, mostly to and from their solicitor. One of them, Elizabeth was surprised to see, was Eric's will. She hadn't realised he'd ever made one. The date was recent, only months before he died.

The will, once she'd waded through the legal jargon, didn't throw up anything too surprising. After all debts were cleared on his estate, the house and surgery were hers to do with as she pleased. He'd actually said that – as she pleased! As if taking full possession of them was something she'd been waiting for all these years. *Oh, Eric.* She shook her head sadly. She put the will aside. There was very little else, apart from a thick brown envelope, which he'd gone to some bother to tape together for added security. Annoyed with the wording of the will, Elizabeth tore open the envelope now, disregarding the time put into securing it all together.

A bundle of papers fell from its innards, a sheaf of pages with various logos all of which seemed to Elizabeth to be very familiar. She rifled through them quickly, catching only words at the top of each. *Overdraft. Term Loan. Credit Card. Overdue. Default.* All of them sent to Eric from different banks; five in all. Elizabeth gasped. She thought for a moment she'd never catch her breath again. Eric had gambled them into hock up to their eyeballs. They owed an absolute fortune, probably more than the house was worth and, if the red underlined numbers were anything to go by, more than the surgery was worth too.

She was penniless.

They were on the brink of bankruptcy. She was on the edge of ruin.

Good God – she could be homeless by the time she had sorted through this mess.

After that, there had been no chance of sleep. She sat for she wasn't sure how long, staring at the pages before her. The will was worthless – there was no house or surgery, not once all the debts had been repaid. There was nothing. She couldn't even sell them, because it was unlikely the bank would allow it. No, they'd be more than likely knocking on her door as soon as it was deemed reasonable to ask her to move out while they put the place up for auction.

In the darkness, Elizabeth sobbed her heart out, once the panic had been driven away by anger. She had cried for the lives she might have lived, for the fact that she might have married someone else. Someone who could have made her laugh, someone who could have given her children; she'd have traded anything for that. So, she mightn't have been *the doctor's wife* and all lah-di-dah, but she might have had a roof over her head to see her into old age.

As the storm pushed back out across the sea, Elizabeth felt her own temper dying down. This was no time to lose her head. For the first time in years, her fate had been placed back into her own hands. It was up to her how she handled the narrow choices that were presented to her from here on in.

She walked through *her* house later that morning with

fresh eyes; seeing everything from an immensely stirred perspective. Now, she picked up vases, assessed drapes and kicked sideboards calculating their value. She cursed woodworm and thanked her lucky stars for the storm that had pushed her from her bed. It was better to find out for herself than to be faced with bailiffs at the door.

An hour later she was driving her little runabout out to Shanganagh Cemetery. Of course, Eric wouldn't care either way at this point, but she needed to let him know that she would sort out this mess. She, Elizabeth O'Shea, was about to stand on her own two feet and if the prospect scared her just a little, in a strange way it exhilarated her too.

Eric's plot, the freshest in the graveyard, showed the signs of a stormy night. Thankfully, the undertakers knew enough to secure the many floral tributes beneath tightly secured netting mesh. The little wooden cross with his name spelled out across a brass plaque sat askew this morning. Elizabeth was alone in the graveyard and it was probably just as well, because she knew that anyone listening would think she'd lost her marbles.

'Eric, I know that you thought what you did was for the best, but...' she began, her eyes drifting across the various wreaths that had been battered by the wind. 'But I found the letters in your desk and now...' She felt her resolve cast off for a moment, her voice cracking with emotion. 'The thing is, if you'd only said...' It occurred to her; she'd done the same thing many times over the years as she'd washed dishes and prepared meals for them. She'd shaken her head, knowing that even if she tried to explain that she understood he wouldn't have listened. 'We could have sorted it all out and maybe...' she stopped, took a deep breath. 'Maybe, there was a way to make things right, maybe you wouldn't have died so suddenly – if you didn't have to do so much worrying. Maybe... we could have been happier.' But of course, she knew that whatever else their union might have been – it was never going to be happy.

Unexpectedly, a rage as she'd never known before reared within her, burning her up from somewhere deep inside her belly.

Her eyes drifted from the plot before her; she couldn't look at it now. Just yards away, the large grave that she'd tended for so many years seemed neglected by comparison. It wasn't fair – none of it was fair. Eric buried here with flowers and all the fanfare of a local celebrity, and her baby was interred in a grave that didn't even bear his name. She couldn't stop shaking, and before she realised what she had done, she was peeling back the layer of green netting, hurtling flower arrangements across the graveyard, as though they'd been scattered by the wind and not the madwoman she'd become. Expensive wreaths of lilies, begonias and hydrangeas, baby's breath and roses – were flying through the air, landing askew and rolling along the path – unwanted; begrudged. She wanted to hurt him. She wanted to make Eric pay for everything he'd done to her – everything she'd let him do... and that made it so much worse.

Eventually, when the grave was empty of any floral

tributes, she marched to its head, kicked the cross that bore his name viciously so it leant sideways as if to make away from her. She stood for a moment, surveying all the damage she had caused. There was no guilt, not one ounce of remorse for wrecking the hard work and the expensive gifts of mourners to her dead husband. Then she turned, unexpectedly convulsing with the sort of grief that comes from years of buttoning up the deepest emotions.

She made her way along the narrow path; too familiar over the years, since she'd spent so much of her time here tending it. *The Grave of the Little Angels* was a large plot, opened long before Elizabeth could remember. It was a holding place for babies who had died before the parish priest had time to welcome them into the Catholic family. Her little baby was here. It was as near as she could get to him now, as near as she'd ever been to him since he was born. She threw herself across the damp earth, not caring that her expensive coat would be covered in wet soil, not caring if anyone came along and saw her. Elizabeth lay prostrate across the nameless grave for a long time.

Eventually, she heard the sound of a curlew far below, playing among the rocks, perhaps being cast about on the windy tide; the sound pulled her from her tears. She drew her scarf tighter around her and turned her collar up against the breeze before kneeling down again and touching one of the may flowers she'd set there just weeks before. It was battered and bruised from the storm the night before, too delicate to survive the harsh weather really, but still, Elizabeth pulled a mound of earth up around it for protection. Then, she gathered herself up. It felt as if she'd cried herself out, this time for the one she'd really lost.

Elizabeth made her way downwards. She would walk to the pier; stand for a few moments with the sea air whipping back against her face. She would shiver and pull her collar closer about her and enjoy the wind on her back as she walked uphill to close the door out on an evening that held only the promise of winds and rain.

Just as she turned back from the pier, she caught sight of her friend Jo parking her ancient car on the road outside her cottage. She had brought one of the fruit cakes from her pantry for her, knowing that Jo had a sweet tooth and there was only so much funeral food Elizabeth could get through before it went off.

'Jo,' she called, but her voice was lost upon a wind that probably picked it up and dropped it streets away, startling some other afternoon walker with its false proximity. Ballycove was like that. The wind blustering through streets carried far too many conversations to ears that might be better off not hearing. 'Hello, Jo...' she tried again, but even without the wind working against her, she was not a woman used to shouting and so her voice trailed lamely while Jo made her way inside, unaware of it. *Bother*. Now, she would have to knock on the cottage door and the last thing Elizabeth wanted was anyone thinking she was calling to visit because she was suddenly lonely.

Sighing, she tapped lightly on the door. Inside, she could hear the door being rattled, as though locks were being thrown back and then Jo stood before her, with an expression that was at once both welcoming and curious.

'Oh, Elizabeth, what on earth brings you here on an evening like this? It's going to pour down at any minute. Come in, come in...' she said standing back into the narrow hall to welcome Elizabeth into her snug home.

'No, no, I really must get back. I just came out for a walk to wake me up a bit for the day and I thought, I have so much food that I'll never get around to eating... so I...' She presented the porter cake, wrapped up in greaseproof paper. It was large enough to treat a family for a few days.

'That's very thoughtful of you...' Jo said taking it. 'You really shouldn't have though. I mean, you might have callers yourself while I...Well, the only ones to call here are Lucy and Niall. Mind you, when they're here, Niall eats me out of house and home...' She started to laugh at this and for a moment, Elizabeth felt a stab of something she couldn't put a name on.

'It's a sort of thank-you present too, you know, for the funeral. You were really kind, and I don't know how I'd have managed without you.' It was true. Jo had commandeered her kitchen and supplied an endless stream of tea, coffee, whiskey and sandwiches for anyone who turned up at her door while they were mourning Eric.

'Isn't that what friends are for?' Jo said easily. 'Are you sure you won't come in for a cuppa? It's going to pour down out there any minute.' With that, the rain began to fall, in hard sheeting slaps against her back. 'Come on, you can't go out in that...'

'I suppose, I can't,' Elizabeth said ruefully, but she

faltered on the doorstep. 'Really, the last thing I wanted was to impose...'

'You won't be imposing. Sure it's only me and the cats here and they're not great conversationalists to be honest.' She laughed at this and closed the door gently behind Elizabeth.

'Here,' Jo bent down, discommoded the fattest cat Elizabeth had ever seen and shook out a cushion on the only carver at the small round kitchen table. The cat, obviously insulted, skulked towards the kitchen door, arched his back and then wound his way out to the hall. Ignoring him, Jo placed a mug of tea before her guest and flopped into the seat opposite. 'Ah, sure isn't this lovely now,' she said as she sipped the strong tea from her own mug.

'It is,' Elizabeth agreed and she meant it. It was cosy here. The cottage, rather than feeling as if it was cramped and coming in on her, felt more like it was enveloping her in welcome warmth. It was homely in a way that she'd never managed to achieve in her large sombre house. Here, it was tidy, but lived in. There were scuffs on the walls in places and a cupboard door that could do with being re-hung perhaps. The whole place was occupied by a meal just gone and one to come. It was a room that had seen happy times and some sad ones too. It was, Elizabeth knew, the heart of this little cottage and everything about it had Jo stamped upon it. It was the kind of room that would fester with emptiness if she wasn't here.

'Yes, it really is lovely.' Elizabeth settled back into the carver. It wasn't a generous chair, but soft cushions at her back and one on the seat made it feel as if it had been waiting for her to sit in it, for her whole life.

'Well, how did you get on for the night?' Jo asked her eventually.

'It was fine,' she said softly. 'Waking up was strange, sensing his space empty.' It was funny. He had died almost a week ago, but today was the first time it felt as if he wouldn't be coming back, although, Elizabeth had no idea how to explain that now. 'The storm woke me, but before that I slept soundly.'

'You'll have been worn out after the last week. It's draining, having to keep a stiff upper lip when, let's face it, all you're going to want to do is curl up in a corner somewhere and have a bit of a cry.'

'I suppose,' Elizabeth said. She looked towards the clock again, but of course, she had no-one to rush home for now, nothing in the world that had to be done or call her away from this moment. 'I'm going to have to make some decisions, amn't I…' she began.

'You will, but there's no rush, not yet.' Jo leant forward, interested. 'People understand, you know. No-one would expect you to…' She narrowed her eyes then for a moment, picking up more from Elizabeth's unfinished sentence than she'd planned to share. 'What happened?'

'I…' Elizabeth wasn't sure where to start, but considering all Jo knew of her life, this was probably not the hardest thing she had to share over the years. 'It's all gone, Jo. Everything – he gambled it all away. I'm probably a hair's breadth from the banks serving me an order to get out so they can sell the house and the surgery.'

'That can't be right.' Jo leant forward, taking her friend's hand. 'There must be some mistake. Eric would never...' She stopped for a moment, trying to let it settle. 'He'd never be that stupid. Surely not?'

'It seems he was. He'd hidden it well from me.' She shrugged. Not that he'd have had to, because after all, she'd never have gone searching it out. 'He's been gambling for years, up to his eyes in debt with several banks.'

'He wasn't very good at that either, so?' Jo raised an eyebrow and in spite of herself, Elizabeth found herself giggling. 'Can't you continue to run it as it is? Get a decent locum in and...'

'Thea Gilchrist isn't likely to come back.'

'No,' Jo agreed. 'That had been a long time coming; I think the whole village cheered you on when you gave her her marching orders.' Again, they started to laugh.

'Not my finest hour,' Elizabeth said, but she had enjoyed it. Thea had been foisted on them from a neighbouring practice when Eric was too sick to work. Eric hadn't been dead two days when she marched into Elizabeth's living room and demanded that she hand over the practice to her. Elizabeth had been in shock, but even she hadn't expected to lash out quite so enthusiastically.

'I disagree. To be honest, I think we were all a little in awe of your extensive vocabulary when it came to telling her where to go. The parish priest had to run into the pantry to hide his smirk.' Jo shook her head fondly at the memory. 'Anyway, she was a horrible woman. We'd all have left the practice eventually for one in the next town over – you did us a favour. Be honest, even you couldn't imagine having Dr Gilchrist as your GP.'

'Anyway, it's not much good to us now. I really don't know what to do next,' Elizabeth said and she buried her head in her hands. The bravery of earlier had evaporated when she returned home – the house, the surgery, the debts, it was all a total mess. 'There is no-one else to cover the practice on Monday morning…' A sudden dry panic was overtaking her now. Monday mornings were always the worst in the surgery. People coming in with Monday sniffles mostly, but often, it was the day people earmarked to pop in and get something off their chest. It could be a worry or an unexplained ache or pain, or it could be something much more serious. 'And I'm not sure where I'm going to find someone. What will people do?'

'Don't worry, you're panicking over nothing. Here's the thing: regardless of whether you get someone to take up on Monday or in a week's time, Doctor O'Shea's old patients will all be delighted to see the back of that awful woman. If there's something urgent, they'll take themselves off to the A&E in Ballybrack and if it's something small, they'll just drop into a doctor in the next town over from them. Don't you see, as long as she was here, they couldn't do that without feeling they were letting down the old man himself. Now at least, you can get someone decent in there and if you get the right person, it will all work out for the best in the end.'

'But that's the thing, Jo: who will I get? I mean, I've looked through all Eric's contacts and there's not one I can think of who'd be able to help me find a doctor to take over. I'm afraid after Thea Gilchrist that they'd foist someone even worse on us.' Elizabeth shook her head. It was useless.

'Why would you ask any of that lot? Sure, wasn't it one of his old "friends" who landed you with that lemon? No, now is the time to find someone you want, not an employee that some other practice just wants to get rid of. Actually...' Elizabeth set her head at an angle, her thoughts crowding over her words for a moment. 'Do you know there might be just the perfect person?'

'I can't see how...' Elizabeth wanted to say more. After all, Jo might be all very good at whipping an apple tart out of thin air, or marvellously making dust and debris disappear, but there was no way she could pull a qualified doctor out of her hat in an instant.

'It's Lucy, my daughter...She needs a change, but she's stuck. She's been stuck for far too long. Maybe, just maybe...'

'Do you think she'd come down here to take over?' Elizabeth leant forward, suddenly interested.

'If we could convince her, it could be perfect for both of you...'

2

Lucy

It had been a moment of complete madness. A night shift on A&E, one drunk too many or maybe just knowing that time was passing and with it any chance of making the most of what time was left with her son before it was too late. She'd fired off an email at four o'clock in the morning. A leave of absence. She would take a year to spend travelling or hanging around the house – being a mother. Maybe just...*being*. Four hours later, an email from the HR department, replying to the single form she'd filled in, dropped into her inbox. They didn't even wish her the best of luck or enquire as to why exactly she felt so burned out that she knew the only way to keep going was to walk away.

And that was that. Lucy didn't know whether to jump for joy or feel a little sad at this unexpected parting from everything apart from Niall and Dora her trusty hound who had been her life for the last couple of years. Really, outside of work and the friends and colleagues she had here, there wasn't much more to her life to leave behind. She stood for a moment, stunned into stillness. She had walked away from her job. Just like that. Dear God – was she mad? And for a moment, she wondered what on earth had possessed her.

Still, she slept soundly when she arrived home, woke after lunch and then it hit her again. What had she done? Thrown in her job for a year? She would have to tell Niall – he'd probably be delighted. It'd mean he could leave boarding school – he hated it, they both knew that. Boarding school had been Jack's idea. He wanted a big future for his boy – pity he didn't want to actually be in the same country as him. Jack was living in Australia now, starting over with wife number two – Melinda Power was nothing like Lucy. She shook the thought of her ex-husband and his new life from her mind quickly; it was time to fully let him go.

She'd have to tell her mother. Oh God. That would be like going ten rounds with Tyson, except her mother would jab with love and care and she'd worry like crazy that everything was all right with her only daughter.

'But that's just so perfect,' Jo said when she rang to tell her the news.

'Really?' Lucy asked, because she still couldn't believe she'd actually done it.

'Yes, really. I never understood why you stuck at it, after...' She was too tactful to say *after the divorce*. 'I mean, you've been killing yourself and for what? You hardly see Niall, you never get to take a weekend off and it's not as if you're broke. I mean...' Again, the divorce and the sale of their old house had left her with a financial cushion – thankfully her mother was too kind to say that outright either.

'Come home, Lucy. Ballycove could be just what you need now and...'

'And?'

'Well, you know I told you about old Dr O'Shea?'

'Yes, I remember. How's his wife? She must be very lonely.'

'Elizabeth?' Jo brushed off the name, as if his widow was unlikely to notice he was no longer about the village. 'Oh she's fine, nothing that a little getting out of herself won't cure, but it's the surgery...'

'No, no, no, I can't...' Lucy realised why throwing in her job seemed like such a perfect opportunity to her mother. 'Anyway, didn't she have someone else running it for her?'

'Oh, that dragon? No. Thankfully, she's gone back to whatever cave she slithered from. No, Elizabeth needs someone new, someone who's looking for a fresh start. Oh, Lucy, you'd be perfect and it could be just the thing for both of you.'

'And what about Niall?' Lucy shook her head. She couldn't imagine Niall being at all enthusiastic about moving down to Ballycove. He was too geeky to fit in with the farming and fishing kids who normally hung about the village.

'Look, just to keep your mother happy, will you come down for the weekend, get a feel for the place? Let's see what you think. Don't decide yet, but maybe when you meet Elizabeth and you have a look around – you never know. It might be exactly what you're looking for.' She ended the call before Lucy could say another word, no doubt off to make up their beds and cook up a storm of pies and cakes.

Lucy enjoyed the drive once she left the city behind; a looming red weather alert meant the roads were tame for now and Niall snoozed gently beside her. He was not a huge conversationalist when they were driving, but then what teenager ever was? Once she hit the midlands, she sank a little further down in her seat. The skies were rolling out a dark metal canvas before her and on either side peaty bogs unfolded purple heather and white cotton into the distance. The land was flat and uncompromising, but it was comforting to see little houses, smoke firing up their chimneys and the occasional stab at optimism where clothes flapped on clothes lines in the wind before the certain storm threatening from ever-darkening skies.

Soon, she was driving into Mayo, its familiar rocky fields and winding roads welcoming her with a soft misty rain that passed not too long after it began. Ballycove sat on the coast, facing off the Atlantic Ocean with its back at the North Sea.

Perhaps she was biased but Lucy always thought it was one of the quaintest villages on the western seaboard. Built into a stony cliff that hung over a stout pier, the streets zigzagged upwards in an angular spiral, until, at the top, the finest houses and the looming limestone church sat proudly overseeing all. Her mother lived at the lower end of the town in a small house – one of a row of workers' cottages.

Lucy had loved growing up here. She'd always thought it was the most idyllic spot. She loved everything about the cottage, but most of all, she adored her tiny bedroom at the front of the house that overlooked the sea wall. She had always treasured waking up in that little room, with the crashing of the waves just beyond her window and the constant call of gulls and curlews floating in from across the waves. It was, she'd once thought, even lovelier at night, to be snuggled in the tiny room, safe and sound while the winter storms crashed against the walls opposite and whistled along the cottages, rattling letter boxes and swinging gates.

In summer, when she left the window open, she slept and woke with the salty fresh smell of the sea in her nostrils and the music of the tide in her ears. It was no wonder that she seemed to eat for four when she was here. Quite aside from the fact that her mother cooked good wholesome food, long walks on the beach or back across the peaty stretch of fields and hills meant she was constantly ravenous. It would be no bad thing, if she could persuade Niall, to stay here for a while and breathe in fresh air and maybe even sit at a table with good food and better company. There was no denying she had always been thin, but now, when she caught her eye in the rear-view mirror, she was positively gaunt. A shadow of the girl she truly was.

Life had shaken the vitality from her. The last few years had kicked it from both of them. She looked across now at her lovely sleeping son, his pale complexion and gangly arms and legs a testament to a young life wasted for too many hours before a computer screen while she raced to keep on top of the demands of her job. The downward spiral of the quality of their lives had begun with the ending of her marriage. Still, there was no doubt that falling into a routine of hospital food that she could hardly face at the best of times and barely seeing daylight, didn't help with making her look or feel any better than some of the patients she tended to. With a stab of recognition, she knew, glancing at Niall, she had neglected both of them. They needed this before it was too late.

It was a huge relief to see that Ballycove had not changed one bit. She drove into town, past huge trees with the promise of new buds glistening on their fingering branches. She sent up a prayer to whatever power might be able to bring soothing to both Niall and herself and then shook him gently. 'We're here, sleepyhead.'

'What, already?' He'd slept soundly for the last hour of the journey.

'Yes, we've made good time. Although your grandmother will probably say we're just in time for dinner.' Lucy laughed then because she knew that her mother would make it her personal mission to get some meat back on Niall's bones for the few days they were here. She reached for her bag from the back seat of her car and swung around to find Dora back at her heels.

The little cottage felt smaller as all places do when you return after a long absence. Everything about the place seemed a little duller: the red door faded pinkish, the nets on the windows a little yellow and in the tiny patch of garden the vibrant plants of her memory were sleeping soundly for a few more weeks. She had hardly touched the knocker when the door swung back to reveal her mother, slighter, greyer, older but still warmly familiar with her great welcome.

'Oh, dear Lucy,' she said as she folded her in a huge hug, which betrayed her gauntness beneath her bulky hand-knitted jumper; then she held her hands and stepped back, gazing at her only daughter. 'Let me look at you…Oh, it's so good to have you home.'

'Come on, let us through the door, before Niall changes his mind and hightails it back to Dublin again,' Lucy joked, keeping her voice normal above the shock of seeing her mother look so unwell.

'Niall, look at you, you must be nearly…' There were tears in her eyes and Lucy knew they'd left it far too long. 'Six foot? You've grown so much.'

'He's not quite that yet, but you know the way it is, Mum, he goes to bed at night a little boy and before breakfast it seems he's grown a few more inches.'

'He's twice as handsome with it.' Her mother reached up to ruffle Niall's mop of curly hair.

'Aww, Gran.' He smoothed it down again, a little embarrassed at anything that might serve as attention on him. Still, Lucy was glad to see he bent down and kissed his grandmother shyly on her cheek.

'Come in, come in.' Jo pulled them into the hall, led them into the snug sitting room where a roaring fire blazed in the hearth. 'Oh, it's just so lovely to see you both,' she said again and Lucy couldn't help assessing her, counting the years on her face. Her mother was veering towards her mid-seventies now. It was not old, but somehow, the years seemed to have crowded in on her all at once. Her normally straight and large frame had begun to droop in on itself, so it looked as if someone had come along and flattened her, just a little more into herself. But her eyes were bright, her smile was warm and if there were more lines on her face, they suited her. Her complexion told of a woman who enjoyed the sea air every day and there was no missing the sense of purpose that came of being interested in her neighbours and friends and lending a hand at any turn she could.

The rain started to sheet down. Half an hour later it seemed to batter all that was holy out of the sky. Lucy realised she had missed this, the feeling that the real world still happened, with rain that was raw and wind that bellowed.

'That'll likely be it for the day,' her mother said softly as she stood looking out the front window towards the pier opposite. They'd had more tea and home-made brown bread, settled in and now Lucy could almost convince herself that she'd never left.

'It's no good,' Lucy said eventually, pulling herself up out of the chair. 'I can't sit here for the night; I need to stretch my legs.' She was too used to walking miles around hospital corridors to settle down just yet. 'I'll stroll to the pier for a breath of fresh air; give Dora a chance to have a sniff about too.' She looked down at Dora then who nuzzled her snout deeply between her front paws. There was no way she was going out in that. 'Niall, do you fancy getting a bit of fresh air?'

'Are you joking?' Niall eyed her from behind a giant wedge of apple pie. 'No, Mum, I'm good here. I'll keep an eye on Gran for you,' he said before swallowing a large mouthful of pie.

'You'll get your death of cold out there,' Jo said gently.

'Don't worry, I'll just go to the wall opposite, breathe in the fresh air. We don't get much of that in A&E. I'm not going to waste it now we're here…' Lucy knew she needed to feel Ballycove wrap itself around her and feel as if she really was home at last. 'Wuss,' she murmured at Dora who only dug deeper into the shaggy pile rug before the fireplace. 'I'll be back in a few minutes,' she said then, putting Jo off coming with her. They both knew her asthma didn't need a shower of rain to start it up again.

Outside, she pulled the door firmly shut behind her. The wind was biting cold and the rain, easing slightly, still felt like prickling stab wounds when it managed to infiltrate any area not covered by the oilskins. She made her way across the empty road, stood at the thick wall for a moment, looking down at the angry water beneath. She picked her way past the boats docked in preparation for the storm. The noise down here was orchestral, the wind and rain fighting against the harsh sea with a backdrop of clanging chains – they combined in an eerie endless symphony. This was what she needed. Why on earth hadn't she realised it sooner?

She turned reluctantly back towards the cottage as the rain whipped about her, as if scurrying from all sides to toss her off balance. Making her way back across the road once more, she was struck again by her mother's appearance at the sitting room window. When had she grown so fragile? Her mother had always been a robust woman, but here, with the light on her outline, there was no mistaking that her mother's presence owed as much to legacy and more to bulky clothing than it did to any real weighty flesh upon her bones.

A strange, terrible recognition occurred to Lucy, only heightening as she passed by the photograph taken of them both a year earlier on the hall table. Her mother was not well. Lucy had seen that look too many times for it to dupe her now. Above all the shock waves that flooded her body, she wondered, a little absently, if her mother realised that she had silently taken a step on a journey that would entail months of treatment – if they were lucky enough to catch it in time.

3

Jo

Jo had never liked Jack Nolan. Not from the very first day Lucy had brought him home to the cottage. Maybe even before that, she had a feeling that he would not be good for her daughter. From the start she knew he couldn't be trusted. He was far too good-looking for his own good or anyone else's and he knew it; a womaniser, it was in his bones.

In the beginning, she'd hoped this thing – whatever it was between them – would fizzle out once they had each immersed themselves in the heavy schedules of being house doctors in a busy hospital. Then, Lucy told her that she was pregnant with Niall and that was that. It was too late to say a word against him and Jo simply had to bite her tongue. Of course Lucy knew it was an unspoken shadow in the corner of their relationship for years. Neither of them wanted to open it up and when the marriage broke down, they both knew that Jo had been heartbroken for her daughter. Regardless of what she thought of Jack, she'd never wanted to see Lucy or Niall hurt that badly.

And yet, Jo still felt it lingered between them. It wasn't an argument or even regret – more a narrow apprehension that might detonate at some point and it meant that for years she'd guarded her words carefully. So, although Lucy only lived three hours away, sometimes it felt as if she'd moved to a different world. They'd drifted apart in some indefinable way; not that they didn't speak every other day, rather, they didn't talk to each other as they had before and Jo missed this dearly.

Three curlews circling stridently above her head brought her thoughts back from things she wished she could change. God, she loved this place. She loved everything about coming down here to swim when darkness closed in on her and freed her from the cumbersome truth of her age and aches and the gnawing certainty that time was running out. She loved the godliness of it all, which was strange, because she'd never been a religious person. Perhaps it was the sense of how completely irrelevant all her fears were in the face of the utter vastness of the sea and sky around her. She loved the silence and the roar of the ocean, the velvet sky and the inky water. Mostly she loved the fact that it made her feel alive in a way that nothing else could. She even loved the biting cold that ate through her skin and into the very marrow of her bones – in some absurd way, it warmed her from the inside out, as if it lit some fire that would never be extinguished.

There was no turning the clock back on what might have been. Out here, with the sea gently embracing her in its icy seal, she could clear her thoughts. It was time to think only of those things she might be able to change for the better.

Elizabeth O'Shea was every bit as lost as Lucy, even if it was for very different reasons. Whatever about the surgery, or her husband's debts or that old mausoleum of a house she was rattling about in – Jo knew that no matter how she tried to set up the dominoes, ultimately Lucy taking over the surgery was out of her hands and she was fine with that. *If it's for you, it won't pass you.* Isn't that what her own mother had said many years ago?

No; she'd done what she could there. Jo sighed, feeling a familiar wave of contentment wash over her – as if she was closing the page on another chapter where she could read no further.

But *this*, an unexpected thought was edging its way into her now; *this* could be the greatest gift she could ever leave with both Lucy and Elizabeth. These days, she thought about leaving a lot, as if some message had long been printed on her DNA and she was responding to its inherent whisper. She sighed deeply now, wondering how she could put into words the nirvana state of joy that swimming each night in the freezing waves brought to her.

She would bring them swimming with her, down here, at night; somehow she would talk them both into it, just once. It would be something they'd remember when she left them; perhaps they would cling to it when she was gone, or maybe, just maybe they could come here together occasionally.

Overhead, the moon stole swiftly behind a swollen

grey cloud and darkness enveloped her further, so it felt as if there might not be a soul about for miles. Then, as if to reassure her, the little church bell far up above her rang out its midnight chimes. Jo closed her eyes. She was too old for making wishes, but one floated up and she murmured it onto the stillness of the air around her. *The Ladies' Midnight Swimming Club*. That's what she wanted more than anything else now and somehow, some deep part of her knew with certainty it would be the answer to so many other questions.

4

Dan

Dan exhaled – a long, ragged sound that felt as if it might fill the whole city. Of course no-one else heard it. He looked out across the rooftops. People were getting on with life, oblivious to the fact that his world was crumbling around him. It was one of those stupid, horrible coincidences, that was all – but Leah Maine wouldn't see it like that. He was quite sure of that.

Leah was head of the studio, parachuted in six months earlier when the new owners decided a more aggressive approach to growing the audience was required. Dan knew even then, neither the Americans, nor Leah, boded well for the sitcom he'd written to be commissioned for a third year. He was right. Still, although he could see the final curtain before they'd even completed recording, it was the unfortunate timing that had finished them off. The red tops were full of it, mind you; it was an easy gambit to make a short and screeching headline of his downfall. The worst of it all was that the show was good. The critics had praised everything, from the writing, to the acting; even the costumes had picked up prizes at the annual awards.

'The problem,' Clive Cooper said as they waited for their final sentence, 'was not with the show.'

'It's not you, it's me?' Dan said, as if that insufferable break-up line covered the train wreck this would make of his career.

'Yeah, something like that,' Clive said and he began to inspect those perfectly manicured hands. Clive would recover. He had fingers in so many pies; he was up to his elbows in work and he'd been in demand since his one big hit, *The Green People*, had bagged every gong going a few years earlier. 'Look, hardly your fault that the episode went out on the same night that a tourist boat sank on the Thames…'

'No, but very unfortunate that the whole episode was one long joke about a modern-day *Titanic* bringing down the whole of Westminster…' In fairness, Dan felt bad for the real-life victims whose faces would probably live on forever in scenes that were televised on all the major news channels. That was it, really. While the news channel was beaming out pictures of the greatest tragedy London had seen in his lifetime, their channel had audiences laughing their heads off at the same story, but in a spoof docu-comedy that suddenly no-one found funny.

'Might as well suck it up, buddy; sometimes timing stinks,' Clive said under his breath as Leah made her way past them in a cloud of expensive perfume and a skirt too short for her skinny legs.

'Let's get this over with.' She snapped her fingers and flung open the door into her newly remodelled office. Throwing her expensive coat across one of the two chairs available for Dan and Clive, the message was clear: one would be staying, the other was going and no prizes for guessing which direction Dan was headed. 'I'm gonna cut to the chase here, boys,' she said, sitting against the side of her desk, so there could be no question of anyone getting too comfortable.

'Leah, it's clear that...' Clive began, but she put up a hand to stop him and Dan knew he wouldn't get the chance to say anything to try and save his bacon. It was a done deal. It had played into Leah's hands and there wasn't a word he could say to change his fate now, except...

'I'm glad we're getting this chance to clear the air,' Dan said then, walking bravely behind her desk so she had to almost contort herself to follow his voice. 'You see, if you're prepared to agree a fair severance package, I'm happy to walk, but...'

'What the?'

'Yes, I've had legal advice.' It was lies, but he was working on only one premise: he wasn't going to walk out of here like the sacrificial lamb they expected him to be. 'It's like this: I have other projects I want to pursue, but I'll need a cushion, so...'

'After the debacle that you're responsible for, you're bloody lucky that we're not suing you...' A look passed between Clive and Leah and it became clear to Dan that he was always going to be the first casualty of the takeover.

'You might want to paint it like that, but there isn't a labour court in England that's going to agree with you. If you're sacking me without so much as an acknowledgement of the good work I've done for this company, long before you came, well...' Dan's voice petered off because he really was walking on the very thinnest of ice.

'How much?' Leah could be trusted to want to keep them out of court. They'd all heard the rumour that she'd lost too many legal battles already with embittered staff who had seen an opportunity to bite back. Dan leant forward, scribbled the first amount that came into his head on the desk blotter and turned it towards her. 'Okay, but you're outta here today. I want your desk cleared, I want your keys handed in and I'll have this sorted into your bank account by the end of the week.'

'I'd like something in writing, too, just in relation to... just to make our severance official,' Dan said calmly. The reality was, he wouldn't trust Leah not to say he hadn't embezzled the company once his severance package arrived in his account.

And that was how he found himself, sitting in a bar, with a condemnatory cardboard box at his feet, getting too slowly drunk for his own liking. It seemed like his only option when he'd slunk out of the production offices earlier. Knowing that he'd be the talk of the coffee room for the rest of the day didn't help to raise his spirits very much either. There were, he tried to convince himself, other jobs. There were other production companies. For goodness' sake, if Leah actually paid up he could probably set up his own production company, on a small scale to start. The problem was he wasn't sure he wanted this life anymore.

None of it.

He didn't want to work in television. He didn't want to live in that crumpled flat that wasn't much bigger than a wardrobe. He didn't want to live in London – he wasn't even sure he wanted to live in the United Kingdom with the way the country had turned out since Brexit. He was a mixed-race, single man, living beyond his means, in a country run by right-wing politicians who cajoled him for a vote so they could legislate against him. He wasn't even sure that England was home to him anymore. In fact, and this was the niggling whisper that his moderate amount of professional success had managed to silence for the last few years, he wasn't sure that this country had ever been his home in the first place.

As Dan became drunker, these were the thoughts that careered about his head. A heavy hand on his back almost made him jump from his skin. Harry. Harry White was everything Dan was not. Everything about him screamed success, from his public schoolboy background to his astronomical success first as a talent scout and now as an agent to some of the biggest names in British media.

'Come and work for me,' he said as he ordered two large glasses of whiskey for them.

'It's not just the job…' Dan said and he waved his hand as if to bat away a thousand other unmentionable worries.

'No?'

'No.' Dan stopped, saw their reflections in the glass behind the bar opposite and in a flashing moment of sober thought, said, 'It's bigger than that. I can get another job in the morning, probably one that pays better than working for Leah, certainly one I'd be happier doing.'

'But?' Harry was watching him now; maybe he already knew.

'I need some time out, to...' Dan wasn't sure what he wanted to do. *Find himself?* Wasn't that what women did? They went off and they ate, prayed and loved? Dan had no interest eating or praying, never mind about loving. 'I want to figure things out,' he settled on.

'I see,' Harry said softly and perhaps he did, but he was good enough not to offer any trite words too quickly. Instead, they both sat in silence for a little while and considered the deep amber liquid in the glasses before them. 'So, you're thinking of taking a bit of time away from the madding crowd, eh?' he said ordering two more doubles.

'Yes, Harry, I think I might be,' Dan said with a lot more certainty than he'd realised he felt.

'Perhaps it's time to finally write that book?'

'That's what I was starting to think too,' Dan said softly, because maybe, for the first time since he left Leah's office, it seemed like there might actually be something he could pull out of this day apart from a hellish hangover.

'Better do it now than leave it too late.' Harry's voice was gentle, but he wasn't saying anything that hadn't already occurred to Dan. 'You could take a few months and who knows, if you don't find what you're looking for, maybe you'll find something else? Something even better?' Harry was trying to cheer him up; still, Dan appreciated the effort. 'Now, less of this maudlin hanging about. Let's drink these and get you to bed.' Harry handed him one of the glasses, they swallowed them quickly and Dan felt as if his whole body had been set on fire from the inside out. 'Come on, back to mine – you can sleep on the sofa for tonight. Dream about this new start until tomorrow.'

The mother of all hangovers – he deserved it of course, but it wasn't helped by the fact that the sun streamed in, scratching his eyes open on the uncomfortable leather couch. He lay for a while, in denial about the stiffness that had set into his back, the throbbing pain in his head, and the dryness in his mouth that made him feel as if he'd gulped down sand instead of too much whiskey the night before. Most of all, he was trying to thwart the overhanging bleakness that he knew marked out his first day of unemployment.

'Coffee, mate – that's what you need.' Harry handed him a mug that must have contained at least four shots of the strong coffee he had imported from some undoubtedly ethical bean farmer in Brazil, via a stopover in Andalucía for roasting and pricey packaging.

'Urgh.' Dan shuddered as he took the first sip.

'You really did hit it hard last night.' Harry slapped his shoulder and grabbed the vintage man bag that held his notebook and probably an array of travel-sized grooming products. He balanced on the edge of the sofa for a moment, drinking the last of his own coffee. 'I've been thinking, you know, what you said last night, about maybe taking time.' He looked at Dan now. 'You should do it. Take yourself out of London for a while, see if you can't write that novel – have a go. If you come up with anything half decent send it to me.'

'You want first dibs at something that I haven't even written yet?'

'I want you to write the bloody thing and wipe the satisfied smile off Leah Maine's face, that's what I want. If it's any good, I'll see if I can sell it for you. How's that for a deal?'

'That's pretty decent of you, mate,' Dan said, although at this point, he was more grateful for the coffee, even if it did taste like liquid tar.

'And you should get out of London, head for the sticks, the proper sticks I mean, not somewhere like the Cotswolds where you'd be tempted to come back before you've finished.'

'Right,' Dan said, although he'd never lived anywhere outside of London in his life, well... not as far as he could remember at least.

'I'm thinking Wales? Or Scotland? You might meet some lovely lass. You never know...'

'Ireland. I could go to Ireland. There's a place there I've always wanted to visit. It's on the west coast, as far away from London as I'm likely to get.'

'Hang on, mate, I didn't mean go into complete isolation.' Harry laughed, but there was an edge to him that perhaps meant he realised that Dan was actually serious about this.

'It's the land of saints and scholars. Where better to find my muse?'

'Yes, but it's hardly the sort of place your mates are going to be able to pop over to for a weekend, now is it? What's wrong with Snowdonia or the Highlands?'

'Ah, come on, Harry, if I'm going to do this, I might as well do it properly.' And even if his head was still hurting and his back was aching, Dan felt as if there might be something to look forward to. He drank back the contents of the mug and stood up – suddenly he had things to do. There were calls to make, perhaps a new future to look forward to and maybe even some closure on what had gone before. 'I'll see about booking something today and I'll let you know before I leave.'

5

Niall

Niall searched frantically in each of the bags. 'How could you leave it behind?' he spat at his mother, his voice almost on breaking point.

'I didn't leave it behind, I just...' He'd placed his games console on the stairs, waiting to drop it in the centre of the large carry-on bag that years ago they'd bought for going to Spain – back when they were a real family and did real family things together. Whoever forgot to pack it in the car didn't really matter, but he was much too angry to admit this. All he could think of was that it was not in Ballycove. He'd only noticed it was missing when he went to unpack his bags on the bed. It added to his frustration that the room was tiny, and that most of his video games would have to be stacked on the floor. Not that those were much use without his console. On a tall locker, he'd placed the huge television he'd brought from his own room in Dublin. The TV was a gift from his father, probably to assuage his guilt at taking off for Australia and leaving him here with his mother. *We can Skype each other; it'll be like I'm still here.* Yeah. Right. Sure, it will.

'Just bloody forget it,' Niall said and he stomped up the stairs leaving his mother probably livid and his grandmother open-mouthed. It was no good though; he couldn't settle in the tiny room. Nothing here felt like home and the only bit of technology he had was the smart phone his dad had given him for Christmas. He lay on the bed, browsing and generally absorbed in the world it led him into. He could hear his mother and his grandmother chatting away happily downstairs. It was all very well for them, catching up; what was he meant to do if they were staying here for a couple of days? God, he could die of boredom here.

He pulled his bedroom window tight, yanked over the curtains, so when his mother peered into the room, she assumed he'd fallen asleep. She closed the door gently with a click and with the finality of that soft sound, her footsteps moving lightly about the hall opposite told him she was turning in for the night. It was early and he wasn't tired yet. After all, if they were at home, he'd often spend twelve hours soaking up game time at the weekend if his mother was called in for another shift. It was nothing unusual for his mother to leave him in his room. It was, he supposed easier than the ongoing argument of trying to get him to leave for anything much more than dinner.

As the night began to pull in around the cottage, he thought he would go mad. There was nothing to do in this place; he missed his games console and the people who passed as his friends. Quite simply, he missed being at home, where he could wander down to the fridge that contained recognisable fast foods and gallons of milk or juice and the special-brand coffee his mother loved and he'd acquired a taste for. He had to get out of here. He pulled on his shoes and jacket and made his way towards the front door, letting himself out with hardly a sound. He almost crashed into an old biddy from up the road. The doctor's wife. He'd met her once, when her husband had fallen badly on his way home from the pub. The old doctor had been a right tosser, but of course, his gran had insisted they help him home. It was only up the road, that big musty house of theirs.

Mrs O'Shea had opened the door for them, led them up the long staircase, uneven steps catching them out occasionally. She'd said thank you at the finish, as if they'd just installed a new burglar alarm for her and Niall had marvelled at her reserve. She was from another age, he supposed, all pearls and set hair and probably afternoon tea and mothballs. She looked different today, walking along the street – smaller, inconsequential, as if the life had been blown out of her. Maybe he spotted tears in her eyes, but he didn't look too closely. He had worries of his own to consider.

He bolted down towards the end of the village. There wasn't really anywhere to go, not like their home in Dublin when he could have taken the bus into town, hung around the city streets for hours on end, before taking the last bus home. He'd been about fourteen the last time he'd done that and his mother had been livid. Deep down, he knew it was partly why they were here now. Maybe it had as much to do with her worries for him as it had with any concern for herself. Ballycove was the kind of place you couldn't hide in. Not really. Oh, there was a beach that stretched for miles, but in the cool temperatures, it wasn't the sort of place you wanted to spend hours on end. There was a coffee shop, three pubs, the local church and a boat house where he'd seen some of the local youngsters hanging out. They were kids who had small boats or surfboards and Niall had zero interest in any kind of sport or anything else in this backward place.

6

Elizabeth

Elizabeth couldn't decide if the lilies added a feeling of refinement to the hall or if it might look as if she'd forgotten to leave them up at Eric's grave. She wanted to make a good impression and the flowers could swing it either way. The thing she had to ask herself: would the positive impression so far outweigh the negative one to be worth taking the risk? The answer, she decided, was no, so she moved them into the kitchen and set them on the draining board where she had no intention of bringing Lucy Nolan.

She would treat her as she'd treated every other colleague Eric had entertained in their home. She would show her around the surgery first and then they could sit and have tea and cake in the drawing room. Of course, she knew it was much too early for cake, but what else could she offer the woman? Sandwiches? Well, at least, that's what Elizabeth thought they should do, but because she was Jo's daughter, Lucy was not like Eric and a completely different species to Thea Gilchrist. Not all doctors, Elizabeth knew, were created equal.

Eric's approach to being a GP was old-school. He was a rather conventional country doctor, a combination of tweeds, scuffed leather medical bag and gruff consideration. He turned up for a house call only if he had to; saw anyone who was well enough to show up, in his surgery. Over the last few years he dispensed decreasing amounts of sympathy and large numbers of antibiotics, muscle rubs and painkillers. He didn't believe in anything that wasn't scientific. The notion of sending people to a yoga class to deal with hypertension elicited a snort at best, and a loud guffaw when he'd read it aloud to Elizabeth from a supplement in the *Times*.

As small a village as Ballycove was, Elizabeth didn't really know Lucy, apart from empty small talk if they met in Mr Singh's supermarket on those rare weekends when she visited Ballycove over the last few years. Elizabeth thought about the way Jo described her daughter. She sounded like a very modern woman; cut of a different cloth to the type that had been available when Elizabeth was a girl. She could imagine Lucy Nolan being a Pilates devotee. That in itself was good enough to promote her in Elizabeth's estimation. Ballycove needed a breath of fresh air and the surgery needed it more than anywhere else.

Still, for all that she liked the idea of Lucy, Elizabeth felt a ticklish, unfamiliar nervousness in the bottom of her stomach as she went about the drawing room, dusting where no dust had dared yet to land. It was early morning now and the sun streamed in through the surgery windows. It gave the feeling that there was some natural warmth about the place, although of course, nothing could be further from the truth. The reality was that the surgery was little more than a lean-to garage. It was in need of a serious overhaul, if not complete rebuilding. That wasn't something Elizabeth had ever given much thought to before and she certainly wasn't in the happy position of being able to afford to give it any deliberation now.

Her mind cast back once more to the bundle of documents that Eric had stored out of sight from her and it brought that increasingly familiar sense of panicky sweat across her shoulders.

Last night, at a late hour, when she should have been tucked up in bed, she had taken down the old calculator that normally hid at the back of the kitchen drawers. She totted up the lot, between the overdraft, the loans and the letter from a private firm who'd forwarded a tidy sum to her husband for his personal use. It came to a grand total of sixty-two thousand euro. Not a fortune; perhaps, if she sold the house, she could easily rent somewhere more modest and pay off the debts, but it would leave her with nothing at the end. She would be cast for her remaining years into a grotty council house if she was lucky, or if not, at the mercy of some harsh landlord who would kick her out as soon as a more lucrative renter turned up on the doorstep. She couldn't let that happen.

She'd realised, later, as she lay in bed, that losing this house, in itself, wouldn't be the end of the world, but she would need another. She would need a home to call her own and one that didn't feel as if it might be snapped from beneath her at a moment's notice.

She'd been surprised, a few days earlier, sitting in Jo's cramped kitchen. It was neither glamorous nor particularly tasteful, but it was more modern than her own and it had a quality that the kitchen here had never managed. It was homely. It felt as if it had been filled with love and laughter and if you sat in silence, Elizabeth had a feeling that the walls would whisper back at you a message that you were always welcome and there, in its warmth, always safe.

The doorbell, when it rang, knocked her from her ruminations; it was not a bad thing, she considered. Too much thinking is not good for a woman on her own, particularly maudlin thoughts and that's what she was verging on. If she wanted to get out of this mess that Eric had foisted upon her, feeling sorry for herself wasn't going to be the way to do it.

'You're really very good to come,' Elizabeth said as she shepherded Lucy in through the hall. Lucy looked younger than she had expected; perhaps the bracing walk up from her mother's house had washed a decade from her tired skin. She was a striking woman, not beautiful or delicately pretty as Elizabeth had once been, but she had well-defined features and an energy to her that probably came from working hard and living clean. She didn't dress like a doctor either, and Elizabeth thought that was no bad thing.

'It was the least I could do; your husband has been very good to people in the village. My mother can't speak highly enough of him,' Lucy said easily, and even if there was only a small grain of truth in the words, it was nice to hear them all the same.

'Shall we have some tea?' Elizabeth asked brightly as she showed the younger woman in to the drawing room.

'Please, don't go to any trouble for me. I'm only going to stay a few minutes. I've promised Mum I'll take her across to the next town for a gander about the shops.' Lucy stood in the doorway, only half committed to the drawing room. 'Oh, what lovely flowers,' she said then, making her way into the back of the house and towards the arrangement Elizabeth had placed haphazardly next to the kitchen sink. She bent to take in their scent. 'Those are lovely. Will I pop them in the hall for you?' she asked, perhaps assuming that the arrangement was too large and awkward for Elizabeth to carry.

'Really, there's no need...' she said and regretted that there lingered in her voice a hint of dejection. She'd been so looking forward to sitting in the drawing room with Lucy Nolan and now, it seemed as if they would pass each other in the hall for a few minutes and that would be it. Suddenly, the afternoon and evening seemed to stretch out incessantly before her, endlessly and lonesome.

'I'd love a mug of tea, if it was going,' Lucy said softly then, spotting the tray Elizabeth had lain earlier with her best china cups and saucers and a round of biscuits and sweet bread. 'You've really set out to spoil me with these.' She nodded appreciatively at the tray.

'Oh, it's not much and I'm not exactly rushed off my feet since Eric passed away,' Elizabeth managed softly as she flicked on the kettle.

'Where will we sit?' Lucy asked now, settling into the idea perhaps that this would not be such a flying visit after all.

'Wherever you'd like. If you're rushing off, don't worry about the tray. I just thought...' What had she thought? That Jo wouldn't have already given the girl a good lunch? Nothing was less likely. Perhaps, she'd thought that things could be the same as they'd been when Eric was here, entertaining in the drawing room – pretending that everything was so very prim and proper.

'Ah, I see you're a twitcher,' Lucy said bringing the tray across to the kitchen table and settling just opposite the window where there was a decent view of the fat balls Elizabeth had hung out for the birds against the wall opposite earlier.

'Well, it passes the time, doesn't it? My husband was never an animal lover, but our garden is such a wilderness; there have always been lots to watch out there.' It was probably the thing she liked most about this house: the fact that they had a constant trail of foxes, hedgehogs, weasels and all sorts of birds passing through at different times of the year.

'You're lucky. My house in Dublin hardly sees daylight, never mind actually allowing a view of anything much more than a courtyard preened to within an inch of existence.' Lucy laughed, but the sound was empty.

'I couldn't imagine living in the city,' Elizabeth said as she popped the lid on the teapot and set it down on the kitchen table.

'Yes, I suppose I sort of fell into it. There was no great master plan.'

'It's never too late to make one, though, is it?' Elizabeth said lightly and she wondered if that was really true.

'That's what I'm hoping at least.' Lucy sat back a little in her chair, sighed softly. 'I should be honest with you, Mrs O'Shea.'

'Please, I'd like you to call me Elizabeth.' This surprised even herself, but the truth was, she didn't feel like the doctor's wife anymore and anyway, it was madness not to be on first-name terms. She wasn't entirely sure who she was now, not with the way things were really, since she'd found those letters from the bank.

'Okay, Elizabeth.' Lucy smiled. 'I know my mum would love to see me work as a GP here. Honestly, she'd love to see me settled down close by with Niall and a job that made me happy, but...'

'You're not sure this is the place you want to settle?' Elizabeth asked softly.

'A lot has happened over the last year or two. Everything I thought my life would become has changed. Niall's world has already been turned upside down,' Lucy said and there was no mistaking the fact that there had been heartbreak. You could so easily miss it, if you looked away, but it was there in spades. Lucy Nolan was giving up her free time because she sensed the utter loneliness that stretched before another human being and that was something that made Elizabeth feel as if she was unexpectedly privileged. 'My mum has probably told you?'

'No, Jo would never discuss anything private, beyond how proud she is of you.' Elizabeth smiled sadly, realising that it was a quality she'd probably overlooked in Jo, but one to be admired.

'Well, she's been a rock, but it's not exactly a secret. My marriage broke up, just over a year ago. My husband met someone else and now...' She smiled sadly, bravely. 'He's moved to Australia and it's hard, you know?'

'I'm so sorry.' And Elizabeth felt she really was, because at least up in Shanganagh Cemetery, Eric may have left an empty space in their home, but he wasn't creating pain in her heart each day by making her feel as if she was somehow less than someone new. 'That's really hard. You're...' Elizabeth broke off, because she wasn't sure what to say next, fearing that she may sound condescending or worse, perhaps a little pathetic.

'It's just the way things worked out.' Lucy smiled then, a brushing together of her features; probably one she used when she needed to face a patient who would have to be courageous. 'I haven't been particularly brave or resilient, but I've tried to be dignified. I think sometimes, that's as much as you can manage.' Her voice had softened and there was no mistaking the vulnerability. 'So—' her smile this time managed to reach her eyes '—shall I be Mother, or do you want to pour?'

They drank their tea in the kind of easy silence that passes between people who may not yet be friends, but if time allowed, they might be.

'When the sun is shining out there, it's really quite lovely,' Elizabeth said eventually. They were both watching a pair of doves tracing their way along the overgrown path.

'I think the rain is gorgeous; everything is so lavish and verdant,' Lucy said softly. 'I never realised that these properties extended so far out the back. It's quite the revelation.' She laughed now. 'Are they old coach houses along the end?'

'I believe they are. There was a line of houses just like this running to the end of the street once. They're Georgian, of course, so the attics would have been home to the servants and the stables and the coach house at the back would have seen the family's livery settled in. I suppose, we've let it go to rack and ruin, but it all takes money and I'm afraid Eric never really saw the point. In the beginning, when I first married him, I tried to convince him to...' She laughed, a gentle sound that held precious fond memories in its marrow. 'I was young and enthusiastic; I thought that they'd make a far better surgery than the old rooms he settled for. Eric liked the idea of being on the main street – whereas I always thought that we could open up the entrance at the back. There's plenty of parking, just opposite, and room for a good size waiting room and maybe an extra surgery too.' She shook her head then; it was a lifetime ago.

'I remember visiting your husband before I applied for medical school.'

'Really? I didn't know that,' Elizabeth said, but of course, Eric never really discussed anything to do with the practice with her. 'Did he encourage you?' she asked.

'In a way, I suppose he did. He was probably late in his career then. I'm not sure it could be considered a vocation, but compared to a lot of jobs, it was clear that he was committed, in a way that other professionals don't really sustain as the years pass.'

'Yes, I suppose he was.' He certainly worked long hours or at least that was what Elizabeth had tried to convince herself of over the years. She'd turned a blind eye to far too much, but then, she'd learned early not to quarrel with Eric when he was drunk.

'And that's it, really, with medicine – you're either committed or you're not. I don't think anyone would sign up for being a doctor based on the working conditions or the wages, but for me and I suspect for your husband, there's the chance to make a difference.' Lucy shrugged now and Elizabeth tried to equate this version of Eric with the one she'd lived with all those years.

'Well, I'm not going to lie and tell you that if you were to come here it would be easy. Eric always said that being a GP was the hardest job in the world, and God knows, the practice isn't exactly a money-making machine.' It was as near the truth as Elizabeth could face telling. 'Still, the village is nice, the people are decent and I have a feeling that if you decided to fill in, just for a week or two, at least you'd know one way or another.' She picked up a piece of sponge cake and popped a crumbling end in her mouth. Life was too short to eat sandwiches when the sun was peeping through the grey clouds outside and the leaves were dripping slowly onto the puckered ground beneath.

'Let's take a look then.' Lucy got up, as if unexpectedly energised with the idea of the surgery. 'It's years since I was there last.'

'Oh, dear, I'm not sure how it's going to look to you so,' Elizabeth said, regret tinting her voice.

It's a funny thing, looking at a familiar place through the eyes of someone new; Elizabeth thought she knew every single inch of her home and the surgery. She had cleaned the place from top to bottom for too many years to count, scrubbing away not just the scuff marks and dust of daily inhabitation, but the imperceptible translation of sickness and misery that she blasted with disinfectant, antibacterial cleaners and stoic rubber gloves. Now, today, with the unforgiving spring afternoon sunshine picking out chipped paint and time-worn tiles, it seemed her life's work counted for very little. The rooms were dated and archaic. They belonged to another age, a time when Eric had qualified, when the GP was expected to sit behind his desk and pronounce his words of wisdom with little more than a stethoscope or a thermometer in his arsenal. The walls held charts that looked as if they could belong in a museum. The blinds that had stuck closed many years earlier had a tatty, neglected air about them. Even the doors creaked onerously as they were opened; it seemed they too were ready to hand notice in.

This was how Elizabeth saw the consulting rooms – cramped, miserable and inadequate – and for all Lucy Nolan's kind words, she knew too that the condition of them spoke volumes about the way her husband held himself and his patients' regard. It was all too much. 'We shouldn't have come here,' she said quietly, closing the door on Eric's consulting room. 'I'm sorry, it's a silly idea. Whoever takes over a practice in Ballycove will have to open a whole new set of consulting rooms...These will never do.' And then something else struck her. This idea, the notion that she could somehow keep the practice going had been her only hope. And now, it was dashed. 'It was silly of me to even think...' a small tear escaped her '...that anyone would want to set up here...'

Lucy Nolan was used to working in a modern hospital with electronic gadgets and state-of-the-art equipment – Eric didn't even own a computer.

'It could be very homely...' Lucy said, but they both knew her words – no matter how kindly chosen – simply could not gloss over the fact that this place was a dump.

'It's pathetic,' Elizabeth said and felt an avalanche of frustrated tears rise up behind her eyes. 'I can see that now, even if I couldn't before.'

'It would need a lot of work, if it was to be a long-term arrangement,' Lucy said gently. She walked over to the little cubbyhole that passed for a reception desk. 'Don't tell me that old Mrs O'Neill is still here.' She smiled fondly.

'Ah no. I'm afraid she retired a couple of years ago.' That had been a day of mixed emotions. Elizabeth had never been keen on the woman, but perhaps it hadn't been either of their faults – rather it was just that she resented her. When she'd married Eric, she'd imagined them being a team. The arrival of Annie O'Neill had placed her firmly on the bench, so her only contribution had been in later years, to come down here and clean the place when it was empty or help out in moments of crisis. Elizabeth had never been good enough to be a full-time receptionist, but she could *do* for the weekends. She'd been the one to hold crying babies when their mothers had an examination or to cajole small children when they needed to get their shots.

'Her daughter took over from her, when she retired. Alice is a lovely girl. She's actually a nurse, so I suppose it was lucky for us. She knows what she's about...' In spite of herself, Elizabeth liked Alice. She hadn't inherited her mother's bossy nature; rather, she was far too harassed trying to keep her family, job and overbearing mother all happy at the same time.

'You were lucky there. I remember Alice from school and she was lovely,' Lucy said warmly. 'And she only does reception?'

'Well, yes, of course. What else?'

'Oh, no, I just wondered...Surely for a registered nurse, there would be opportunity to use her skills to save on time for the doctor on duty?' It was an offhand remark, but so thoroughly sensible that it sounded as if a decision had already been made.

'I suppose you're right,' Elizabeth said evenly; not that it mattered now, because suddenly, it was obvious that this couldn't really be a surgery for much longer. Even the examination table in Eric's office was being held together with a couple of nails and an elastic bandage.

'Oh, my goodness,' Lucy murmured. She had walked back behind Eric's desk now and was looking at his old medical bag. 'That's such a lovely piece of history, really, isn't it?' she said softly and it occurred to Elizabeth that perhaps they were seeing the place very differently. Whereas, all Elizabeth could see was how forlorn and antiquated everything was compared with the surely bright and modern hospital Lucy was accustomed to, Lucy was seeing the place with the rose-tinted view of pastoral nostalgia. 'You'd have to wonder, how many people have been made well as a result of the contents of this bag, wouldn't you?' she said, holding it up now and tracing her hand along the soft leather and the blackened, dull clasp lock.

'It was a gift, from Eric's mother when he graduated from medical school. I'm not sure it was new, even then,' Elizabeth said a little fondly. 'He's hardly used it these last few years. He hated doing house calls. I suppose, the only people he's actually gone out to are... well, people who couldn't possibly come in.' That was the truth; you had to be literally on death's door before he'd make an appearance. So, his house calls the last couple of years had been predictable. They were to the dying or the already dead, if he was running late.

'I suppose, one man, on his own, it's hard to get to everyone.' Lucy shrugged, too young yet to be dragged down by the fact that eventually, as Eric had said once, everyone dies, regardless of what you do. Elizabeth shivered.

'It's cold in here; we should probably go back upstairs.' Elizabeth knew the cold had little to do with the temperature of the place and everything to do with the realisation that her options had drastically narrowed. She couldn't ask this young woman to pin her future to a sinking ship. That would be unforgivable. She wasn't even sure, when all was said and done, that Eric had been making enough wages to pay a doctor and clear off his debts – wasn't that probably the reason he'd buried his head in the sand at the end?

She made for the door, assuming that Lucy was following behind. She was almost at the stairs when she realised that she was alone. She stood for a moment, feeling as if she was about to fall from a precipice into the unknown. She would have to think of another way to sort out Eric's gambling debts. She was quite sure that employing a doctor to take over the surgery was not going to be the answer. It was a funny thing, but all these years, she'd believed them to be well off; not just because she hadn't realised they were in debt far over their heads and not because she'd been blithely unaware of her husband's gambling habit. Rather, she'd thought that they were financially comfortable because her husband was a GP. It was a good job, a career that had income flowing into their home on a daily basis, but what if she'd been wrong?

Looking at the surgery now, with the fresh eyes of an outsider, she could see it was in a shambles. All of it. Everything about the life she'd believed they were living, it was all a shoddy, ill-constructed mess and now, she was faced with finding a way to move forward and make some kind of future from its ashes.

'You're not ready for this, yet, are you?' Lucy said softly then at her back.

'No, I don't suppose I am, really,' Elizabeth answered, but she pushed through the door and walked back into the kitchen where, only such a short time earlier, it had seemed as if the future ahead could yet be a little brighter than the past.

'It's a lot.' Lucy shook her head. 'A big responsibility, to feel that if you don't keep this place running, there is no other local doctor to take over...'

'You're very kind, but it's not just that.'

'I know, you've lost your husband. I can't imagine what that's like, after so many years of marriage. Death – it's so... final.' She broke off, because of course; they both saw the other woman's situation as somehow worse. 'But, you know, if there is no surgery here, people will find another doctor and I'm sure, given a month or two, you'll probably manage to source a young doctor eager to take over,' Lucy was saying now, but they both knew, the words were only being said to smooth over the emptiness of everything.

'Oh, look, don't worry; you don't have to try to make me feel better. The truth is I'm not as honourable as you might think.' Elizabeth felt the tears now. There was no holding them back anymore, but Lucy Nolan had been candid with her, the least she could do was offer the same in return. 'The truth is... my husband was not only a drinker, it turns out he was a gambler too.' She sighed. 'He was a really bad gambler, the sort who loses far more than he wins and perhaps the sort who just didn't know when to stop.'

'I'm sorry,' Lucy murmured.

'It is what it is, now. I hadn't realised. I really had no idea – what on earth does that say about me, eh?' It was the reproach that kept rising up in her thoughts: how could she not have known? 'Anyway, this place, the surgery, everything we've built up over the years, I can't see any way of hanging on to any of it. I'm not the kind of woman who can carry on under a cloud of debt. I'll have to clear it and then… well, I can't see there being much left over when I've seen all the bills off.' There it was. She shrugged. Somehow, saying it out loud was not as terrible as she'd have expected.

'That's awful. I'm not sure what to say to you, but…' She made a face, an inscrutable expression that was a mixture of condolence and hopefulness. 'Look, you've just buried your husband; you can't make any huge decisions here and now. These are things that people mull over… This is your home, your life…No-one is going to come in here and demand immediate repayment in the week after the funeral.' She caught Elizabeth's eye. 'Are they?'

'No, I shouldn't think so. All of the debts that I've come across so far are from reputable lenders – banks and so on.'

'That's good, at least.' Lucy leant forward, reached her hand towards Elizabeth's arm. It was a simple gesture, but Elizabeth felt it was an act of kindness, as if someone really cared. 'Does anyone else know?'

'Good God no, apart from Jo. I don't think I could bear to have the whole village talking about me now. I'm not even sure how I've told you, to be honest; I think I'll die of mortification when word gets out.' In spite of herself, probably due to a touch of nervousness, her tears mingled with an edgy laugh, so it sounded as if she gently snorted out the words. 'Oh, dear.'

'Look, you're in no fit state to make any decisions yet. I haven't anywhere I need to be for another few months. I was going to take Niall out of school until September to travel and pack in quite a bit of living before I return to my job in Dublin. But that still leaves us a little time to help out here, if you'd like.'

'So, you will go back, eventually?' Elizabeth asked, and she wasn't sure why, but part of her couldn't quite fit this woman in with a soulless city life.

'Yes, I suppose we will,' Lucy said briskly. 'Here's the thing though: if it helps, I'll open up the surgery tomorrow morning for you. I'll run it for the next two weeks and by then, maybe we'll have an idea exactly how it's running and what it's worth. At least, you'll be able to make an informed decision and not one based on what you *think* is the right thing.'

'You're very kind. Are you sure?' Elizabeth had to ask, because she knew that when Lucy Nolan had agreed to come here today, neither of them had truly expected her to say she'd come back another day.

'I'm not really sure, but I think Mum has been certain since the moment she mentioned it on the phone to me and who am I to disappoint her at this stage?' She took up her mug and they toasted the next two weeks. It was, Elizabeth knew, just a reprieve, but already, it was one she was looking forward to.

Later, when the day had mellowed, in spite of the gushing overflow of water racing down the cliff face and the constant drip of gutters and eaves, it was decidedly warmer than anyone could have predicted. Elizabeth decided on a walk. She would only head to the end of the village, perhaps look out across the pier and thank the heavens for the fine evening it was turning into one way or another. There was, Elizabeth knew, an unmistakable lightness in her step after her conversation with Lucy Nolan earlier. She hardly noticed walking past the familiar houses, so caught up was she in the glorious blue skies and the notion that there was room to breathe.

Soon she was turning onto the road where the fishermen's cottages stretched off into the end of the village. Jo's little house sat stout and proud and she remembered the afternoon they'd spent there, when she'd felt the warmth of another person's home envelop her in a way her own had never managed. It struck her as odd, this feeling that somehow she'd never really thought about it before, but her house – for all its faded elegance – had never been homely.

At the very end of the row, she stopped for a moment, looking back up the hill from Jo's house, and then she looked back at the cottage. It was the only one with a gable wall and wide entrance lane running about its side. It had its own tiny garden, squaring it off, making sure that everyone knew it was just a little different from the rest. A plaque said the row had been built in the 1920s. There were narrow windows either side of the front door.

Jo had lived her whole life in that house. She tended the roses around the door – ready to bloom again in time for summer and she polished those brasses every single Saturday morning that the weather would permit.

Elizabeth leant against the low perimeter wall for a second. The sky overhead had pushed back any hint of cloud now, a clear blue vista, with a soft, end-of-day sun intent on drying out the land; it was inviting her to walk a little further.

'Elizabeth.' Jo's voice at her back startled her. 'Just the person I was thinking of.' She was making her way down the path. 'Lucy told me – it's wonderful news.'

'It's only for two weeks, but...'

'Initially. Let's see how it goes first,' Jo said softly and of course, Elizabeth knew her friend would love nothing more than to have Lucy here full-time. 'But that's not what I wanted to talk to you about.' She stopped now, as if assessing Elizabeth for bad news.

'What is it?' Elizabeth felt her stomach turn over with the inevitable nerves that come before hearing the very worst.

'Oh, it's nothing bad, it's just...' Jo bit her lip for a second. 'Don't say no immediately, but I was wondering, if you'd like to come swimming with me tonight. It's...' Her voice trailed off, perhaps registering the look of horror in Elizabeth's eyes.

'It's rather cold for that sort of malarkey for me, but...' God was there any way out of this? 'I...'

'Of course, of course,' Jo said quietly, 'it was silly of me. I just thought you might really enjoy it – something to knock off a bucket list, if you had one.' She was laughing now, but Elizabeth could see that she'd let her down somehow.

'Maybe next month? When it gets a little warmer. You know what they say: never swim when there's an R in the month!' Elizabeth said lightly, but the thought of going into the freezing waters now didn't particularly appeal to her. She didn't even have a swimming suit for heaven's sake.

'Right, that's a date. We'll make it May Day, or rather night,' Jo said, happy now that she'd tied her down to a specific time.

'Right.' Elizabeth agreed, a little shocked. Dear God, what had she let herself in for?

7

Dan

Dan's parents never made a secret of the fact that he was adopted. Mind you, his mother was such a typical English rose and his father still burned to a freckle if he so much as looked at the sun, it wouldn't exactly have come as news to anyone, with Dan's dark skin, pitch-black hair and heavily lashed brown eyes. Being adopted had never been a thing for him. Even at that stage, when other kids rebelled, Dan just counted himself lucky. He was an only child, lavished with love and he adored his parents. If he'd wondered at other kids, searching for their birth parents, he'd have probably supposed that they mustn't have had the same happy home he'd had.

So why on earth did this gaping hole seem to have opened up in him now? Just when he needed it least? It woke him in the early hours of the morning. Of course, he knew it probably had a lot to do with the fact that he'd booked his ticket, sublet his flat and he was headed for the one place that might be able to give him an answer to this question, that for so long hadn't meant as much to him as he supposed it should have.

He should be getting a new job, well, probably a new career once the media had finished with him. He should be finding a partner to settle down with, getting his life sorted, looking forward rather than looking back for parents who clearly didn't see themselves in his future. He told himself these things a million times, during the night, when sleep had played a game of chase he wouldn't quite keep up with. He tried his best to talk himself out of the notion, that out there somewhere, there was a connection like no other to him – his mother. Perhaps he had siblings, or half siblings, perhaps he could find his father.

The more the notion niggled at him, the more reasons he seemed to come up with for finding out who he actually was. He could list backwards a dozen inherited diseases that could show up in the next generation. Didn't he want to know if there were markers there before he set off on a road that might be too painful to consider once he'd stepped on it?

There was another thing too, and it was probably this that really worried him the most. The notion that his mother could be alive today, but by the time he found her, it could be too late. He'd seen too many documentaries, people just missing each other by the thinnest thread of time. The more the idea festered, the more he realised he didn't want that to be his story.

The only problem was, he had nowhere to start. It wasn't that his parents were being evasive, he knew them too well for that, but rather it was the whole system that seemed to be in place in Ireland for when it came to tracking down anything to do with a parent who simply did not want to be found.

It could drive him crazy if he thought about it too much, and so, by the time he was sitting on the ferry, he'd already talked himself out of making this trip all about tracing his roots. Instead, he would prioritise clearing his head, maybe settling into writing something so he could at least pretend to have been productive and then, if there was the time, or the inclination left, he might just see if there was anything he could learn about his past.

Dan surprised himself by actually falling asleep on the crossing over. He'd woken to the sight of land, the sun driving slowly towards the west and it filled him with a giddy optimism, something that he realised he hadn't felt in a very long time. He hadn't been fully sure about the journey on unfamiliar roads to the other side of Ireland before he'd left, so he'd booked a room in a small B&B on the outskirts of the city.

It was a tired little house on the deep end of an estate that looked as if it was on its third generation of occupancy, having become unfashionable for the bright young things. He noticed the houses here looked as if they were owned only by the elderly or inhabited by people who couldn't afford something better.

'Ah, you're going to Ballycove, are you?' the old lady who welcomed him asked. She seemed to be a little deaf and if the carpet stairs were worn, it certainly didn't take the fulsomeness from her welcome. 'First time in Ireland?'

'Yes, that is...' He stopped, because how could he possibly explain? 'The first time I can remember.'

'Oh, you're in for a treat in Ballycove, especially this time of year. Mind you, it can be stormy. You'll want to bring a good rain jacket, but if you get the weather... well, it's a little bit of heaven,' she said before offering him half her own dinner, which was sitting on the stove, because he looked like a *boy* who needed feeding!

'You're very kind,' he said softly, because he had a feeling she was, 'but I have to meet someone now and then I'll be straight into bed for an early start tomorrow.' He'd seen a greasy café just along the road. It would be good enough for dinner and tomorrow he'd explore the capital before heading west to start on this self-prescribed sabbatical that already seemed to be filling him up with a sort of nervous and unfamiliar optimism.

8

Lucy

Her mother had been over the moon and even if Lucy wasn't sure about her decision, perhaps that was enough for now. She'd spent the last two days worried sick about Jo and the fact that her mother seemed to be completely oblivious to the reality that she had lost almost two stone in weight and her skin had taken on a grey tone that Lucy recognised even if she didn't want to.

Dora was happy too. She ran about the beach early the next morning with an abandon that seemed even more excited than ever. Niall had been predictably sullen with the news that they would be staying put for another two weeks. He'd been expecting to head back for Dublin and his games console first thing on Monday morning – to say he was not impressed was putting it mildly. Lucy wasn't sure how she really felt about filling in for Dr O'Shea for two weeks. The surgery looked as old as the ark and as for poor Elizabeth – well, it was pretty obvious she wouldn't be a lot of help in terms of any real hands-on input.

Lucy told herself, sternly, none of that mattered. It was only two weeks. She'd be giving the woman a bit of breathing space, doing what she'd been trained to do and maybe getting some idea of what was wrong with her mother. It would give her a chance to sort out the house in Dublin and perhaps make some travel arrangements for the next few months.

Lucy drew in the fresh salty air and looked across the beach towards the butty grey pier. She turned then, a full three-sixty to take in the village at her back. In the distance, she could see Ballycove yawn into life for another day. At the top of the village the sun danced across the blue-grey slates of the remaining Georgian houses at the top of the town. Lucy remembered walking past them as a teenager, even then admiring their grace. It always seemed to Lucy that they were the kind of house she'd love one day to live in. Had they been the prompt that sent her into medicine? Had she always wanted to live in a large Georgian house, with a walled in garden, an Aga and rooms filled with children and dogs? She did want all those things – once. She'd wanted them with Jack, but now, that dream was over and she was, whether she'd have chosen it or not, beginning on a new path.

She sighed, determined that she would see only the silver lining, no matter how hard she had to squint to find it. The world was going to be, she decided now as the crisp sun dazzled her on her approach to the slipway, her oyster. Now, all she had to do was rid her mother of this crazy idea that they were all going to form this Ladies' Midnight Swimming Club. Hah. *Saints preserve us*, was all she could manage to answer when Jo had pressed her earlier, but they both knew, it was a done deal. She'd traipse down to the cove on the first of May, just to keep her mother happy, even if she'd prefer to do anything but.

The surgery looked even more dilapidated in the early morning light. How on earth could a building that had windows facing both east and south be so depressingly dark? Of course, she knew, it wasn't a question of sunlight, rather it was the overhanging miasma of the man who'd spent a lifetime barking at patients and probably demeaning his wife; that was what lingered in the core of the place. Eric O'Shea had not been a nice man. The words Lucy had uttered yesterday had not been to polish his character; rather they were to soothe his widow. Lucy had a feeling that the whole village felt a release of something close to relief when he'd finally gone. Ballycove was too small a village not to visit your local doctor. There was no guarantee that a practice in the next town would even fit you in. Better the devil you know. The general consensus was that while he may have been a distant and crotchety man, he was a fair doctor and there was no danger of him not looking after his patients as well as the next.

Alice greeted her with the familiar warmth of their shared past. They'd been in secondary school together, and even if they weren't close friends, they'd liked each other well enough to get along. This morning they greeted each other with genuine warmth as if the years that passed between them had somehow melded them closer rather than further apart.

'You've caused quite the stir,' she said that first morning when Lucy handed her a cup of instant coffee that she'd made at the tiny sink in the old man's consulting room. 'The whole village is buzzing with the news that you're taking over. They absolutely hated the last one,' she said, wrinkling her nose as she tasted the coffee. It was cheap and nasty and a new jar was mentally added to Lucy's shopping list at lunch time. 'Thea Gilchrist?' She said the name as if every doctor knew every other doctor in the country. 'Never mind, a total cow.' She shook her head, glad to be rid of the woman.

Alice had aged a little unfairly it seemed to Lucy. Probably four kids, a husband in the guards who worked overtime too much and a mother who would always be a simpering bully; the combination would have aged Cleopatra double quick too.

'We are going to have fun here,' Lucy said brightly. 'You and I are going to be a team and we'll make this a place people want to come to – even if they are sick coming in, they're going to feel lighter leaving.' She meant it. She'd seen the value of creating a culture of positivity around people who felt unwell. Sometimes a few kindly words and a bit of encouragement went further than any painkiller. 'But first, you're going to have to tell me how this place works…' She tapped the bruised and slightly tragic narrow bench that stretched along the wall of the waiting room.

'I'm not sure I can tell you a lot. It's a version of

organised chaos, mostly. I do the receptionist duties—' she threw her eyes up to heaven at that '—and Dr O'Shea saw the patients. My mother set up the filing system, such as it is, and to be honest, even though I've been here a couple of years, I've never actually been brave enough to sort it out properly.'

'It's busy?'

'I suppose it is, but a village this size, it could be a lot busier. I think he just got set in his ways. He wasn't the sort of man you could suggest changes to, you know?'

'And his wife?'

'Mrs O'Shea? She's a total kitten. I'd say she'd go along with anything, just to keep him happy. She and my mother were never exactly bosom buddies, but I like her. I think she's quite... well, I wouldn't want to have been married to *him*.' She nodded back towards the open surgery door.

'So, talk me through what happens. Is it all walk-in or are there appointments?'

'Dr O'Shea didn't believe in appointments. He believed that if you needed a doctor badly enough, you'd sit it out here with everyone else...'

'So, small babies, winter vomiting bug, old dears waiting to get their heart monitors checked?'

'What heart monitors?' Alice laughed. 'I'm afraid, when you look around here, this is it. Old Doctor O'Shea didn't do anything modern. He saw patients with either his stethoscope or his tongue prod. He didn't do heart monitors or ultrasounds or...' She shook her head. 'He didn't put any weight on the whole idea of keeping the vomiting bug at home or making sure that the old dears getting their flu injection didn't pass on their septic throats to the pregnant woman sitting next to them. He didn't believe in alternative therapies or referring anyone for counselling. I'm sorry, Lucy, but consider yourself stepping into the TARDIS and re-emerging somewhere in the early 1970s.'

'Dear Lord.' Lucy shook her head sadly; suddenly the romantic nostalgia of the creaking doctor's chair and the vintage wall charts was beginning to dull. 'Thankfully, I've got some of my own equipment in the car. I'll nip out and bring in what I have and then we'll see what we can do from there. How long have we got before patients start arriving?' Just as well, she'd come prepared.

'About half an hour,' Alice called after her as she made her way out to the car. It wasn't nearly long enough, but the first patients were going to have to be...*patient* while she got the run of the place, Lucy decided.

The morning flew past. Once her first appointment was sent through it seemed to be an endless stream of spring colds, aching muscles, back pains and a run of ear syringing. The work was straightforward and Lucy thought at lunchtime, it was more diverse than she was accustomed to in many ways in the A&E. Mind you, the fact that she'd mainly covered night shifts since the divorce had a lot to answer for there. Over the course of the morning, she met people she remembered from her youth, old and young. People she'd been in school with and a boy she'd fancied like mad when she was about fifteen. He was still handsome, in a slightly squidgy way now. He'd gone on to be a priest and even if he was in denial, she had a feeling he might be gay.

She'd enjoyed every moment of the morning. When Alice finally poked her head around the door to say that the waiting room was empty and they could break for lunch, Lucy realised she was hungry and tired in a way that she hadn't felt for a very long time. It was satisfying. They popped the kettle on for another cup of substandard coffee when Elizabeth arrived down with two bowls of hearty home-made soup and thick buttered brown bread.

'I'll bring down some proper coffee,' she said eyeing the unfortunate jar. 'I'm not sure where that came from, but I have a cafetière upstairs and a decent coffee after your morning is the very least you both deserve,' she said before disappearing back into the main house once more.

'Don't you miss being a nurse?' Lucy asked Alice as they devoured the bread and soup.

'Yes, very much, but beggars can't be choosers. There aren't any nursing jobs going around here, so I took the next best thing,' she said between mouthfuls.

'We are lucky to have her,' Elizabeth said a little regretfully as she returned. She placed a tray before them with a steaming pot of coffee, two large china mugs and a delicate jug and sugar bowl. There were biscuits too, but Lucy wasn't sure she'd have room for much more than the coffee. 'Don't go trying to turn her head on us now,' she joked.

'And you've never been keen to come down and help out, Elizabeth?' Lucy asked.

'Oh, me?' She reddened slightly. 'I'm not sure what I could do. I'm not sure I'd be any good at anything down here really.' She was blushing now as if she'd been caught out in some embarrassing way. 'I come down and tidy up about the place, in the evenings, when everyone has left, but... well, Eric was never keen on me working.'

'That's a shame. I'm sure you'd have been brilliant front of house,' Lucy said and she meant it. She could imagine Elizabeth O'Shea being highly organised, business-like, but sympathetic. She was refined enough to give confidence to anyone she had dealings with, but unassuming enough to make them feel comfortable.

'If you find yourselves over-run, I'd be happy to help out in any way I can.' She smiled, the embarrassment fading a little from her cheeks, perhaps believing the offer would never be accepted.

'Really?' Alice asked. 'You'd come down here and help out?' She looked a little wide-eyed towards Lucy and they shared a smile that counted for a lot more than the words they'd passed between them. It was obvious to them both after the morning they'd put in, they could halve the work with just a little better organisation. Quite a number of the patients Lucy had seen could as easily have been taken care of by a competent nurse. Indeed, a quarter of them need never have come near the surgery to begin with, if they'd had a nurse who was prepared to travel out and do house calls.

'Yes, I suppose, if it would help, although, I really can't see what I could do that might actually take any work out of this place for either of you...' She smiled thoughtfully then, looked down at the tray. 'Well, maybe apart from making lunch for you.'

'And believe me that is very much appreciated,' Lucy said and she meant it. She looked at her watch then: almost two thirty. 'Gosh, it's hard to believe we're halfway through the day,' she said as she poured coffee for them.

'You're kidding, right?' Alice laughed. 'We're not even a third through the day yet; the afternoon is our busiest time.' She shook her head at Lucy's happy naivety.

'Really?' Lucy asked and she knew that they were in for an even busier afternoon when she saw the two women share a smile between them. 'In that case, I think we definitely need to look at reorganising how we do things around here.'

By the time Alice opened the front door of the surgery twenty minutes later, they had cleared away their lunch dishes and set the surgery to rights for the afternoon round of patients. Lucy had carried a heavy carver dining chair from the main house and placed it next to Alice's behind the poky reception desk.

'Consider yourself on work experience,' she said to the slightly surprised Elizabeth who found herself perched there to learn how to run the reception area of the practice when Alice would be taken up with nursing duties once they got organised.

'It feels a bit odd.' Elizabeth giggled and there was something faintly giddy about her expression, as if she'd been let off to explore in a toy shop. Alice had run off to the loo before heading out to open the front door. 'What will people think?' Elizabeth asked conspiratorially.

'What does it matter what they think? The main thing is, you're giving us a hand and in a week's time, it won't matter who's working as the doctor, you will know as much about this practice as anyone.' Lucy gave Elizabeth a final smile of encouragement before heading back into the depressing box room that served as the main surgery office.

By seven o'clock, Lucy was completely worn out. They let the last patient of the day out into the cooling evening air and it was with a sense of achievement that she pulled the bolt closed on the outer door and switched off the porch light behind her. She had to admit, tired and all as she was, it had been a good day.

'I'm not sure what I'd expected,' she said to her mother later as she sat down to a hearty casserole that had been kept warm in the little stove. 'But it was a good day. The villagers are lovely, every one of them; you couldn't get nicer.'

'They're probably mightily relieved that it's you in that chair and not Thea Gilchrist. That woman was enough to drive us all to an early grave.'

'Ah, Mum, I'm sure she wasn't that bad.' Lucy shook her head.

'They were all raving about you in the shop earlier. Mrs Clarke said it's the first time she's come out of that surgery without a prescription for antibiotics and she's delighted with herself. She said, just feeling that someone had listened to her was enough to know that you knew what you were doing.'

'That's nice to hear,' Lucy said as neutrally as she could

manage – she'd been a bit shocked when she glanced at Mrs Clarke's file. The woman had more antibiotics in her at this stage than the nearby chemist. She had a feeling that there wasn't a lot wrong with Mrs Clarke that a regular walk and moving a few inches further from the table wouldn't sort, but the woman was lonely. She needed to connect with people and feel that she had more to talk about than just her imagined ill health. 'Is there a women's group here in the village?'

'A women's group?' Her mother smiled.

'Not for me, but you know, I'm just interested in what's going on in the village. It's useful, when you meet people, to know what's happening,' she said managing to keep a slightly disinterested tone in her voice. The fact was, that there were four women who'd turned up to the surgery today and she had a feeling that if they had something productive to do with their time, they mightn't notice the pains and aches that took up far too much of their attention.

'There used to be one, but these last few years, it's died off a bit. You know how these things go; someone starts them up and well… every dog has its day,' her mother said gently. She looked across at Niall who had hardly said a word since she got home. With that, he pushed back from the table and left the kitchen, slamming the door behind him.

'Oh dear,' Jo said softly. 'I'm afraid he's not very impressed with Ballycove. I tried to get him out for a walk today, see if he could meet up with some of the other kids around the village? I'm afraid he wouldn't go much further than the pier with Dora.'

'Don't worry about him, Mum, he'll get over it; if anything, getting out of his comfort zone might be the best thing that ever happened to him.' Although Lucy knew it would be better if she got to spend a little more time with him while he was adjusting to village life. She moved towards the kettle and took down a mug for each of them. 'Actually, I wanted to talk to you on our own anyway.'

'Oh?'

'I'm worried about you.' Lucy knew there was no point in beating about the bush with her mother. She'd see right through her. 'When were you last at the doctor?'

'There's nothing wrong with me,' her mother said sharply.

'Well, there's no denying that you're fading away and I've heard you trying to catch your breath while you're going about the house.'

'I'm perfectly fine. I go swimming every day; I'm looking forward to seeing you do the same. Hah,' Jo said getting up from the table, but she stopped when Lucy reached out and touched her hand.

'Just let me do a blood test, okay? It'll only take a minute and I'll send off the samples tomorrow through the surgery.'

'Fine, but just so you know I'm as healthy as an old trout,' Jo said dropping into the chair and rolling up her sleeve for the inevitable.

The night was beginning to toss up a northerly icy wind and after Lucy had cleared up the kitchen and placed the blood samples in a bag for the following day, she figured she'd better get her walk with Dora over with before it decided to turn into a fresh storm. The village streets were empty as she wound her way back up and away from the pier. She wasn't sure she wanted to walk all the way to the top. The wind would be biting and raw up there now. It was hard to believe as the rain began to fall in spiky barbs that it was only twelve hours since she'd walked along the beach, with a bright and cutting sun spitting into her eyes. Still, there was something in the silence, a fullness that held within it a treasure bigger than any city could ever hope to touch. It was a medley of community, small-town history and the rushing energy of the sea, collapsing together within the very fabric of this little village. There was something soothing about it.

She turned back when she reached the point that she'd always considered about halfway up the town. She was opposite one of the village's three pubs. The Weavers was a small bar that had only shrunk as the years had passed. It was housed in what might have been someone's front room once, but now the little terraced house had been given over entirely to the business of selling porter and making traditional music at the weekends. Tonight, the place was quiet. There would be the regular round up of patrons, sitting or standing at the bar, counting down the hours until they had to return home to their cold houses and perhaps neglected spouses.

Over her head, high up on the hill she heard the church bell ring out: nine bells. She imagined, in the little houses along the way, people resting up in their armchairs, tuning in to hear the nine o'clock news of the day. The headlines a melody of prison strikes and foreign wars – Ballycove seemed to be insulated in some ways from those terrible atrocities. This thought, while it unsettled, also made her feel a little more at home, as if, by some happy miracle *she* had settled into a comfortable chair before a roaring fire and here, everything would turn out well in the end.

It was with the intention of catching the evening news, or at least the tail end of it, that she decided to move more quickly. She called to Dora, who was dawdling by a lamp post. 'Come along, we can't stay out all night.' She was looking back, when she should have been looking forward, not expecting to run into someone else on the empty street. But that is exactly what she did. She turned the bending corner, half aware that she was following the uneven footpath, mostly feeling slightly punished at the notion that she too would like to be sitting in the front room of her mother's cosy cottage watching the day's news unfold on the slightly too large TV screen. When Bam.

For a moment, she wasn't entirely sure what had happened, but then, she felt steadying hands upon her shoulders. They were large, strong hands that seemed to anchor her in spite of herself. Behind her, she heard Dora, suddenly, too late, spring to her defence. The little dog came trailing bravely, if a little uncertainly, yapping her loudest bark in defence of her treasured mistress.

'I'm sorry.' The voice was local. She stood for a moment, looking up, perhaps a little dazed, until she realised, it was Alan – the local parish priest. They sidestepped about each other for a moment, but she had the overwhelming feeling that if this was the worst that could come to you on an evening walk, then surely Ballycove was exactly the kind of place she should be rearing her son.

The cottage was even cosier when Lucy pushed in the front door than it had been when she was leaving. There was the faint aroma of home baking in the air and the low drone of her mother's snores before the television in the sitting room. Niall had taken himself off to bed, according to her mother, with a wedge of apple pie and a tall glass of milk – probably still angry with Lucy for bringing them here.

They spent the rest of the evening in front of the fire, half dozing off while a current affairs programme played out with only a passing interest for either of them. At eleven, Lucy felt her eyes begin to close and she knew she needed to be in bed because soon she would drift off to sleep and there was nowhere in the whole world that seemed more inviting than her little bed, snugly made up in the cosy room of her childhood. It was as she was just getting in between the sheets that her mother tapped lightly on the bedroom door.

'Can I come in?' she whispered softly.

'Of course,' Lucy said and she could feel the warm drowsiness of sleep rest upon her words.

'It's just... I'm sorry, this time of night, to be bothering you, but I've been thinking of it since earlier, and I wasn't sure...' Her mother's words faltered and something in her eyes made Lucy stop. Something was wrong. This wasn't about tucking her in and making sure she had everything she needed.

'What is it, Mum?' she said softly but beneath the calm she felt a prickling panic rise from deep within her.

'It's probably nothing, and I should have mentioned it before, probably, but... well, it's not the kind of thing you just say... but since you've taken that sample, I...'

'It's okay, just tell me.' Dear God, the panic was beginning to overtake her now. There was something really bad coming; she just knew it.

'I found a lump,' Jo said softly and her eyes began to fill with tears that might have been sitting behind them for some time, but now they cascaded down her cheeks. 'About six months ago, but Dr O'Shea, well he said it was nothing, just a cyst. Then, when you took that blood sample earlier, well I haven't been feeling right for ages. Oh, Lucy, I'm so afraid,' she said finally, the sobs now taking over her whole body so she was silently shaking with the overwhelming emotion.

'It's okay; it's going to be okay,' Lucy said softly, putting her arms around her mother and knowing, only too well, that there were no guarantees that anything would ever be okay again.

PART 2

May

9

Jo

Not being particularly religious, Jo wasn't sure who to thank when the first of May turned up warm and blue-skied. She woke with the expectant thrill of summer on her windowsill; the swallows had arrived late the previous evening and on the air was the irrefutable contentment that a new season was upon them.

She had always loved May Day, she told herself as she waited for the kettle to boil for her morning cup of tea. It was not just that Elizabeth and Lucy had finally agreed to swim with her at the cove tonight. She had circled it in red on the kitchen calendar, just so Lucy would know how important it was to her; as if by osmosis it might sink into her daughter's bones and then transfer onto Elizabeth.

She rang Elizabeth at eleven in the morning about absolutely nothing more than the excuse to remind her that they had made an arrangement for later. It gave Jo an unexpected lift to hear her friend answer the surgery phone with a bright new ring to her voice; being busy suited her far more than Jo might have ever imagined.

'Maybe we should make it a little earlier?' Lucy said later as she finished eating dinner.

'Do you think Elizabeth will be too tired?' Jo hadn't thought of that before; after all, Elizabeth could be worn out after her day at the surgery.

'No. No, not at all.' Lucy stopped and then the silence that hung between them left Jo in no doubt that her daughter's worry had not been Elizabeth but Jo. She had sent off a fresh blood sample the previous day after the hospital had called to say that there had been a mix-up with labels and to be sure, it was better to run the test again.

To her credit, Elizabeth knocked on the front door at precisely eleven thirty. The night was not yet entirely dark. The clouds had moved aside and a full moon rippled silver across the soft movement of the water.

'It's going to be bloody freezing down there,' Lucy said, handing the two women heavy coats from the hall. The last thing she wanted was any of them catching cold.

'Oh, don't be such a Mary Ellen,' Jo said and shook herself out of the oversized coat. She was at the gate before any of them.

The sea was unusually calm, as nice as she could have wished for it to be. In the cove she threw off her clothes and waited while Lucy wriggled out of her jeans and then stood there shivering. Elizabeth carefully removed each garment with great care and then folded them in a neat pile.

'You're making it worse on yourself with all that shivering.' Honestly, Jo thought, she sounded the same way she had when Lucy was a child.

'Don't laugh,' Elizabeth said from behind them. 'But I didn't think we'd actually go through with this, so...' The women turned around to see her standing in her underwear, a sturdy Doreen bra and large knickers that came well above her waist. 'I couldn't find a swimsuit and...'

'For goodness' sake, Elizabeth, who's looking at you? You could take the lot off and no-one's going to see.'

'R-right,' Elizabeth said and gently peeled off the remainder of her clothes. 'Oh God.'

'Come on, ladies, it's now or never.' Jo tore away down the beach, hoping that when she hit the water Lucy would be at her side. She knew for sure Elizabeth would be, because she knew her well enough to know the only thing worse than jumping in, would be standing there in the altogether! The shrieks on either side of her made her laugh. Suddenly she remembered the first times she'd come here as the weather had grown colder. 'It's better if you swim out a little bit. Hanging about only makes you colder.' She swam out until she was certain her feet could no longer touch the seabed and then she flipped over onto her back. Soon, Elizabeth and Lucy were next to her. 'Look.' She waited while they turned to take in the sky above them.

The moon had turned out in all its satisfying fullness, a great silver-white orb for the occasion and now that the last of the day's light had finally faded away for the night, the sky shimmered with what looked like a million stars over their heads. In the distance, the village rose above them – a zigzag line of streets chasing upwards to the church spire, which was gently illuminated at its crown.

'Oh, Mum, I can't believe it's so beautiful,' Lucy said and she sounded like the child Jo remembered so vividly more often these days.

'It is. I wanted you to see it, just in case...' Jo reached out her hand towards Lucy and for a moment, they grasped each other in the silence and it felt to Jo as if they would never let each other go.

'It puts everything in perspective,' Elizabeth said after a moment.

'It certainly does,' Jo murmured.

'You know, my mother never let me go swimming with all the other village kids,' Elizabeth said softly now. 'I was always kept apart; they were never quite good enough. She always had big notions for me.'

'She must have been over the moon when you up and married the doctor.' Jo snorted.

'Actually she was, even though he was older and it was all a bit quick...'

'A bit quick?' Lucy said.

'Back then, it was all a terrible shame, but I was... you know...'

'She was pregnant.' Jo cut to the chase. The water temperatures would gnaw at them too quickly to spend time beating about the bush here.

'Oh, I didn't realise.' And then Lucy's voice drifted off, because of course, there was no child.

'The baby died.'

'That's terrible,' Lucy said, keeping her gaze firmly on the sky, because perhaps they all knew that if it wasn't for the fact that they were here and Elizabeth weren't so very vulnerable she would never have spoken about the child she had lost.

'It's all so long ago now,' Elizabeth said, her voice echoing strangely on the water. 'I thought he saved me, you know? Eric. I thought he'd saved me from the unthinkable.' She laughed then – a funny, hollow sound – and Jo closed her eyes, because she knew what was coming next.

'Eric saved himself more like.' Jo couldn't help herself.

'I don't understand,' Lucy said.

'It wasn't his baby,' Jo said.

'No. I went to have a pregnancy test – this was long before you could pick one up in the chemist's here in Ballycove and then and there he proposed to me. He didn't go down on bended knee exactly, but by the time I left the surgery that day, I had a fiancé and a baby to look forward to.'

'He just asked you to marry him?'

'Out of the blue. It suited both of us, he said. I didn't understand then what he meant, but I was just so grateful to have a way out of telling my mother. It was such a shameful thing then, different times to now when every baby is celebrated.'

'And the father?'

'He was long gone. A boy I met, Vano Birt.' Elizabeth let the name sit between them for a moment. 'He came with the carnival and then he was gone and I was left with just the memory of our time together.'

'Yes, well, Eric got the best end of the bargain,' Jo said sharply.

'He saved me from Saint Nunciata's,' Elizabeth said softly. 'Anyway, it's all a long time ago now.' The starkness of that time, so long ago, when girls were hidden away and their babies taken from them lingered for a while. From here, Jo knew, if you really strained your eyes, you could probably make out the faint outline of the old convent just beyond the village. Jo had always hated the place. She'd been delighted when it closed up. Even now, they didn't know the half of what went on in those places, but they knew enough to know that any unfortunate who ended up there would have given their eye teeth for a life as a doctor's wife instead.

But of course, that kind of escape comes with a high price and Elizabeth had paid it many times over. 'The point is that, tonight, it feels a little as if I'm making up for being held back all those years ago. I almost feel as if I'm taking up from where I left off that night I met Vano. It was the most wonderful night of my life, if I'm honest, but this...' She shuddered and Jo knew she was crying, but it was a joyful sound. 'This is simply perfect.'

IO

Niall

Niall played the dinner conversation over in his head again and again as he sat looking out at the rough seas. It wasn't that they'd argued, not by a long shot. Rather it was the fact that it felt as if they'd just settled into something out of the blue and it was so far from everything he knew. His mother and this job had dominated yet another dinner conversation and it felt like he was little more than spare baggage beside it. In fact, his mother hadn't even been angry with him. She understood what it meant, days down here – unplugged – it wasn't exactly the kind of relaxing break he'd signed up for.

He had slipped noiselessly from the cottage while his mother dozed before some boring political programme on the telly – even Dora had not heard the front door click softly as he'd left.

Niall sat for a long time on the fat stone wall that kept the sea at bay, but it was cold here. There was no getting away from the fact that the rain clouds that had settled overhead were intent on drenching everything for miles around. The sea beneath his legs had taken on a black and greenish colour, as if it might throw up the contents of its belly in ever angrier roars. It was epic, no doubting that, but it was frightening too. Occasionally a resounding roar would culminate in a surge of water that rushed over the wall alongside him. There was a storm on the way, and he'd seen before that the waves could wash away anything in their path.

After one awesome wash, he jumped back from the wall. Far off, he noticed the old cottage dug into the cliffs. He remembered it from his last visit, always empty out of season; it looked deserted tonight. He set off walking for the cottage, with no great plan in mind. Maybe it was empty and he could stay there for the night? That would teach his mother a little lesson. If he let them see that he could as easily disappear here as he could in Dublin, his mother might just decide to go home sooner rather than later.

He darted along the blackening roads, leaving the lights of Ballycove behind him quickly. Soon, he was on the narrow boreen that led to the only house overlooking the sea from these cliffs. The owner, an old man who Niall had never known, had put in a road at some point. Over the years, the peaty foundation had knotted and buckled it so it was uneven under foot and it slowed him down as he ran to escape the light rain that promised to turn into a ripping shower at any moment.

Once he reached the door of the cottage, he stopped

for a moment, taking in the silence of the place. It was only now, as he stood with his hair slapped wet against his face that he considered the possibility it might be rented out to a new tenant these days. He trod softly around the perimeter, peering in each black window, but there was no-one here. He pulled out his phone. This was a village where everyone left a key out; in fact, he wouldn't be surprised if they had left the door open. He pushed it just in case, but no, a quick search turned up a heavy black key that slipped easily into the lock and in a minute, he was inside the cottage.

He wondered about switching on a light, but decided against it for now. It was a tiny place, one main room that was kitchen, living room and lounge and off this, a bedroom. To the rear, there was a larder and then to the side a small bathroom with a walk-in electric shower that owed a lot more to considerations of access rather than design. A small smile crept up through him. It was warm. Whoever owned the place had left the heating on a timer and so, with closed-up doors and windows and walls that were almost two foot thick, it was as snug as a nest, perched high over the crashing sea below. Of course, there was no Wi-Fi, no real television service, but there was coffee in the cupboards, water in the kettle and familiar staples from home like pot noodles and a tube of Pringles.

Yes, he thought as he flicked on the kettle, this would do very nicely indeed. If he tidied up after himself and kept a low profile he could pop in and out of here again... This place could suit him perfectly. If he disappeared often enough and for long enough, knowing his mum as he did, it wouldn't take long until she realised the best thing for all would be to go back to their real lives in the city where they belonged.

Niall spotted the vodka when he'd finished the pot noodles. It was almost a full bottle, stashed top out over the old dresser. He climbed on a chair and reached in. Lovely. And behind it a bottle of whiskey sat nestled for another day. Niall never really drank, apart from an occasional half glass of wine his mother poured for him on special occasions with dinner. It just hadn't been interesting to him. It had, he knew, quite a bit to do with his father not taking a drink. His father had talked often about the life his own family had endured at the hands of his grandfather's alcoholism. Niall couldn't remember his grandfather, but he'd seen enough photographs to know that they were made of the same stuff. The notion of ending up anything like the old man had steered his dad on a completely sober path his whole life.

Damn it, what did it matter if he drank the whole bloody bottle? Who'd know about it anyway? Another voice, a cruel and twisted voice, muttered something else in his brain – and who would really care?

The cups and plates in the heavy dresser were all very old-fashioned. It was a choice of either fat builder's mugs with logos that had long gone out of use or delicate gold-patterned china that was too effeminate for real rule breaking. Niall settled on a mug and wiped it out roughly with his fingers. He poured a more than decent measure and gasped on his first gulp. God, this stuff could poison you. All the same, it wasn't about the taste, was it? Vodka or any kind of drink was all about getting smashed.

He settled the bottle on the floor beneath his feet and sprawled across an old sofa that probably was cosier if the fire was lit, but Niall was content enough in the darkened room, with the lighthouse in the distance giving off an occasional flash of light.

Funny, but once he found a grungy playlist on Spotify, he sipped the vodka steadily and soon, he'd finished the whole mug. As the night fell heavy and black around the cottage, he raised the volume on his phone until he heard a rumble of something right outside the cottage. A blinding flash of light sheeting across the sky and reflecting on the water for miles out to sea heralded the arrival of the storm. Niall was glad to be safe and warm. A part of him delighted in the notion of his mother frantic, wondering where he might be.

At around three in the morning, after he had made a sizeable impact on the bottle of vodka and when his legs could hardly hold him without the threat of buckling, he decided he might as well try out the whiskey. He pulled the chair over clumsily before the dresser. It took two attempts to get his drunken body standing up so he could reach the stash. He felt around the dusty top, blindly and drunkenly having an idea that it must be there, when suddenly the most terrifying snap grabbed his hand.

Pain shot through him so quickly, he didn't have time to register the mouse trap on the end of his fingers. It sent an electrifying current of fear and shock through his whole body. It knocked him back, throwing his already wobbling frame off balance. He felt himself, hands waving in the air, his whole body like a wind sock, being blown out against forces of alcohol and gravity that were too fine for his fuzzy brain to conquer. He seemed to fall, in slow motion, the chair moving away from under his feet, the soles of his feet, pushing against it and then, slowly, slowly, his body sailing like a grotesque puppet to the flag-stoned floor.

He thought he heard the crash of his head on the stones, imagined he felt warm blood seep about the cold stone. He knew that he was going to be sick, very sick. And then, as a heavy weight pounded against the back of his head, someone switched off the power and Niall fell into unconsciousness. The worst thing was, not a living soul knew about it.

II

Dan

Dan caught the last of the fresh sea breeze before the downpour began to spit in tiny spiteful daggers from the hooded clouds overhead. He wasn't sure what he thought of this place yet. So far, all he'd seen was rain, green fields, and grey skies and seas that might easily be mistaken for each other, such was the depth of colour in them both. The people were nice. He'd only met a handful, but Mr Singh, the shopkeeper and the doctor's widow, Mrs O'Shea – their welcome was genuine. He could sense it and it warmed him when he'd picked up enough provisions to do him until the following morning. All the same, he probably couldn't have picked a more depressing day to arrive back in Ballycove after taking a short trip back to the city for little more than distraction and printing supplies, There was a storm pulling in over the Atlantic. He could feel it, in that shop, when the sergeant had arrived in to ask about the missing boy.

'That's right,' he confirmed gruffly for Mr Singh, 'Jo's grandson, a city boy, he has no idea of what a strom in Ballycove can do. Mind you, it's probably half the reason he's missing. If he'd known what he was about and made some friends, he mightn't be sitting with his legs dangling over the sea wall in an oncoming gale.'

'Poor Jo and Lucy.' Mrs O'Shea shook her head. 'She's taken over from my husband, you know, in the surgery,' she said filling in blank spaces that really made no sense to Dan who'd only just arrived.

'That's nice,' he said rather uselessly and then caught the shopkeeper's eye.

'Her husband was the GP. Poor Doctor O'Shea – unfortunately he passed away and we were all so sorry, but we've been lucky enough to get someone to fill in. Of course, we all still miss the old doctor,' Mr Singh said diplomatically.

'Thank you, dear,' Mrs O'Shea said before turning her attention to the sergeant. 'So there's still no news?'

'They think the boy has gone into the sea?' Mr Singh whispered.

'It looks that way. Last time he was spotted was sitting on the wall opposite his grandmother's cottage. You know what those winds were like last night: one swell and he'd be washed out in a flash.'

'That's terrible,' Dan said.

'I don't know how a kid can sneak out a doorway and no-one notices until hours later. It makes you wonder, and the mother a doctor too. It goes to show you...' The sergeant might have been up for a bitching session about some of the locals, but remembering Dan was standing there made him stop up short. 'Well, let's hope that he moved off beforehand and he's met up with some kid and lost track of time,' the sergeant said although his expression was enough to know that he thought this was unlikely. 'It's a lot of time to lose track of, since last night, mind,' he grumbled before heading off into what remained of the storm.

'Is there a search party?' Dan asked as his few groceries were run through the checkout.

'There won't be tonight. It's too dangerous to put a boat out in that and, let's face it, if he's out there, he's already lost.' The shopkeeper sighed.

'I suppose if there's something organised tomorrow we can all give a hand, right?' Dan said paying in euros before heading out in the darkening evening.

It caught him up, the idea of such tragedy occurring in a place that seemed to be so far removed from the violence and crime of London life that he'd become accustomed to seeing on his news every night. Over here it was different; from the way the shopkeeper had taken the news; the loss of one of their own, it was personal. It turned out that they hardly even knew the boy, in the end.

It may have been dark and overcast, but there was no denying the drama of Ballycove. The coastline sat in a jagged crouch, leering out across the Atlantic. The cottage on the headland might be the centre middle seat, looking down on the most spectacular theatre imaginable – the living, breathing ocean. Dan knew it was just the weather that made the place feel as if a foreboding character was lurking somewhere just out of sight. He put it down to the missing boy. Something like that stirs a place up, filling even the emptiest of places with impending tragedy. It set Dan's imagination on end, a bristling sense that there were ideas, if not always very happy stories lurking just beneath the surface.

Soon he was turning off the main road up the narrow track. When his headlights skirted across the rough patchy land, he spotted a dozen rabbits scattering away into their burrows in response to his unwelcome intrusion. The cottage was not big. Rather, it seemed like a bent geriatric, pinned to the hillside, facing off the Atlantic stoically. Dan pulled up at the front door. There was a small window either side of a deep porch and a whistling chorus of rattling shells hanging from the gate caught in the ferocious wind. There wasn't a soul about for miles, and yet, it didn't feel lonely here – an odd thing, since he'd felt tragically isolated so recently in the middle of London.

He walked about the property first, taking in the rattling wind, the sea air and the freezing drops of rain that fell in spikes on his shoulders and were cold enough to penetrate his jacket. A narrow paving led right around the house. There was no place here for livestock or any kind of farming venture. The owners had seen to it that this place was low on maintenance and uncomplicated. After walking all about the house and glancing through the windows, he knew he would have to go inside. Not that he was putting it off exactly, but probably, it was the idea that once he was in, that was it; he was tired after the journey. There would be no going out to get wet and blown away again. He would settle down with his cooked chicken, his bottle of burgundy and his thoughts.

Going back to the car again, he pulled out his groceries and key for the cottage. He slid it into the keyhole and the door opened easily. The rental agents had emailed a list of instructions to him and he remembered them once more. He already had a mental to-do list for when he got in the door: everything from turning on the central heating to checking that water was running clear before he filled the kettle for a cup of tea. There was a whole paragraph about how to manage the well should he find himself without clear running water. Apparently, there were pumps and electrics involved and if the worst happened, they had included a plumber's mobile number with a good luck shamrock by its side.

Inside the door, he reached for a light switch. The bulb threw a weak glow about the porch and as he pushed past the next door. It opened into a warmer than expected room. The heat was not the only thing that surprised him.

The boy was half sitting on the hearth rug, his back against the couch. He smiled lazily, as if he wasn't sure if he was seeing things or if Dan was actually there before him. Dan couldn't take in much more than the gash that ran along the side of the boy's head, but in his periphery vision, he caught the half bottle of vodka, the overturned chair, the empty pot noodles and the bloodstain on the rug. This apparition pulled Dan up short for a moment – perhaps he was in the wrong house? But then quickly, he went over the details of the key in his pocket, the description of the journey and the fact that everything about the cottage was exactly as he'd remembered. He knew that the mistake had not been his.

'Hullo,' the boy said and there was the unmistakable sound of drunkenness in his almost breaking voice.

'Hello, yourself,' Dan said, dropping his bag down on the floor and pushing out the door. 'I suppose, you're the welcoming committee?' he asked, not entirely sure what else to say.

'Yup, you're welcome. Fancy a… drink?' he managed between hiccups.

'How many of those have you had exactly?'

'What are you? My mother?' The boy's features turned suddenly dark.

'Hardly, but let's face it, you've had enough – coffee, that's what you need,' he said and turned back towards his car to carry in more of the provisions he'd just picked up in the supermarket. It was as he was switching on the kettle that something dawned on him. 'You're not Niall? Are you?'

'How'd you know that?' The boy looked as if Dan had just divined some rare truth.

'How did I know?' Dan blew out an exasperated breath. 'Because half the village is out looking for you, that's how. Your mother is probably beside herself with worry and they're going to deploy a lifeboat out on the bay to find you as soon as the storm dies down.'

'Well it's nice to hear I've been missed,' Niall slurred.

'I'm sure it is.' Dan bit down on the anger that was rising up in him. 'Anyway, it's time to ring your mum, and then we'll see about getting you into some shape and back to her.' He picked up the kid's mobile from the chair at his shoulder and handed it to him. The boy scowled at him from beneath knitted eyebrows. 'Seriously, she's going to be in a bad way. The whole village is up to ninety worrying about you...' He let his words peter off, but the boy just stared at him. 'Look, make the call; do you really want to be responsible for someone being drowned out in that sea while they're searching for you? Don't be a complete ass,' he said, shoving it into the boy's hand.

Dan turned and listened while the boy rang his mother, busying himself preparing coffee, divvying up the half chicken between two rolls so at least when he returned the kid, he might not be quite so badly hung over. He handed him the coffee when the call was finished. 'Well?'

'Yeah, you were right, she was worried.' He sipped the coffee then, pulling himself up a little higher against the chair at his back. 'I must have blacked out.' He rubbed his head then. 'I didn't realise. I've been here since... yesterday.'

'You fell, I'd say.' Dan pointed to the chair and the stain that had dried into the rug. 'You've got a matching patch on the side of your head.'

'So, this headache might not be all about the...' he picked up the almost empty bottle from the floor '...vodka?'

'Alcohol won't help – I can tell you that much.' Dan dropped into the chair opposite the kid and handed him one of the rolls. They both began to wolf down their food.

'So, are you here on holidays or are you going to live here, now?' Niall asked when he'd finished and wiped away the crumbs from his sweatshirt.

'For a while, I suppose, yes,' Dan said and it surprised

him, because it wasn't just a holiday now that he was here. He did not have a return ticket booked. In a week someone else would be living in his flat, sleeping in the bed he'd so recently slept in while he pottered about here on a cliff side overlooking the ocean.

'Mental.' The boy looked around the cottage now, taking it all in again. 'You're English?'

'That's right. London – I'm just having a bit of a break, looking to... research, and a few months in peace and quiet.' Dan smiled; he liked that idea.

'Yep, like I said mental.' The boy looked at him now. 'What would anyone want to come here for when you could be in London? What kind of work do you do?'

'I'm a writer, so the quiet will be good – less distracting.' Dan wasn't sure why he told the boy that. His writing job with the BBC was gone now and after what happened there, he knew the chances of finding another were thread-thin.

'Right.' Niall looked thoughtful then for a moment. 'What kind of books?'

'I write for television.'

'Christ, even worse. My grandmother will be bloody all over you. She used to be involved in amateur dramatics back in the day – still harping on about it now.'

'I'm not sure Am Dram is my thing.'

'Too good for it, are you?' Niall scowled.

'No. Not at all. Any kind of theatre is worthwhile. It's just I've only come to the end of a project and I want to start something different. Being here is all about...' Dan sighed. What in God's name was he doing making excuses to this kid?

'You're here to chill?'

'Yeah, I suppose, something like that.' Dan thought, perhaps taking time to catch his breath might be as much as he'd need.

'Yeah, well, I suppose this place will be good for unwinding. You can sit outside, put your music on as loud as you want and watch the seagulls all day long if you feel like it,' Niall said and there was an unexpected softness to his voice. 'You won't be... It's very isolated up here.'

'I suppose it is – maybe the quiet will send me back to London more quickly than I'm planning.' He wouldn't add that he had an endless selection of books and music to keep him going for at least a year if he felt like it. 'I'll probably hunker down with a decent movie, a good dinner – that'll be enough to start.'

'This whole village is a bit... out of the way, if you ask me. It's full of auld ones and everything about it is backward, but if it's quiet you're after you'll get it in spades. Probably be bored out of your brains by next week though.'

'You're new here, right?' Dan remembered the conversation in the shop earlier.

'How'd you know that?'

'They were talking about you in the supermarket when I dropped in to pick up supplies.' Dan smiled. 'You could always come back and visit me, for a coffee – not vodka, mind – some days, if you fancied it.' He had a feeling the kid didn't have much else to keep him out of trouble.

'Yeah, all right, maybe.' There was a hint of enthusiasm in Niall's answer, but not enough to give away the fact that he might actually turn up.

'You might even help me find the best beaches about the place for swimming.'

'I might, but you'll be the only one getting wet, mate. I'm not likely to put myself through that torture until we hit July at least.' Niall pulled himself up. It was time to head back to normality and maybe the coffee and the chance to sit and gather his thoughts was enough to galvanise him. Dan didn't ask why he'd come to the cottage, or why the sergeant seemed to think that he might have thrown himself into the ocean, but he knew enough to realise that the kid needed something more than he already had in life.

Even in the hammering rain, the village was handsome. Perhaps the bleakness made it more striking. Dan clocked the mileage at just less than three miles from its centre – not a bad stroll if he fancied it on a bright day. He could imagine the narrow streets, come summer, filled with the scent of the ocean, flower baskets tumbling over with brightly coloured petunias and lobelia, a sea of river daisies waving from window boxes. It was a village that graduated from the simple fishing cottages, with remnants of sea-rusted chains about their doors up to a gothic church whose spires reached towards heaven, lit by strategic soft cannons of sepia golden glow.

'I'll probably be grounded for a month.' Niall's words cut into his thoughts.

'I'd say you'll be lucky if you're not grounded until you're twenty-five, at least.' Dan laughed. 'But still, your mum, well, she's just going to be so relieved to have you home. If you play it kind of cool...'

'How do you mean?'

'I mean, don't go off on one. Don't be stroppy. Put your arms around her and tell her you're sorry for making her worry, but it wasn't entirely your fault.'

'Of course, it wasn't my bloody fault,' Niall said.

'You see, that's what I mean: try and chill a bit, let her do the talking.' He nodded towards the raging sea. 'Try to imagine what's been going through her head.'

'Yeah, well, if she didn't drag me halfway across the country – who knows...'

'Look.' Dan stopped the car. 'Listen to me. I don't know what's happened between you and your mum, but I'm telling you this: if you want to come out of tonight without paying back for the next year, you need to be smart and you need to grow up. I know, you're a kid, but if, like you said earlier, your dad's not about, that leaves a fairly big space to fill and it's up to you to fill it.'

'You don't know my mum.' Niall laughed. 'Sorry, but she's too busy working to notice who's the man about the house.'

'There's one thing you learn as you get to be an *old* man like me.' Dan smiled now at Niall. Old is relative, especially when you're a teenager. 'It's never too late to be the man you can be, nor is it ever too soon.'

They stopped just short of a couple of old fishermen's cottages, solid and modest. Niall's house was at the very end. Dan could see two women inside clearly, sitting together, as casually as if they were part of a book club.

'Wish me luck,' Niall said gingerly.

'You won't need it.'

'Come in with me, just for a minute.' Niall looked at him now and even here in the hushed darkness, it sounded more like a plea than an invitation.

'Okay, but only for a minute. Your mother will want to get back to normal. I'm sure it's been a nightmare for her.' He followed Niall and waited while the door was pulled back.

'Oh, God.' Niall's mother grabbed him by both shoulders and clasped him as if she'd never let him go again. 'Oh, thank God,' she said, over and over again. 'I thought you were…Oh, I can't believe… you're not,' she said and the words probably only covered a tiny fraction of the emotions swarming within her. Niall stood there and managed to put his arms around his mother and embrace her in return. Soon, a torrent of tears began to flow without any embarrassment between them.

'I'm sorry, I didn't mean…' Niall stood back from her, for a moment; raised his hand to his head. 'I must have conked out and then…' he nodded towards Dan '…he found me and… Mum, I had no idea that…'

'Let me see you.' She walked him slowly towards the centre of the room, holding his shoulders, eying his gait and then, she angled his head to peer at the wound that had almost dried now, the blood caked in spurts around the yellowing bruise. 'Yes, that could have knocked you out for a while all right,' she said, but her nostrils sniffed the air and there was no denying the smell of alcohol. She was wise enough to know this wasn't the time to take on that conversation. 'I should bring you to A&E, just for a scan, to be on the safe side, but at least you are at home.' She looked now at Dan. 'How do I ever thank you...'

'Dan.' He stuck his hand out, the introductions to Jo and Lucy, quickly made. 'There's no need, I'm just glad he's safe and well. He's a good lad. This was just an unfortunate series of events.' He smiled at that.

'Ah.' Lucy smiled now. 'That was one of Niall's favourite books when he was younger.'

'Mam,' Niall said, obviously embarrassed now.

'Of course,' his grandmother said then, 'you're here on holidays. I was telling you about him earlier. Elizabeth met him in the supermarket. He's taking over Victor White's place,' she said now to confirm the village grapevine was correct.

'You've got me,' he said smiling and he liked very much the idea that here, as far as these people were concerned, he was doing just that, taking a break – not running away from the failure that his life in London had become.

12

Elizabeth

The two weeks they had agreed on had turned into a month and now, it looked as if they might make it to two months since Lucy had agreed to take over the practice just to help out. There was energy about the place, something that Elizabeth couldn't quite put her finger on, but there all the same, since Lucy had arrived. Of course, she was efficient. She had completely reorganised how the surgery was being run within the first couple of days. There was no doubt that they had saved time by simply freeing up Alice to take on house calls to the very elderly who had routine bandage changes, heart and blood pressure checks or simply had come into the habit of popping in for a chat in the waiting room and a brisk check-over with a doctor who barked at them.

Lucy filled Eric's old medical bag with a blood pressure cuff, a pin light, thermometer, his old stethoscope and a plethora of gloves, bandages and dressings. Elizabeth told her to keep an eye on her mileage so they could set up an expense account and they'd see her at lunchtime. She was armed with little more than a list of house calls on that first morning, her surprisingly able qualifications and the effortless charm of one who knows how to handle patients of all ages and temperaments with ease. Mornings, they'd agreed would be appointment only, with enough space between each to ensure that everyone was running almost on time and there was a brisk movement through the little waiting area so it never had more than one or two patients in the queue.

They had set to – Lucy, Niall and Elizabeth – together one evening, emptying out what had been little more than a junk room off to the side of the practice. It seemed, when they entered it, that it was the kind of space where Eric had never really crossed the threshold. Elizabeth imagined him, standing at the door, then hovering briefly and throwing what he no longer wanted towards the far wall, before turning the key on the little room firmly again. It took two evenings to clear it out and although it was full mainly of junk, beneath it all, was an ancient examination table, a beautiful roll-top desk and a generous apothecary cabinet that mightn't have a whole lot of practical application but filled a corner and if they'd had the manpower to shift it, would have looked gorgeous in a proper waiting room with a huge vase of flowers on top.

Over two nights, they'd managed to clear out the junk, wash down the walls and Niall gave the place a quick lick of paint one afternoon when the rain outside meant that he had no excuse not to. Alice was thrilled with her new consulting room where she would provide triage and basic medical care and shorten the queue for Lucy after her house calls were complete.

'I love it,' Alice said when Elizabeth led her into the little examination room once it was ready. 'It's just perfect.'

'Oh, dear, I'm afraid it's a bit of a mishmash,' Elizabeth said because apart from the few bits of furniture that had been buried beneath the trash, they'd hauled down carver chairs from the dining room and hung old prints from a spare bedroom on the walls. Lucy had picked fresh wild flowers – gorse and enormous happy dog daisies on her morning walk – and a view of the overgrown garden completed the easy, if not exactly sterile feel to the place.

'No, she's right, it's perfect; exactly what we're going for,' Lucy said expertly. 'It's an old practice. We can't compete with the shiny new medical centres in the bigger towns, but the reason you're going to get patients coming back here is because we're offering a top-class medical opinion, in a small village atmosphere.' She smiled then. 'We want the place to feel welcoming and relaxed, the kind of place that downplays the bad news and makes people feel like they're a little lighter leaving.'

'I think between you, you're already managing that,' Elizabeth said.

'Between *us*,' Lucy corrected her softly.

The thing that really surprised Elizabeth, apart from how busy the practice was, was actually how much money flowed through the place. On her first morning, the small drawer filled up with fifty-euro notes so quickly that soon she was tucking them beneath the drawer to keep the thing looking tidy. At the end of the day, they'd taken in far more than she assumed was made in a week. Again, Lucy had changed things around when she arrived. Rather than patients handing over their payment to the doctor, they set up a proper area so a receipt could be issued and a record made of all payments at the reception desk. This, she told Elizabeth, would make it a lot easier for her to see exactly what the practice could be worth before she went about making any decisions to sell it on in the future.

By the end of that first week, between the actual work of the place, knowing what the income was like and enjoying being part of it all, Elizabeth had begun to feel very differently about the future of the practice.

'It's not a golden hen, but it's a very good income,' Lucy agreed at the end of a long day, where the practice had been brisk and steady. 'You'll still have to pay for insurance and supplies and...' She lowered her voice then, aware that Alice was next door. 'You should probably look at Alice's salary. Eric was paying her a pittance. She should at least be paid a community nurse's wage, since that's the work she will be doing.'

'I was going to ask you about that,' Elizabeth said, closing the door softly behind her. She had been shocked when she realised what Alice received for a full week's work; it was verging on slave labour when you divided it out at an hourly rate. 'Will you let me know what the rates are? She's worth every penny that's due to her for her qualifications,' Elizabeth said softly. 'There needs to be mileage too, for that little car of hers. She covered a lot of ground this week.'

'She won't be expecting a raise.' Lucy smiled.

'Probably not, but even so...' Elizabeth felt embarrassed at how miserably her husband had treated her. It turned out, when you looked at the weekly takings and the money that he managed to fritter away between the pub and bookies, he'd treated Alice every bit as shoddily as he'd treated Elizabeth. 'We'll set things straight and then I can start thinking of the future,' Elizabeth said softly.

'It's too soon to go making any big decisions yet,' Lucy told her. 'Just sit tight for a few months. Certainly, you'd be mad to go handing the place over to the likes of that awful woman who covered for your husband.'

'Thea Gilchrist? Not likely, not now.' Elizabeth smiled, thinking of what a near miss she'd had if she'd been foolish enough to let the other woman take the reins of the place from her.

It seemed to Elizabeth that once she began helping out in the surgery the weeks just fell into each other, like a lazy train of dominoes, each day following easily and happily from the last. She quickly managed to build up something like a routine. Arriving bright and early to open up the surgery, she brewed fresh coffee before Lucy and Alice arrived. The days were filled with meeting people and maybe counting her blessings too. Then, for that last delicious hour, she went about all the little jobs that tidied away her work for the day.

It surprised her just how much had to be done, from lodging the takings, replacing the files and finally tidying up generally, so they were ready for the next day.

Arriving back in her own kitchen, the silence after such

a frenetic day was suddenly a welcome bliss. Dinner alone – looking out onto the garden – was not the empty, lonely affair she had expected it to be since Eric had passed away. Rather, she was very often entertained by the busy wildlife at play outside her window. If anything, she wondered if it had been lonelier when he'd been alive, when she'd had the expectation of so much more knocked out of her.

Sitting here, watching a tiny robin peck about the ground, with the weariness and fulfilment of a busy day behind her, she realised that she was very much at peace with herself.

13

Niall

Considering how long they'd been here, Niall thought it was time to put things straight with his mother.

'Look, I'm not saying that there's anything wrong with it, I just need to know when we're going back to Dublin,' he said, because the truth was, even if he hated school and hadn't a friend to call his own there, at least he felt invisible during the summer holidays. He could hole up in their anonymous house and play games all day long. Here in Ballycove, it was painfully obvious that he was just an outsider, killing time with not much more to do than walk the beach or help his grandmother with her shopping.

'Listen, Niall.' She switched on the bedside light and sat down on the side of his bed. 'I've been thinking, I want you to be happy and if you think that your father could make you happier than being here, well...' She said the words softly, but there was a grief to them that was immeasurable.

'You're saying that I could live with him?'

'I suppose I'm saying I could ask.' Her voice was as gentle as he remembered it to be when he was a tiny kid and for a second, he felt overwhelmed with the kind of love he'd forgotten he had felt for her all those years ago. It seemed like a lifetime away, but of course, it was probably only four or five years earlier.

'He'll say yes,' Niall said and it scared him a little that the confidence that shot through in his voice didn't quite reach his heart.

'I have no doubt he will want you, but that doesn't mean you can book your flight just yet.' She smiled bravely then. 'There'll be things to consider, like school and visas and...' She didn't add his dad's new wife, but *she* was always hanging there between them all.

'My flight?' Niall couldn't keep the excitement from his voice. 'So, it'd mean me going out there to live?'

'That seems like the only way we can make it happen for you now, I suppose,' she said and he wondered what she would do without him, because he knew that even if she started a new life down here in Ballycove, his leaving would be like losing his father all over again.

'I think,' Niall said, making some effort to look into his mother's eyes, knowing that he was going to cast a heap of pain into her heart, 'I think it might be good to find out if I could. I think it would be better than...' he said softly.

'Okay, well, leave it with me for now,' she said. 'It's a lot to take in and a lot to get organised. Nighty, night, my darling,' she whispered before kissing him gently on his forehead and stealing out the door, leaving only the faint trace of bergamot and a lingering sadness in her absence.

As he drifted off to sleep, maybe, Niall realised, he was sorry too. He was sorry that his dad had left and that the lives they'd thought were guaranteed forever had come to such an abrupt end. Niall shuddered. He turned over on his side, facing the window. Reaching out he pulled the curtains back silently. The night sky was patchy blackness. There were no stars catching the clouds tonight. There was no moon peering in at him. He would have to make do with the endless tattoo of spiking rain that cut against the old window.

Soon, he was drifting off, thinking of that unexpected warmth he felt when he'd returned to the house after they'd thought he'd been lost in the storm. Niall had liked it. Perhaps, this place wouldn't be so bad, if they had some measure of the life he'd remembered when his father had been here. Back then, his parents had friends, people who came over for dinner at the weekend, people who drank wine in the garden and joined them for walks in the Dublin Mountains when the snow was on the ground.

Of course, he realised now that his parents' friends had divided into two camps – the bigger of which fell on the side of his father. Niall felt it was hardly surprising at the time. Back when it had all gone wrong, his mother had been a wreck. There was no point visiting their house then and expecting a good time. His mother hadn't been up for entertaining or mingling or even trying to pretend.

With that thought, Niall felt himself drift off into a deep sleep. Only in the morning he'd wonder at the notion that his father had managed to carry on as if nothing much had changed in the world and for some strange reason, over a year after it had all happened, this seemed like a fresh revelation.

The next day, his grandmother didn't call Niall until after two and then they sat down to brunch together. They spent a leisurely hour, between readying their meal and then sitting at the small kitchen table overlooking the rocky garden that fell away towards an old brick wall at the end. Amid all of the emotion since they'd arrived, the one thing that had registered with Niall was his grandmother's appearance. She had become old-looking. It wasn't that her hair had greyed more or that she walked with a stoop, it was something more abstract, and yet weirdly more profound. She was tired. Niall wasn't sure if that fatigue was all about the drama that had kicked up around him, or if it was something else, just the amalgamation of all the worries of the last few years, all coming together to wash the vitality from her. The realisation added to a new emotion that Niall had become aware was beginning to sit somewhere at the back of his conscience. Was it guilt?

'It's not that bad, is it?' she asked as they sat finishing their coffee. He could see that fatigue hadn't dulled her ability to see right through him.

'What?' Part of his brain was thinking, *please, not the big heavy conversation now.* He had actually thought they might get away without this at all.

'Everything, I mean, you know, we're all doing our best, but... well...' she said. 'I know that you're a bit thrown by your mum taking up the job at the surgery, but it's only to see how things go. She hasn't jacked in her job or your lives in Dublin. Do you know, I don't think I've seen her as happy in ages?' Of course, she was talking about his mother's job.

'I know you're right.' He did. He'd seen it, compared to when she came home from a shift at the hospital; she was enthusiastic, as if suddenly she was doing something that meant something to her. 'It's just... I feel like it's come out of the blue...'

'And it has,' his grandmother agreed. 'For both of you, but that doesn't make it a bad thing. Once you start making friends here, it'll be different, you'll see.' She smiled kindly at him and he wondered if his mum had mentioned the idea of him going to live in Australia. He had a feeling his grandmother would be every bit as bereft if he left as she had been when they thought he'd fallen over the pier wall. He decided it was best not to mention it, no point in upsetting her. Instead, she sent him on an errand to deliver an apple pie to a shop on Garden Square.

Niall hadn't noticed Mr Huang's piano shop before; well you wouldn't, would you? It was faded and shaded and a sign in the window said if you were interested in looking around you could ring the doorbell and someone would come to let you in. Niall rang the bell and waited, holding the warm apple pie close to him and enjoying the smell of freshly stewed fruit and warm cloves.

'Hi.' A young girl, about his age, answered the door.

'Oh, hi, hello, um, I mean...' he mumbled, because he had forgotten exactly what he was meant to be doing here, talking to a pretty girl in the middle of the afternoon. 'I mean, here.' He held out the pie. 'My grandmother asked me to send this over for Mr Huang.'

'That's my dad.' She smiled, taking the pie. 'I'm Zoe and you must be Mrs Harris's grandson... Neill?'

'Niall,' he corrected her a little too formally.

'Oh, okay. Well, Niall...' She waited for an uncomfortable moment, when neither had very much to say. 'I suppose I'll be seeing you around; that's if you're staying on in town?'

'I um, I suppose you will,' he said and backed away from the door, trying and failing miserably to pretend that each step wasn't achingly self-conscious. Then, from a small distance, he shouted, 'I'll see you around, Zoe Huang,' before racing back to his grandmother's house.

For some reason the rest of the day seemed to pass by in a lazy haze; perhaps he was getting used to not having his PlayStation, but it was late in the evening before he even began to think about it again. And then, his mother had returned from work and it seemed he had more pressing things to think about.

'Did you get a chance to talk to Dad?'

'Yes, I asked him.'

'And?'

'There are some things he has to figure out. Of course, he likes the idea, I knew he would, but there are practicalities. He said he'll ring on Sunday,' she said neutrally and Niall wasn't sure what to read into that, because the words alone led him to believe that it could be a possibility, but the tone cautioned him not to set his heart on it. 'So, have you plans, for the weekend?'

'Maybe,' he said disinterestedly, because he didn't really have any plans, except that Dan, the guy who had managed to pick him up off his living room floor, clean up the mess he'd made and then smooth things over with his mother, had texted an hour earlier and invited him to go for a hike and a cookout if the weather was fine. Niall surprised himself when he realised that he wouldn't half mind going for a hike with the guy. It certainly beat knocking about the village on his own, or worse, hanging about the house while his grandmother tiptoed around him, trying to walk the fine line between spoiling and stifling him.

'You won't...' she said softly. 'You won't do anything stupid, will you?'

'Mum, I've never considered doing anything stupid. That was an accident, but no, I have no intention of jumping into the sea in a bid to end it all any time soon,' he said sarcastically.

'Please, don't talk like that,' she murmured, because after a long day in the surgery, she was too tired to fight with him.

'Sorry,' he said and he meant it. He must have, because he couldn't remember when he'd last apologised for one of his cynical comments. 'Anyway, I might go for a hike, tomorrow, with Dan.'

'Dan?' she said a little vaguely, perhaps trying to picture some local kid. 'Saturday? I was going to ask you to come over to Ballybrack with me. There's an exhibition and...'

'Why don't you bring Gran and Mrs O'Shea? I'm sure they'd love all that stuff.' He wasn't sure what that stuff was, but his mother's idea of an afternoon out generally involved looking at some scruffy artist's work, hanging in a coffee shop where a sliver of cake set you back a fiver and they still expected a donation on top of that.

'Hmm, maybe.'

Niall closed his eyes that night, knowing that the response from his father could go either way, but maybe that didn't seem as terrible as it might have a week earlier, or even just before he'd run into Zoe Huang.

14

Elizabeth

The improving weather also brought more people down onto the beach. Youngsters had set up a barbecue the previous day. Jo had rung to tell her that she might need to think about buying a swimming costume. Elizabeth knew her friend was probably right, but at the same time, she surprised herself by not wanting to give in.

'It's too dark for anyone to see very much,' she said as they made their way further down the beach than usual. 'And, let's face it, at my age, they're not going to spend a lot of time gawping at me.' She threw her head back and laughed at this.

'Who is this brazen hussy and what have you done with dear old square Elizabeth?' Jo looked at her and there was no mistaking the amusement in her eyes.

'Yes, well, I haven't completely lost the run of myself; we're still the *Ladies*' Midnight Swimming Club. No mention of harlots there!' Elizabeth said without thinking too deeply about it.

'I like that,' Lucy said simply. 'Wouldn't it be wonderful if we could get more of the village women down to join us? I bet it'd halve the number of aches and pains we see in the surgery if we did...'

'That would be lovely,' Elizabeth said.

The following night, they were racing down the darkening beach. Elizabeth couldn't wait to get to their perfect spot and the delicious feel of the ocean cloaking her whole body and soul. Lying on her back, with the icy waters about her, looking up at the stars dotting the black sky was her release. For the ten minutes of capering about in the stinging cold, she felt altogether and utterly more alive than she'd ever imagined possible. Her whole existence had somehow transformed into a life with meaning far beyond what she could have ever expected. She talked to villagers every day that once she would have hardly known. She knew that as much as she liked Lucy and Alice, they were every bit as fond of her in return.

The icing on the cake was this: swimming with Jo and Lucy, here in the darkness, occasionally in silence, sometimes talking about nothing important but, more often sharing their deepest worries and *always* finding something to laugh about.

'It's nice having a writer living in Ballycove, isn't it?' Elizabeth had said as they ran out into the cold waves.

'Is it?' Lucy asked, diving in.

Elizabeth looked across at her friend. It was hard to

know how far out they were swimming in the darkness, but the moon spilling across the water gave enough illumination to see each other. 'It's cultured, isn't it? The idea that we have a man of letters in the village.'

'Oh, dear, listen to you, still hankering after old Mr Abbott's bookshop.' Jo whooped. She held little store on what people did for a living and more on what they did for their neighbour.

'I remember Mr Abbott's bookshop,' Lucy said fondly. 'Did you love it too, Elizabeth?'

'I worked there, as a girl before...' Elizabeth sighed. She thought about old Mr Abbott often these days, more so now that Eric had died.

'When she married old Eric, he didn't want her to work anymore, so that was that, although you did visit regularly, didn't you?' Jo asked. 'I often wondered if he and Eric had... you know?'

'Stop it!' Elizabeth squeaked. She caught her friend's eye and they both howled with laughter.

'What is it?' Lucy turned about to tread water. She was watching the two women intently now, perhaps aware that some great secret had been shared between them.

'Jo is wondering if Eric and old Mr Abbott were more than friends,' Elizabeth said diplomatically. She waited a beat for the penny to drop and when it didn't, said: 'They were both gay.'

'Oh my God, I never knew that your husband was gay,' Lucy said after she recovered her balance again in the water. Elizabeth and Jo laughed at her reaction. Had she really no idea that Eric had been gay?

'In the beginning, neither did I.' Elizabeth found herself laughing at the absurdity of it. 'Why am I laughing?' She gasped then, but the other two women were laughing just as heartily. 'It's absolutely not funny.'

'It sort of is, when you think about it now.'

'I suppose he was very neat and precise and... Oh my God, I can't believe I just said that – it's such a stereotype. I'm so sorry. And that's why you never had any more children?' Lucy said softly as if some invisible piece of puzzle was slotting into place.

'Yes. My marriage was completely empty. Eric saved me from Saint Nunciata's, but he condemned me to an empty marriage so he could save face in the village. Back then people wouldn't have come near a doctor who was gay – it was actually illegal at the time, as if the government could legislate against something so intrinsic in a person. Of course, there was no chance of ever having a family of my own after my little boy died.'

'Was he stillborn?' Lucy began.

Elizabeth nodded sadly. 'It had been a terrible labour. The midwives were all nuns. The same order worked in the hospital that ran the convent and the babies' home. One of them took him from me to clean him up and I never got to see him, never mind hold him. He died as she was wrapping him up in blankets.' Elizabeth shuddered. Even now, thirty years later, she cried when she thought about her little boy passing so softly through this world. 'I knew from the moment they took him from me that something was wrong with him. The matron actually gasped when she saw him.' She felt the familiar sting of tears on her cheek as she remembered. 'It was the longest ten minutes of my life, when they took him away and then came back with the news that…'

'It was how things were done then. There was none of this bonding with the baby or the father being present at the birth. Elizabeth's little boy was taken from her and buried without ceremony in the plot of the angels up in Shanganagh Cemetery. They wouldn't even put a name on the grave in those days. He died before being baptised, so as far as the nuns were concerned he remained in a state of original sin,' Jo put in quickly.

'That's terrible,' Lucy whispered. 'I'm so sorry.'

'It was just the way of things. We went along with them, because there was no point in expecting anything else. I was one of the lucky ones. Many of the girls who were committed to that place spent years in it. Some of them only got out as old women when the convent closed down. They were literally forgotten about.' Elizabeth had made a point after she lost the baby of going into the home. She visited once a week with parcels of food and clothes and a healthy financial donation for the nuns to keep the place heated. She was the doctor's wife, one of the few who could reasonably expect to be allowed in.

'I often wondered if perhaps you should have married *him*, instead of Eric,' Jo said and Elizabeth couldn't be sure if she was making fun of her.

'I'm not sure Mr Abbott was the marrying kind,' she said a little sadly.

'And Eric was?' The words were pointed.

'You have a fair point, but I think he did the best

he could,' Elizabeth said quickly. He had saved her; it was as simple as that. Even after her child had been stillborn –Elizabeth had always known it. Eric had rescued her and no matter how things had turned out between them, she'd always known she could never repay that debt to him.

'Bloody Stockholm syndrome,' Jo muttered in a familiar refrain. 'That's what they call it, you know, when you can't see your jailer for what they are...'

'Oh, Jo, you have no idea, not really.' Elizabeth would never forget Maureen Duffy. Poor Maureen Duffy; she was driven demented with the grief of her child being taken from her. She knew only too well; she'd seen girls her own age sent to the convent and they'd never left; not really. Their babies had been shipped around the world, while those girls had spent a lifetime mending other people's clothes in an effort to make some payment for their *sins*. By the time the last of the women were turned out in the early nineties, most of them had become so institutionalised they were hardly able to care for themselves, never mind set about finding the child they'd given up all those years earlier. Those spirited girls she'd known decades earlier had long since died to be replaced by women who were little more than empty, broken shadows of themselves.

At the end of the day, Eric had rescued her from that. Even if he was a drinker and a gambler, he was, she knew, at his core a good man for doing that single act of saving her. 'I know what Eric was, believe me. I know it even more now, but how can I blame a man who had more to fear from life than I had? His life in Ballycove would have been over if anyone then had known that he was gay.

We were both making up for our own shortcomings. It's just a shame that our limitations couldn't have been more compatible.'

'At least you weren't hiding the truth from yourself,' Jo said eventually.

'How do you mean?' Elizabeth swam closer to her, sensing that what she was going to say next was not going to make either of them smile.

'Oh, Elizabeth, I've been such a stupid woman. I found a lump, in my breast, months ago...'

'No.'

'Yes. You know me, always pretending that everything was fine. I buried my head in the sand... It looks like I might have left it too late...'

'Oh, no, don't say that, Jo, it can't be. Did you know about this, Lucy?'

'Only because I forced her to take a blood test,' Lucy murmured.

'So, it's confirmed? You're quite sure?' Elizabeth asked.

'She's gotten my blood samples back, but even from them, she can tell, it's going to be quite the battle. She's made an appointment for me with a top consultant. We go this week...'

'Well then, we will have to wait and see and you will have to stop thinking the worst now,' Elizabeth said fiercely. She knew for sure that giving up before you started was no way to win a war.

'My mum might have to book a few sessions with you, only taking life as she finds it,' Lucy said softly.

'It didn't do me a lot of good, did it? An empty marriage

and an empty bank account.' The vast darkness reverberated its own kind of silence around them, with only the waves to hear. Elizabeth knew life somehow levelled things out here – there was no hiding between real friends.

'Don't say that,' Lucy said.

'Lucy, the bailiffs could arrive at the front door any day. I'm just hoping I can make some clever moves before they realise exactly how bad things are.' Of course, all of her worries were nothing now compared with Jo's news. Elizabeth turned over onto her back, stared up at the clouds peeling back above her head to reveal a velvet black sky punctured with a horde of silver stars. 'We're a right lot, aren't we?'

'Maybe, but we have each other; I have a feeling that might be enough to pull us through.'

'I hope you're right,' Elizabeth said softly.

The news of Jo's cancer came as a curve ball into the vista of Elizabeth's contented existence, because in spite of the financial worries, she realised, she was quite happy. They had been friends for a long time with a shared bond and when the chips were down, it was Jo who had always been there.

The plain truth was that even if they were very different women, Elizabeth loved Jo. The idea of her going through what she'd watched happen to so many other women in the village over the last number of years was unthinkable. She went home that night and sat in her kitchen, dumbstruck. What could she say? But of course, she realised later, there were no words to make things better. If there had been they'd have come automatically, wouldn't they?

What struck her later, more than anything, was the notion of having something to look forward to. She wasn't sure what exactly could set the tune of a drum that Jo might want to march to, but she knew that Lucy was right. They needed to be positive now. Jo needed something to aim for beyond the path of treatment that would probably lie ahead. Perhaps the gurus would call it purpose, but at their age, she had a feeling that purpose was a bit boring and she preferred the idea of being propelled out of bed by something that made her heart sing. For her, for Jo and she suspected for Lucy now too, that was swimming in the deep waters under a star-filled sky.

She wasn't sure if it was the whole experience of rushing along the beach in the altogether and feeling the water envelop her body in a way that was all at once intimate, thrilling and exhilarating. It might just be the simple physicality of the whole exercise. There was no denying the feeling that in some way, it was overwhelming. When she swam out far enough to feel as if she was being swallowed up in the vastness of the waves above her head, she felt as if suddenly she was at one with something far greater than she'd ever felt before. Crazy as it sounded, it was as if the sky, the ocean and the unfathomable depths below her all blended into one and she was as intricately linked to this vastness as she was to the tips of her toes or the tiniest molecule of DNA in her body.

There was, she knew, the link to Jo, also. She couldn't forget the fact that her friend had walked down to that spot on the beach every night of her life, and tore off into the sea for a long swim. Of course, it turned out, in the end Jo was the more modest of them both – which seemed at odds with all they'd believed themselves to be over the years. Jo had been the one to wear a necklace of shells, whereas Elizabeth always favoured her pearls. Jo had discarded her bra in the 1970s and spent the last forty years with her boobs hanging somewhere around her waist, whereas Elizabeth stuck to a solid girdle to keep her shape in place beneath her smart skirts and cashmere twinset – well she had until recently at least.

Yes, they might well be chalk and cheese, but there was no denying that when Elizabeth lay back on the icy water, the giddy rush that went through her was as warm as any emotion and that made her feel as if they were connected by far more than just time spent in the same village.

15

Dan

It was one of those rare things, this place – always changing, so even though he'd stepped on the sand only minutes earlier, the disappearing sun, the incoming tide, the shadows of the clouds cast over the sea, it all made a hugely dramatic difference to everything. If this was in London, he'd have to cross four or five postcodes to affect such a profoundly different view. He would walk to the second open cave, he decided. It was less than half a mile along the beach, where the land almost turned back on itself to welcome the shallow, rushing river that fed into the sea in a blistering constant backwash.

The caves, which were hardly even that, were dug into the land, the sea lapping up a little further towards them in every storm. Dan imagined if he were a child he probably would have explored them and made them his own, secret – though not at all hidden, clubhouses. They had the potential, in a child's imagination, to become the setting for mysteries and adventures. All you needed add to the mix were a couple of friends, an energetic dog and lashings of lemonade and spam sandwiches.

He was whistling the theme tune to the *Famous Five* by the time he reached the second cave. Dan picked out an enormous flat rock, just sheltered from a light breeze that was whipping up from the south-west. It was not the raw winds of other days, but it was enough to make him feel more alive than any saunter about London would have managed. The excitable cocker spaniel that'd joined him on his walk was now worn out; she flopped down at his feet and he rubbed her damp ears absent-mindedly.

Almost on the horizon, a boat bobbed along towards home, a spray of eager gulls dotting the skyline above it. Dan watched it as it made its way back to the pier, perhaps so the captain and his crew could make it home for dinner before darkness fell. It was almost hypnotic, that gliding movement, easing home after a long working day, so much so that when a giddy shriek cut through the silence of his little hideout, he wasn't sure if he'd imagined the alien sound.

He walked to the corner of the cave, just the point where it headed off before turning into the next one over, and looked out along the strand. Then, a second excited shriek warned him that he was not alone, although it did not prepare him for the sight of Elizabeth O'Shea and Jo Harris running from just a few feet away towards the freezing waves that ebbed ever closer to his hiding place. Dan drew back immediately, not entirely sure why; perhaps it was the junior sleuth in him kicking in. There was something lovely about it. There was something right about Jo Harris swimming in the open waters, but Elizabeth was the last person he'd have ever imagined tearing off her cashmere and pearls and ripping into the icy Atlantic waves.

He peered out towards the water again. They were submerged, just bobbing heads among the surf; from here with the advancing twilight, they might be seals or porpoises swimming a little more closely to the shore than you'd expect. He stood for a moment, a small smile playing about his lips, listening to the sounds of the ocean and occasionally, just above it a shriek of excited laughter. What harm could it do to wait here, with his back to them and listen to their joy?

Now and then, he caught their words on the breeze; mainly Jo's guiding them out into deeper water at first. He heard them, cavorting through the waves like children on summer holidays. Impervious, it seemed, to the cold, to any self-conscious notion that someone might come along. Their eager delight... well, it was contagious. It was as if their giddy happiness had infected him and his smile, for the first time in weeks, perhaps months, was actually real.

He dropped down to the ground, sat on one of the flat rocks, leaning against the cold stone that was at least dry at his side. He could sit here for quite a while, happily, watching the sea glinting orange, purple, silver and gold against the back of the cave, like an old movie projector casting faint shadows from the outside in. He could stay here forever listening to the starlings fly in perfect formation across the water. He tried to catch them every night, just as the sky was sauntering to a deep French navy.

There was something absorbing about watching from his little cottage, the birds' murmuration in wild excited patterns across the sky finally calling an end to their day. They ranged noisily across the sky in droves towards nests that would hem them in until they were ready to call out the morning chorus. It was almost as if they'd cut the corners on the end of the day, only to sing loudly in the early hours so they stamped their mark on either end of each day before anyone else had the chance.

He could not watch them now; the last thing he'd want was the village to think he was a peeping Tom! He kept his back to the sea and his eyes firmly on the cave wall before him. But he imagined them, as they cast, like an inky net only just flirting over the waves, as if gathering momentum before shading the town and letting anyone who dared question the hour that it was time to call halt.

It was time to go home and put an end to another day. The action stirred something in the dog at his feet. Before he had a chance to grab her collar, she was gone like the clappers, headed out towards the beach to bark excitedly at the birds overhead. 'Damn.' He had no choice but to follow her. He hoped the women were still in the water, or perhaps already changing in the cove next to him. He needn't even pretend he'd seen them if they were already hidden by the dark overhanging rocks. 'Here, girl,' he shouted, more to alert the women that he was about, than to call the dog. 'Come back, girl,' he shouted again, louder and more urgently.

He emerged onto the beach, hoping it might look as if they'd just turned the corner having walked from the furthest end of it. It was too late; the worst possible timing. Elizabeth was at that halfway in, halfway out stage; Jo at least was covered with a thin towel. There was no chance of dipping into the ankle-height water to save Elizabeth's blushes and no hiding within the cave because Dan found himself awkwardly standing in her path. It seemed to him, the only thing to do was to turn his back and shout a cheery hello, giving her time to make her way up the beach and wrap up in towels or whatever clothes were nearest to her.

Dear God, how had he managed to find himself standing on a beach with two near-naked pensioners and a yapping dog at his feet? How would he look Elizabeth O'Shea in the eye when they next met in the supermarket?

'Hello, hello,' she shouted gaily back and he imagined her running; a white streaking sliver of a woman, the vision of her naked torso and limbs still too fresh in his memory to quite erase.

'You're a bit late for our swim,' Jo hooted.

'Sorry,' he shouted then and prepared to tell his biggest lie of the day. 'I didn't see anything, don't worry. I've... got terrible long-distance vision.'

'Well that's good.' Elizabeth laughed and he had a feeling she was right behind him now. Still, he didn't dare turn around. 'For you at least, I suppose; the last thing you'd want is to see me in all my glory traipsing about.' She giggled then – a girlish, infectious sound that if he hadn't met her before would have portrayed her as someone very different. 'It could be enough to put a man off his dinner, entirely,' she said warmly, although he had a feeling there was a slight shiver to her voice. 'Almost there,' she said then.

He could hear them, scrambling into clothes, probably still wet. There was a jumping sound to their voices as if they were hopping about, trying to get dry and pickle themselves into clothes that were not meant for this kind of carry-on.

'Isn't that Lucy's dog? Dora?'

'Is it? She joined me halfway along the beach for a little stroll and we got a bit carried away, I'm afraid, but it's such a lovely night and even when it gets dark here the lights of the village are enough to guide us back.'

'She normally comes with us, but Lucy had to cry off tonight so I assumed she would stay back at the cottage,' Jo said. 'Dora will walk for miles with you, but she won't come near the water when it's dark.'

'For my money it's even nicer in the dark, otherwise there wouldn't be much point in being the Ladies' Midnight Swimming Club,' Elizabeth said softly. She was at his back. She tapped him on the shoulder to let him know he could turn around now. She was dressed for home, the only tell-tale sign of her swim a faint wet shadow about her shoulders where her hair dripped in a snitching patch of moisture. 'It's funny, because when my husband was alive, I'd never have come down here at night-time. I'd never have gone swimming, certainly not...' She smiled then – a playful twist of her lips. 'This one...' she nodded towards Jo '...she's a terrible influence, always was.' She bent to pat the dog's head. The little dog sat quietly, as if she knew that this bit of attention had to be savoured. It was unlikely it would come her way if she was not well behaved.

'My hat, just because you look like butter wouldn't melt – don't be heeding her. She's the one who's out here as naked as Gypsy Rose Lee on a Saturday night at the Palladium.' The two women giggled again. 'Even Lucy when she comes has the decency to wear a swimsuit,' Jo ribbed her friend.

'It must be…' he tried to think of a word that could capture the essence of joy that seemed to envelop everything about her appearance now; he settled on the perfectly inadequate: 'bracing… in these temperatures.'

Elizabeth turned and they fell in step together as they headed back for the village. 'I suppose it is, but it's more than that.' She looked out to the water, as if giving some kind of secret salutation to it at the end of a long journey. 'It has made me feel more alive than I've ever felt before.' She smiled, turning her face towards him. 'Those probably sound like the words of a woman on the edge of madness, but it's the only way I can describe it.'

'It doesn't sound mad at all,' Dan said softly. 'In fact, it sounds completely reasonable to me.' And it did. Somehow, he could feel the aliveness of it, the sea breathing in its fresh full body towards the waiting shore and at this hour, the cold and the sound of crackling rocks and shingle only added to the energy of the place. 'Still, I don't think I'll be following you in, just yet.' He laughed at that and they walked on a little in silence.

'You probably already feel as if you're living life to the full,' Jo murmured and she glanced at him shyly. 'I mean, you've done so much. I've looked you up. You're all over the internet.' A nervous laugh fell out on the air before them. 'Is it okay to say that?'

'Of course. It's what people do, isn't it? Look each other up? See exactly what the global village has already shared on the bush fires.' He smiled at this. He had looked up Lucy – Jo's daughter, no particular reason, just curious. 'I hope you didn't unearth any dark secrets I've been hoping to hide.' They all laughed at this.

'Only one,' she said and her voice had a tinge of something in it, which sounded like compassion, but that was such an outdated quality where Dan had come from that he almost missed it amidst the tide racing in towards their slow, easy steps. 'And I've told everyone in the village – you've written scripts for every English heart-throb we've ever heard of.'

'Stop it, Jo – you're going to embarrass him,' Elizabeth castigated her friend. 'You might have the decency to embarrass yourself too, if you had an ounce of decorum about you.'

'Yep, if only their sex appeal wore off on me,' Dan said self-deprecatingly.

'See,' Jo said triumphantly. 'We're as bad as each other.' And they all laughed as they made their way back towards the village.

'Niall says you're writing a book next.' Jo looked at him expectantly.

'That's right. I came here to get away from the madness of London and maybe finally start that novel I've been hoping to write for years.'

'Well,' Jo said stopping at her gate. 'Tell us – what's it about?'

'Yes, is it all about Ballycove and the scandals that secretly lie hidden behind our pristine net curtains?' Elizabeth laughed. 'What?' She looked at her friend. 'You know it's what we're all wondering…'

'Is it about the old convent?' Jo asked then.

'Sorry,' Elizabeth said touching his arm, 'but it's just someone mentioned you'd been up there, looking about the place, so naturally, we assumed that you might be…'

'Researching?' Dan finished for her. He took a deep breath. 'Yes, something like that. I'm looking into a few things as well, and yes, you can rest assured that the novel will be set here in the west of Ireland, but don't worry, I have no intention of scandalising any of you with secrets that have been kept hidden.' Then he laughed. 'Although, if there are secrets that I could work into a subplot, I'd be delighted to hear all about them.' He was only half joking and half telling the truth, because aside from getting away from London and starting the novel, he wanted to come to Ballycove for more reasons than just peace and quiet. But, nice and all as these two old ladies were, he was nowhere near ready to share any more of his reasons with them than he had been with Harry before he'd left London.

'Well, you're talking to the right women if you're interested in village gossip.' Jo laughed.

'Jo!' Elizabeth bristled. 'I never gossip.' She leant in closer to Dan now. 'But if you're interested in the convent I might be able to help a little.'

'Actually, she's probably one of the only people around who will help. Apart from Elizabeth, there's only a handful of nuns left. Most of them are going gaga and none of them are inclined to talk about what went on there,' Jo said.

'And the women who lived there?' Dan asked.

'I'm afraid that the few who were left when it closed down are scattered to the four winds now. Mostly, they'd become so institutionalised they ended up in some sort of sheltered living. None of them wanted to come back here; you couldn't blame them really. They felt abandoned by the people of the village. They'd been thrown in there as young girls and forgotten about. That leaves a sort of scar that isn't healed just because the prison door is swinging open.'

'God, I suppose,' Dan hadn't realised that women had stayed on there after their babies were born. 'And the ones who left after…'

'They've all but disappeared into the passage of time. Mostly they left here as quickly as they could; tried to get away from the shame that was attached to… well, you know. Ireland was a very different place then,' Elizabeth said sadly.

'Anyway,' Jo said more brightly, pushing in her gate and effectively locking Dora inside to put a finish on her night's adventure. 'If it's Saint Nunciata's you're interested in for your novel, Elizabeth is the very best woman to talk to. She visited there every single week when no-one else in the village was allowed to so much as look through a window.'

'I hated going there, every week,' Elizabeth said softly, 'but I couldn't just turn my back on those girls.' She shook her head sadly. 'Thank goodness times have changed so much since then.'

'Yes,' Dan sad softly, 'thank goodness indeed.'

PART 3

June

16

Jo

Far from giving them hope, the second opinion was bleaker than the first. Jo couldn't help but think it must have been a strange thing for Lucy to be on the other side of the medical transaction that passed between doctor and patient. She found herself thinking odd thoughts like that throughout the day, as if she was looking in on them both, somehow immune to the reality of what it was all about. The day they sat together in a private consulting room, waiting for a prognosis that Jo knew in her bones couldn't be much better than the first, was probably the scariest day of her life. It overwhelmed her in a way that made her feel as if she was somehow beyond it all.

Here in the austere bleakness of the oncology ward, she felt as if she had shrunken to a shadow of herself, as though she was already beginning to fade from life. To be fair, there was very little to be found in the fabric of the place to encourage any real hope or confidence.

Of course, she knew that they probably did their best, but there was no papering over the cracks of what it was all about here. The waiting room was punctuated with pretty prints of flowers and everyone was not only lovely, but there was a gentle efficiency about the place that even if it would not dispel the fear of the disease, it certainly fought bravely to contain it. Jo felt as if the nurses here could just about fold up anything neatly and crease it into a far more compliant form, whether that was sheets, bandages or indeed cancer.

They delivered tea and biscuits and left them sitting next to a window with an uninspiring view of the car park below. Still, she managed to smile and thank the nurse, before ignoring the tea and diving deep into her own thoughts. Jo was new to the idea of being ill. But she had seen it often with other women in the village. It didn't take long for people to fall into the role of patient. She had every intention of taking her time about it.

Dr Badero was a lot older than the other doctors they'd met; with his grey-white hair and gentle Nigerian accent came a sense of calm and confidence. Even Lucy felt she would trust this man's judgement. He took his time reading every single file, scanning through the tests that had come back showing the same but worse. He pushed his glasses to his forehead at the end, all the better to really listen to Jo.

'So, you've already had the cancer confirmed and a prognosis from the regional team.' He left the files down, turned his chair so they were sitting in a perfect triangle. It was intimate; they might have been friends chatting.

'They are very thorough, you know,' he said a little sadly, perhaps to prepare them.

'So, you think that they are right, that I've...' Jo took a deep breath '...a year at most.'

'I think, dear lady, they are being most generous.' He put his hands together, closed his eyes for a moment. 'There is no good way to give this kind of news, but if I were sitting in your seat now, I would prefer someone to be honest with me,' he said kindly and the only part of Jo that had not become numb with fear felt her heart drop to somewhere in the pit of her stomach. 'You have a year if you agree to treatment, but that year will be spent feeling very unwell and when you're not in hospital you will be dreading the next time you have to come for more treatment.'

'And without it?' Jo said now, her voice remarkably steady.

'Without it, I'd say with a little taking care of yourself, eating well, not trying to do too much, I think you could have maybe six months, but that is being optimistic.'

'It sounds as if I can go about my normal life and then...' Jo's voice began to break.

'No, dear, I'm sorry if I gave you that impression. No, this will be with pain management and there will be days when you will be so tired your body will just not be able to do much more than lift a cup of tea.'

'I've already been taking medication.' Jo looked at Lucy a little guiltily. 'Eric wrote me up for whopping painkillers and I've just kept repeating the prescription, but they're not working anymore.' She shook her head now a little sadly, passing a bottle of pills across to Dr Badero.

'Oh, they are working,' he said examining the bottle. 'You just need a much stronger medicine.'

'So, what's next?' Lucy asked with a lot more gumption than Jo felt.

'Next your mother needs to think about what is right for her.' He looked at Jo now. 'Do you want treatment? It is available and it will add maybe months onto your life.'

'No offence to the oncology teams, but I don't think the kind of time it's going to add on is the sort I want to be around for, Doctor.' Jo shook her head sadly, then she looked at Lucy. 'I'm sorry, darling, but I couldn't imagine spending my last weeks going from one hospital appointment to the next. I'd just like to live, as normally as possible, the time that's left to me. Is that terribly selfish of me?'

'Oh, Mum.' Lucy reached out and put her arms around her. 'You've never been selfish in your life; you wouldn't know how to think of yourself first.' Lucy was failing miserably to keep the tears from her eyes, and then she squared her shoulders bravely and said in a wavering voice, 'You must do whatever feels right for you. I'll be here, no matter what you decide.'

'Oh, darling, I know that. I've always known that.' When she raised her hand to Lucy's face, she took a small mental picture to keep her going for a time when she would no longer be able to reach out and touch her daughter.

17

Elizabeth

Elizabeth was delighted when Lucy knocked on her door early one Saturday morning and invited her to an exhibition over in Ballybrack. Jo was too tired and Lucy needed the company, she said. Elizabeth loved art, well, she loved the idea of it; she really hadn't a clue about what was current or what might be valuable. There were a few paintings hanging about in the house that were as old as Methuselah, but only one of these actually made her heart soften when she gazed at it. Was that appreciation? She wasn't sure, but she'd tag along at any rate.

She had paid herself a modest wage over the last few weeks from the surgery. She deserved it, Lucy told her. She could treat herself, if she saw something worth buying that she liked. It would be nice, to have something in this house that she had chosen, as opposed to things that meant so very little to her. Lucy had to see her son off before they left; apparently, he was going hiking with Dan.

'That's good,' Elizabeth said softly.

'Is it?'

'Oh, yes.' Elizabeth tried not to gush. 'He couldn't be going off with anyone nicer. Dan is a good egg.' She smiled then, thinking of that evening only a few days earlier when he'd happened upon her and Jo as they were racing up the beach from the water. That sort of engagement creates a funny kind of connection. They may not know each other long, or on some levels very well, but he'd seen her at her most vulnerable and somehow she didn't resent him for it. On the contrary, it felt as if they'd allied in some way that went beyond mere words. 'And he did find him for you, that time, when... well, you know...'

'I've tried not to think about it.' Lucy shook her head, indicated and steered the car away from the kerb. Soon they were coming towards the end of the town. She slowed as they passed by the pier, but she was not looking out at the water.

'Jo?' she asked softly.

'She's told you, about...'

'No. I haven't heard from her since the appointment yesterday, but I know she's scared and I figured that she needed time to let whatever they'd told her settle in.'

'She's...' Lucy said softly and a small tear made its way down her cheek. 'I'm sorry, I can't let her see me like this.' She laughed an empty hollow sound. 'Too many years of training.'

'The consultant didn't have good news so.' Elizabeth thought her voice sounded like a distant echo. She didn't want this to be real. Not cancer. Not Jo. She'd tried to convince herself they'd gotten it wrong, that it might be some kind of food allergy, like coeliac disease, and once she sorted out her diet, the weight would pile back on.

'Six months, maybe a year if she's lucky.' Lucy was sobbing now, moving the car forward, automatically going through the motions of driving. 'And of course, she won't hear of treatment; not that it would give her much longer.'

'Oh, God.' Elizabeth felt as if her whole world had just caved in around the little car. She couldn't be losing Jo; it just didn't make sense. Jo simply couldn't be dying. 'Could you get another opinion? You know, even the best doctors make mistakes.'

'Biopsies and scans don't lie. I've seen them for myself; it's taking her over as surely as that tide is coming in this evening at six o'clock.' They drove on for a while in silence, each of them trying to digest what this meant.

'Look, Elizabeth, I'm not even sure if she planned on telling anyone yet,' she said as they neared the town. 'You know what she's like.'

'I do indeed, only too well, but I'm glad you told me. It's not something that you should be carrying about with you alone.' She squeezed Lucy's shoulder to reassure her they would get through this, although she couldn't quite see how.

It was almost lunchtime when they arrived in Ballybrack and they rambled along the narrow streets, each lost in their own thoughts, until they came to the old parochial hall that housed a craft market each weekend. The hall itself was almost dilapidated, but the locals and the craft workers had worked hard to paint over the worrying cracks with a leafy motif, which ran along whitewashed walls.

Over the constant hum of shoppers and sellers Elizabeth caught the soft melody of piano music drifting from one end and creating an ambience that carpeted over the individual sounds that might otherwise have been harsh in the overhanging emptiness of the high ceilings and bare floors. There was an unmistakable lingering dint of must and mothballs undercutting the heavy overbearing aromas of scented oils and waxed candles on the stalls. Perhaps, it was just as well; although Elizabeth was not keen on artificial fragrance, they might be better than a hundred-year-old damp. At the centre of a medley of brightly coloured stalls, there was a pop-up coffee shop with a wide selection of craft coffees and delicious pastries. They mooched about the stalls for a while, admiring a selection of crafts from silver jewellery to farmhouse jams. Lucy picked up some conserves and pickles, which she thought might give a little exotic flavour to their breaks at the surgery. Then she purchased a few bottles of locally brewed beer for Dan, who she supposed would enjoy something a little different after his long hike. It was a thank you for taking Niall under his wing for the day.

At the very end of the hall, on a slightly raised area, what was probably the speaker's corner or a pulpit many years earlier, a few canvases stood on easels. More hung against the bubbling plaster of the whitewashed walls.

'Shall we have a look first and then have coffee?' Lucy asked, although she looked as if she could do with sitting sooner rather than later.

'Of course, then if we see something we like, we can have a little think before we make an offer,' Elizabeth said, although from here everything seemed too modern. None of it would sit easily in her staid and somewhat jaundiced faded house. They moved through the canvases with ease. Elizabeth was right; they were all very avant-garde. Almost self-consciously contemporary in their aspect and colours, a ferocity about them that spoke more of anger than of anything that Elizabeth would admire in a piece of art.

'Nothing here for me, I'm afraid.' She smiled at a girl who stood to the side, chewing gum and occasionally twisting one of the many hoop earrings that adorned her ears, nose and upper lip. 'Although, it's all very... energetic,' she settled on before they moved off towards the coffee shop.

The coffee shop served home-made cakes and a pretty decent Italian coffee; it was a pleasant surprise. The seating area spread out from a little stall that emitted a fresh aroma of ground coffee and heavy chocolate. Garden chairs with soft padded cushions around neat wooden tables wound away from the stall and towards a rather bruised and dull-looking grand piano. They had only chosen their table when Elizabeth spotted one of the village children taking up a seat at it and gently unfolding a soft rendition of 'Clair de Lune'. It suited her mood perfectly and brought tears to her eyes easily, being surrounded by such beauty and yet, having this overwhelming feeling of impending loss.

'That's heaven,' Lucy said as she sank back in her chair and allowed the music to wash over her. She was right, Elizabeth agreed. The trip and wandering about the market had hardly been wearing; it was the news of Jo's diagnosis that had worn them out, but sitting here, the chairs were surprisingly comfortable, and listening to the soft piano music felt almost soothing.

'She's from Ballycove,' Elizabeth murmured. 'Young Zoe Huang.' She remembered the day her family had moved into the old bookshop. Everyone in the village had expected a Chinese takeaway, but it turned out Mr Huang bought and sold pianos. 'Her family have the piano shop. They do a brisk trade in buying old German pianos, doing them up and selling them on.'

'German pianos?'

'Apparently, they moved here from Berlin. Her mother is German. She played in the Berlin Philharmonic, but then I suppose, kids and all sorts of things, they arrived over here with the Celtic tiger and they managed to survive the downturn, so...' Elizabeth waved across at Zoe. 'She's a lovely kid.'

'She's probably around Niall's age.' Lucy closed her eyes for a moment, leant back in her chair as the music drew to a harmonious close. They sat for a while, enjoying the diversion of looking about them. Zoe popped over for a little chat and explained that the local chamber of commerce had offered her a Saturday job if she came in and played the piano for a few hours each week. Elizabeth figured she was making more than some of the stallholders, especially that awful art exhibition.

'God, they *were* awful, weren't they?' Lucy whispered; they had sat as far away from the exhibition as they could manage. 'It's just as well that there are other stalls here too to drift about,' she said as she tucked into a deep wedge of apple pie.

'I was actually afraid that they'd be right up your street.' Elizabeth giggled.

'Oh, dear, no, I'm not that brave.' She shook her head laughing. 'I see there's a little antique shop just across the street from here. How would you fancy going there next?'

'Perfect.'

They ate their pie in companionable silence and then sat back in the surprisingly comfortable chairs to people-watch and sip their coffee. She was not going to let worries about the debt hanging over her cloud out the lovely day she was enjoying. She had decided, earlier, that if she saw something nice, not too expensive, she would treat herself, because after all, she had earned the money in her pocket and no matter what may come, she knew that there was very little in the house she'd shared with Eric that really had ever counted as hers. 'It's nice here, isn't it? Watching the world go by.'

'This is heaven, just being able to kick off my shoes and relax. It's as if all the worries of the world are out there somewhere.' Lucy waved her arm towards the exit, perhaps trying to keep the tears at bay.

'It's okay to cry about your mother, you know?'

'But that's the thing, Elizabeth, it's not just Mum, it's Niall too. I'm losing him and I'm not ready to let him go yet.'

'Go on, a problem shared is a problem halved. Isn't that what they used to say?'

'I'm not so sure there's any halving this one.' Lucy looked at her now, then closed her eyes and said softly, 'Niall wants to go and live with his father in Australia.' She opened her eyes now. 'Don't laugh, but I thought coming here, taking time out, it might be just what we need.'

'That sounds reasonable.'

'That was the idea and starting in the surgery, working with you and Alice, I'm really happy here, but he's just not settling in...' She smiled sadly. 'I was beginning to think, I could enrol Niall in the local secondary school next term. Maybe spend the next year or two here, with him, forging some kind of family around him. In a few years' time, he'll be heading off to college, and then...'

'They say that time flies once they start in secondary,' Elizabeth said, because she had no real experience of the kind of worries that weighed so heavily on Lucy. 'Would it be a bad thing, if he went to Australia, made a life out there, with his father and his new wife?' she asked softly. She didn't want to upset Lucy, but she'd learned something in the last few weeks and it was this: happy ever after may be very different to how you could possibly have imagined, but that didn't make it any less happy.

'Honestly? If all things were equal, maybe I'd be okay with it. You know, it's going to break my heart anyway, if he takes off for good, but the truth is, I have a feeling he'd just be in the way out there. His father has a new life there with a woman who was never going to sign up for kids. There's no warmth there, not for Niall, at least. Deep down, I think he knows that, but naturally he wants to be with his dad.'

'Perhaps they'll just say he can't come?'

'That's the thing; my ex-husband has never once played the bad guy. He's always left the dirty work to me. It's not that he's spineless exactly, but he'd rather wriggle out of any kind of situation that paints him as being anything less than perfect.'

'He sounds a bit cowardly to me.' Elizabeth huffed. 'Sorry, but you know, I'd much prefer people who say it as it is. I suppose I spent my married life with someone who swept so much under the carpet that since he's died it's as if I've found an entire continent of secrets and lies and it could all have been so different.'

'It's one of the things I love about my mother.' A flicker of a smile drew up Lucy's lips now. 'But of course, Niall is much too young to see that as a real quality worth valuing.' She shook her head now.

'What will you do?'

'I've already done it.' She clapped her hands together; it was a fait accompli, but not one to celebrate. 'I've asked if Niall can come out to Sydney and his dad has, as I expected, said yes. All we have to do now is book the tickets and they will have to sort things out from there.'

'Oh, dear. Does he know?'

'No, I'll probably tell him tonight. He asked yesterday, but I just wanted one night, the two of us together, without it hanging in the air between us.' She laughed now, but it was a hollow sound. 'And then, I was so tired, I just fell into bed and Niall disappeared up into his room, so I probably should have told him. Maybe it'll make him happier. I don't know anymore.' She shook her head, as if it was her last stand and she was just about to concede the battle.

'Look, maybe if Niall gets to spend the summer down in Sydney – winter there, I suppose – he might be delighted to come home in September and settle into village life here in the west,' Elizabeth said lightly. She hoped she was right. The idea of Lucy returning to Dublin wasn't one she even wanted to think about.

They spent over an hour in the little antiques shop. It turned out they had unexpectedly similar taste when it came to a lot of things. At four, the little town of Ballybrack would yield no more so they decided to head home and soon they were trundling back into Ballycove again.

'You know,' Elizabeth said mildly, as they were approaching Jo's house, 'I've always loved these cottages. Years ago, I used to think it would be lovely to live down here, next door to your mother...' It was the truth. On many of those days that she'd spent happily cocooned in Jo's kitchen, she'd have given anything to have a little cottage all to herself rather than return to the depressing mansion on the hill.

'Yes, I could see you here all right, with roses about the door and a wild flower garden at the back.' Lucy smiled. The springtime sun was inching out across the land, as if it had somehow stood on its tippy-toes so it could reach a little further to cast off the winter cold that clung stubbornly in darkened corners still.

'It's such a pity they never come up for sale anymore...'

'You know there's no guarantee you're going to lose your home,' Lucy said gently.

'But that's the thing, dear – after all these years it's just dawning on me, I'm not sure it's ever really been my home.'

18

Lucy

'What is it?' Lucy's antennae were already on high alert. It had been a busy morning in the surgery and she hadn't slept properly any night since the visit to the oncologist with her mother. She was too drained not to pick up on even the slightest little cue.

'Oh, nothing. Not a thing at all,' Elizabeth said a little too brightly.

'There is something and if you don't tell me now, I'm going to assume the worst, so you might as well just say it.' She smiled at Elizabeth. They had met each other when they were both, to say the least, at low ebbs of their contentment scales. It broke down some of the usual nuances around blunt honesty.

'There's absolutely nothing wrong.' Elizabeth was smiling now, but there was still a trepidation playing around her eyes. She took a deep breath. 'Really, it's nothing, well, not on the scale of the worries you've been carrying about the place for Jo and Niall.' She stopped for a moment, perhaps trying to fix the correct phrasing in her mind for what was coming next. 'No, it's just I got my first payment demand this morning from one of the banks.' She passed the letter across the table to Lucy, topping up their coffees while she read.

'Oh, dear, they're not exactly subtle, are they?' Lucy said.

'I'm not worried about it– no more than I was a week ago, anyway.' She sipped her coffee. 'It's addressed to Eric, so they're not talking about drawing down on his *estate*, such as it is.'

'No?'

'Well, no, and you see, I've been looking about the village and there are plenty of small houses I could pick up for very little. They're not exactly what I've set my heart on, but at least I'm fairly sure that I wouldn't be without a roof over my head. For now, if we can just keep ahead of the banks, perhaps I can make some small dint on the repayments with the money from the surgery, just to keep the wolves from the door for long enough for a cottage that I'd like to come up and then…'

'You're thinking of moving?' Lucy said and she clapped her hands. 'But, that's the best news ever.' It was exactly what Elizabeth needed: a new start, a place to call her home. And it would be an actual *home* – as opposed to the mausoleum that the grand old Georgian had become around her.

'Yes, but that leaves this place…' Elizabeth said, meeting her eye levelly – they both knew the score. Her husband had left a thriving practice behind him and a huge house, but both were on the brink of ruin. He had also left gambling debts that would swallow any cash made on the sale of either and so Elizabeth was in many ways as trapped now as she'd been when he was alive. 'That's why I wasn't sure if I should mention it, just yet. You have so much already on your plate,' she said softly.

'I suppose I have,' Lucy said, 'but all the same, that shouldn't stop you from moving forward with your life. Remember, me being here, it was always only going to be temporary.' That was the truth; it was what she'd signed up for. She had come here for at most two weeks to keep the surgery moving until a locum could be found to slip into the role in a more permanent capacity. Those two weeks had stretched, so soon she would be here almost three months – how on earth had that happened?

'I suppose, with Jo and all...' Elizabeth smiled a little sadly. 'Well, all that you've done here... you've really done far more than I ever expected. You've transformed the whole practice.' She shrugged. 'I thought maybe you'd changed your mind.'

'Oh dear,' Lucy said. 'Honestly, I can't think about anything past Mum and Niall at the moment.' They were everything to her. They far outweighed any desire to travel or even the notion of heading back to her old job in the real world. 'Look, at least now you can go to an auctioneer, show them the house, take their advice, and see how it would stack up against what Eric owed.'

'Yes, I'll have to make an appointment,' Elizabeth said faintly.

'You know this place...' Lucy said. 'The surgery, you don't have to sell it with the house. It's a separate building entirely, if you block off that one connecting door.'

She looked at Lucy now. The idea of selling on the practice seemed a bit crazy to her. It was being here, meeting people, having some kind of purpose that had really brought Elizabeth out of herself. Why on earth would she want to turn her back on that?

'I don't really want to cut my ties with this place,' Elizabeth said as if she'd been reading her thoughts, but then she lowered her voice. 'You know, even if I sell the house, big and grand as it is, anyone buying it is going to have to put a new roof on it and do major work inside with replacing the electrics and looking at how the whole house is heated. It's like an ice box in winter time... in some ways, all I'm selling is an address, a view and maybe, at most, original period details.' She smiled sadly at that. 'The thing is, we both know I have to clear off Eric's debts first and I'll be lucky to make enough from the sale of the house to do that. Prices down here aren't what they are in Dublin. If this house was in the city, I could probably set myself up in Monte Carlo for the rest of my days with what it would make.'

They both laughed at that, but of course, she was right: Dublin prices were rocket high. If Lucy sold her own it would probably bring in enough to buy out Elizabeth entirely and leave her with a tidy profit after clearing Eric's debts. By comparison to the east coast rush to market, houses down in Ballycove had not been bitten by the property madness this time round. 'At the same time, there's something liberating in knowing that I can leave the house behind, you know?'

'Well, I hope that the house you set your heart on comes up at exactly the right time then for you,' Lucy said softly.

'Let's hope so.' Elizabeth began to clear away their dishes.

'It'll be a sign.' Lucy didn't really believe in all that angel or sign nonsense. She'd seen too much of what could not easily be explained by the hand of goodwill or a benevolent God who always managed to turn things out for the best. Children's oncology wards tended to knock any of those notions from you, early on in medicine. 'You don't want to go jumping in and selling the practice without giving it a good bit of thought though. I mean, it's a job for you at the moment and...' She broke off. 'You're too young to settle into an early retirement at the back end of the village.'

'That's very nice of you indeed, but we both know, the way Eric has left me financially, I may not have the luxury of choosing.'

The following week was probably the longest Lucy had ever put in since she'd arrived in Ballycove. It was not that the work was any harder than usual or that she didn't enjoy it, rather it was that constant background worry of Jo in her mind. Was she making the right choice by not having chemotherapy? The consultant had explained a week earlier that first they could attempt to shrink the cancer, buy them back a little time. This would mean heavy blasts for two weekly sessions over the next four weeks. If at the end of this, the cancer had been affected in the way they hoped, they would review her and make a plan from there.

The consultant had lowered his voice when Lucy had enquired about operating first, and popped up an image of her mother's chest and side. He didn't need to explain. Operating now was out of the question. They would have to take too much. Their only hope was shrinking what was there and then they would see what would follow.

The wind was whipping up an eerie melody as Lucy made her way out of town, along the scenic Atlantic walk that would bring her up to Dan's little cottage. Lucy loved this walk. It meandered from the village overlooking the thrashing sea. It was even nicer in the evenings, with the sun sinking into the distance at the far end of the ocean. The horizon, this evening, was burnt orange: the sort of colour that Lucy always associated with Kenya – deep skies and rustling land, teeming with vigorous scurrying, if camouflaged life. Except of course, there was nothing scorched about the earth beneath her feet this evening. The land here was lush and green – a velvety carpet that rolled back towards the scraggy cliffs in the distance. In places, as she moved nearer the cottage, the soil squelched – a giveaway whisper that the land beneath her had shifted to a soft bog.

In a matter of months this place would brown and erupt in a mist of white cotton to replace the purple heathers punctuating the land like determined smiles in the wintry landscape. The little cottage sat nestled in a cute garden, cordoned off with a square-capped wall and a narrow gate at the end of a short path. Dan had parked his car outside the gate and to Lucy's eyes, at least, it looked as if it had hardly been moved since he arrived. He was sitting on one

of two wooden chairs close to the front door, a beer in his hand and a smile on his lips that reached all the way up to his eyes.

For a moment, the sight of him pulled her up. There was a familiarity about him, but it was mixed up with a complete otherness, as if something about him had completely changed since the last time she'd run into him. When was that? She wondered, and she realised, she couldn't remember because she'd become so consumed with worrying about Jo that everything else, apart from work, had become quite meaningless. When she opened the gate, Dora rushed from her side and hopped into the chair next to him. Lucy found herself laughing, the first time she'd actually laughed in days.

'What brings you out this way?' he asked, shading his eyes from the sun.

'I come bearing gifts.' She held up the craft beers she'd bought for him a few days earlier in Ballybrack. 'Just a small thank you for taking Niall hiking. I really appreciated it.'

'You didn't need to do that. I enjoyed it – he's a great kid.' Dora placed her head on his knees and gazed up adoringly at him.

'Well, you look the picture of contentment,' she said as she stood before him.

'Ah, yes, it seems I've finally found the girl of my dreams.' He laughed and patted Dora on her head. 'She's quite happy to do all the things I like to do and never drinks my beers from the fridge or steals my toothbrush.'

'Probably just as well.' Lucy turned to take in the expansive vista ranging out beneath the cottage, ending

only on the horizon where the sun was edging towards its final ebb. 'Gosh, it's so beautiful here.'

'I love sitting here and watching the sun go down when the weather is being reasonable.'

'Living the dream, eh?' She looked at him closely. 'You do actually look like the cat that got the cream,' she said, because there was something almost self-satisfied about his expression.

'I suppose I am.' He reached down, took up a can of beer and handed it to her. She opened it gratefully and sipped a long cool mouthful. She couldn't remember the last time she'd had a can of beer. 'I've just started writing my novel... well; actually, I started it a few days ago.'

'And it's going well?' she asked.

'It is when you're inspired, apparently,' he said. The smile stitching up the corners of his lips had pinpricked two small dimples that she hadn't noticed before.

'Well, I can see why you'd be inspired here.' It really was the most breath-taking view.

'It's not just the place,' he said softly. 'It's the people too. Everyone is so...' He shook his head as if the right word would never come. 'Well, decent, as some of the old boys down in the pub might say. Everyone is so decent and they have time to talk and welcome you...' His words drifted off and she began to wonder how many cans he'd drunk already. 'And they have stories, even though... I'm not sure that they realise their stories are actually worth anything.' He shook his head at that.

'So, you've made their stories into your book?' she asked.

'Not exactly, but I've taken what I've seen and heard in the village and made it into something different.'

'So, what's it about?' she asked, sipping again. 'Your book – or can't you tell?' Her mother had told her that Dan was quite accomplished, having worked on a couple of big TV adaptations over the last few years.

'Well, it's the story of…' He shook his head and smiled easily. 'It's always the hardest part, putting it into a couple of sentences.' He patted Dora for a moment, probably didn't even realise he'd done it. 'It's the story of a woman, widowed and once downtrodden, who begins to get her mojo back.'

'I like it,' she said and her eyes drifted to the top of the village opposite, catching the last rays of the fading sun off the cathedral spire. 'Is it based on anyone I might know?'

'Uhh.' He blew out a long shaft of air that was filled with a kind of shy dread. 'That's the thing, I'm hoping that you won't recognise her, but yes, I've built her up based on a few of the local ladies about the village…' He waited, because of course, she was a doctor; she was good at keeping her mouth firmly shut. She kept silent, even when she wanted to rail at the unfairness of things or sing from the rooftops that there was good news. Of course, she couldn't tell someone else's news – that was buttoned into her over a lifetime of practice. 'Yep, you'd be good at keeping it to yourself,' he confirmed. 'It's loosely based on your mother and Elizabeth. I mean, I haven't put in any real details, not so you'd know who inspired her, but…' He lowered his voice. 'I've put in the Ladies' Midnight

Swimming Club...That's the bit I'm really hoping they won't mind.'

'You know about that?'

'Yes, I'm afraid so. They didn't tell you that I bumped into them one night?' He threw his head back, laughed a loud and contagious sound that Lucy picked up as a giggle at the daftness of it all. Then he looked at her, perhaps realised how much in the dark she was. 'I think it's great – they both seemed to get so much out of it.'

'Yes, well we're simple folks around here,' Lucy joked. She couldn't tell him that her mother's days for swimming or any other kind of adventure were drawing to a close. She shivered, trying to shake that familiar desolate feeling from cloaking her once more. Instead she thought of Elizabeth and she knew she couldn't tell him that the reason she had bounced back so quickly after the death of her husband was because his passing had been a bit of a relief. Nor could she mention that he had left her, not a merry rich widow as most of the village assumed, but rather almost destitute, subjugated, with a bleak past and an uncertain future. The reality was: if Elizabeth had not come across her husband's outstanding debts, there was little doubt that none of those lenders would have revealed themselves until it was time to foreclose. No doubt all of this would add to the dramatic impact of Dan's story, but it would not do a lot to preserve the social standing that Elizabeth so badly wished to maintain. 'Have you told them that you're writing about them?'

'It's not exactly about them...' Dan said now a little defensively.

'Maybe you should let them be the judge of that?' She had a feeling her mother would be tickled pink; she wasn't so sure about Elizabeth.

'They probably won't even see themselves in it. I mean, I've changed names and everything about their physical appearance is completely different. I'm even toying with setting it over on the east coast.'

'Still, if you think there's any chance...'

'It's just...' He shook his head, turned to look at her, catching her eye. She had a feeling, he wouldn't write anything that would hurt Jo or Elizabeth or anyone else. 'People can be a little disappointed, because I'm seeing them through my own eyes, not through theirs...That can be a big difference.'

'Not always a good one?'

'In this case, I'd say, just different.'

'Still...'

'I can show it to them, but honestly...' He drained the last of his can of beer and sat forward. The sun was just on its final step down before disappearing. 'I enjoyed that. I don't know when I last had a beer.' He shook his head. 'Will you come inside? I'm just going to have a bite to eat.' And he disappeared through the door, leaving it open after him so she could follow.

Inside the cottage had that same mix of functional and pretty that marked the outside of the property. It was essentially one large room with a door at either end and what she presumed was a narrow pantry or porch at the rear. It was cosy and even though there was the end of a fire burning in the stove, Lucy had a feeling it was the kind

of place that stayed warm long after the fire had died out. It was tidy too. Dan was an organised sort of guy, not one of those men who needed a woman to come in and sort out his laundry or manage his store cupboards. He seemed almost too big for the kitchen, as if he could reach from one end to the other in a long stride, but he moved with an ease that spoke of how much he'd completely settled into the place.

'Sit, sit,' he said as he pulled out a large pizza from the oven and placed it on the scrubbed kitchen table. 'Do you need a plate, or will you just help yourself?' he asked, placing a bottle of red wine and two glasses on the table between them both.

'I can't just gate-crash your dinner.' She laughed, but the pizza smelled as if it had been smoked and she couldn't help but notice it was loaded with a mixture of cheeses and a hefty fusion of fresh fish and shellfish. Suddenly Lucy's stomach grumbled loudly – it had been too many hours since lunch.

'You were saying?' He raised an eyebrow in mock horror and set about cutting the pizza into slices. 'You can talk about Jo if you want, or don't if it's too upsetting,' he said gently, as if reading her mind.

'You know already?'

'I'm a writer; I pick things up. It's not always a blessing, let me tell you.' He shrugged. 'Apart from which, you look as if you could do with offloading some of that worry you're carrying about behind your eyes.'

'I won't deny that this last week took far more out of me than I'd ever have expected,' she said between delicious

mouthfuls. 'You'd think, well, I thought at least, that being a doctor, being used to hospital environments... I mean, it's madness really. I've worked in busy A&Es for years, but...'

'It's not the same thing at all,' he said gently.

'No. It turns out it's nothing like it.'

'I don't care how often you see that; it's bound to be different with your own mother – nothing could prepare you for that.' He poured out two generous glasses of merlot for them.

'But, that's it – I knew that, but still...' She sipped the red wine, sat back for a moment, savouring the taste. 'That's really good,' she said.

'Happy accident – I picked a bottle up on my first day here and I struck lucky. I'd say I've all but bought out their entire stock in the local supermarket.' He smiled easily. Simple pleasures; maybe they were alike in that. 'I think you're being a bit hard on yourself, expecting to be far stronger than anyone could possibly be. Of course, you're going to be worried sick. The fact that you're there, well—' he smiled '—here in Ballycove, is quite enough.'

'Is it though? Because I feel as if I'm looking at her just fading away before my eyes and there's just nothing I can do about it.' There: she had said what she'd been afraid to give voice to since they'd had her mother's prognosis confirmed.

'It is, of course it is. If you were outside, looking in, you'd see that as clearly as I do.' He leant forward and topped up her glass. 'Another bottle of this left, if we need it,' he said easily and they both laughed.

'Anyway, this isn't doing either of us any good. Tell me more about your novel,' she said as she polished off another slice of pizza. 'This is delicious too by the way, although, a bit messy.' It dripped as she took it up, but the fish was cooked perfectly and the cheeses – a mixture of cheddar, Italian soft cheese and strong Parmesan–melted in her mouth when she tasted them.

'Oh, it's just made from a whole lot of stuff I threw together. Most days, I pick up fish from the men coming in off the boats; there's always unwanted, unusual catches in the bottom of the nets. This evening…' he made a face and threw the tea towel across his forearm as if he was a waiter in a fancy restaurant '…we have prawns, trout, bass and flounder.'

'Very impressive.'

'Well, any writer has to put time in waiting tables or helping out in kitchens before they get a break.'

'So, is that how you got your break?'

'Not exactly…' He sat back and smiled. 'Do you really want to know?'

'Of course – I wouldn't have asked otherwise.' She knew, from what she'd read, that for every writer who made a living from their words, there were probably a thousand others waiting tables all across London, hoping for that lucky break.

'It's not exactly the stuff of fairy tales, but it does have a happy ending, I think.' He smiled and his eyes took on a sort of faraway glaze. 'I managed to get a first in my degree and the university put forward two candidates that particular year to a screenwriting course run by the BBC.

It was only a couple of weeks long and, to be honest, it was as much about networking as it was learning how to write.' He caught the look in her eye then. 'Any writers I know have been writing since they were in school. You don't just walk in the front door of the BBC and say: *I'm ready to start now.*'

'Okay, fair enough,' she said and she had a feeling that she'd enjoy his book once it was published.

'I was only there a few weeks and I ran into Sir Roger Oxley one afternoon. He'd popped in for a radio interview and some angel had sent me on coffee rounds. When I plopped his coffee down before him, I hadn't a notion who he was, but we got chatting and one thing led to another and by the time he was leaving, he'd given me his email address and asked me to send on a script I'd written the year before about the Paralympics in London.'

'And the rest, as they say, is history?'

'In a nutshell, I suppose it is. Sir Roger liked my script. There was more work to do on it, but by the time we were in the lead-up to the next games, it was ready to go and again, we were very lucky, because he managed to secure a fairly big name from the soap opera circuit.' He waved his hands as if conducting a light orchestral chorus.

'It sounds like the stuff of fairy tales to me,' Lucy said and probably, she thought, to plenty of starving, success-hungry writers all over London.

'I suppose so. The show went on to be a critical smash – the people in the *Times* and the *Observer* loved it...'

'And the ratings?'

'Oh, no, they loved it too, but halfway through the

series, our leading man ended up before a magistrate for being drunk and under the influence of drugs behind the wheel of his Range Rover.' Dan shrugged his shoulders. 'You win some; you lose some. It turned out from then on, we got more publicity in brackets behind his name as he walked into court each day and then was sentenced to a stiff turn of community service and a lifelong ban from the soap opera that he had planned to return to later that year.'

'Ah, it still managed to roll around okay for you in the end.'

'Yes, I suppose it did. My next script was the one that really set me up and the rest, as they say, is history...' His voice drifted off, as if the notion of London had robbed him of his enthusiasm. 'So, that's me.'

'And then you decided to come here to write your novel...'

'Yes, that's the plan.'

'Why here, of all places?' she asked.

'Excuse me?'

'Most people, well, the rock stars and the Hollywood faces, all settle for nice tame locations on the east coast. How on earth did you settle on this end of the country?'

'Oh, I don't know, I suppose, it just sort of popped out at me.' He looked away, as if he was embarrassed. 'Here, we shouldn't let this wine go to waste,' he said draining the bottle into their two glasses.

'I really shouldn't have any more. I'm not used to alcohol – too many night shifts; you get out of the habit.' She laughed, but still, she thought, one more glass, not so much to drink, as an excuse to stay here a little longer. It was comforting and relaxed, sitting here, with the wind beginning to howl up outside. 'You know, I can't remember the last time I felt so chilled out,' she said softly, as she turned to look at the stove where a flame had taken flight and now, a river of sparks rushed up towards the chimney. She watched as Dan bent before it and opened back both doors so they could watch the flames dancing around the long sods of turf in the grate.

'Here.' He patted the wing chair before the fire. 'Sit here; you won't believe how comfy it is.' Lucy brought her glass with her and watched as Dora made short work of a remaining pizza slice before coming to rest against her leg where she sat half dozing off before the fire. Lucy found herself almost dozing off too, as they sat in companionable silence with only the glow of the flames throwing light and shadows about the walls.

'I can see why you've stayed here.' She wondered if she were in his position whether she would ever want to leave. No, she decided, she would never leave this place for the bustle and clamour of London.

'What?' he asked her and she realised he'd been watching her.

'Oh, nothing.'

'Go on, a penny for them.'

'They're not even worth that,' she said softly. 'But, well, I was thinking of you here and something struck me.'

'I'm almost sorry I asked now,' he said, but his smile was easy and his voice gentle.

'No, it's not about you; it's actually thrown up something I hadn't thought of.'

'Right, now I'm interested.'

'It's just, I've had this thing in the back of my mind, where I assumed that when I took time out of work in the hospital that I'd travel. See the world? You know, I never really got much of a chance before; I was in college and then we settled into jobs and there was a mortgage and...'

'We?'

'Oh, sorry, my husband and I...' She paused for a moment. 'But since the divorce, well, that's bothered me. You know, the idea that life is passing me by and there's so much more that I'd hoped to have done by now.'

'Ah, far-off fields and all that jazz?'

'Maybe.' She smiled then, sipped some more of her drink. She could feel it making her woozy, but it was a pleasant, happy feeling. It was almost as if she had sunk into a cradle and a gentle loving hand was lulling her into a lovely feeling of repose. 'But then, I thought of you and...' She laughed. 'Why would anyone want to leave here? What on earth could be better than here?' She shook her head at the realisation. 'I mean, you said it yourself, even the people, there's just decency about everything and it...' She nodded towards the meal they'd just shared.

'It rubs off on you?'

'Yes, I think that's it. It infects you so you're a part of it, without actually meaning to be and soon, you've been weaved into the middle of things and there are... relationships.' She nodded towards Dora. 'You know, since

I've come here, I've probably met three-quarters of the whole local population and all I've met with is kindness and a warm welcome.'

'That's it.' Dan shook his head. 'That's what I've been trying to put words on.'

'For your book?'

'No, not so much, more for my parents and my friends in London. They want me back over in London again. This…' He waved his hands about the room. 'This was only meant to be temporary, to get me through… I just needed…' He shook his head. The smile that had faded earlier when they'd stood on the threshold of this conversation didn't disappear this time. 'I needed to breathe, I needed to think, I suppose and now… I feel as if I've drowned in oxygen and there's no going back to that life.' He was smiling broadly, sitting just next to her on the old fender, his empty glass on the floor at his feet.

'I love it here,' she said softly and she felt, for a moment, as if she glimpsed a chink in the life that she had always believed would unfurl before her. That life had been snatched away when Melinda Power had sauntered in and caught Jack's eye two years earlier. And maybe, she had needed until now to see that there were other ways forward, or maybe she needed to be sitting here, with the wind howling down the chimney and the fire dancing in the grate. It felt as if something had clicked into place and it wasn't something she could quite put her finger on, but it was the feeling of coming home, what it meant to really come home, and maybe that was as much as she needed for now.

19

Dan

It was the stark beauty of the place –that was what had caught Dan unawares. It was the biting cold of the rain and the fulsome warmth of the people. It was the fact that the more the one seemed to shroud the land around his cottage; the other enveloped him when he wandered into the village. And he wandered into the village every evening now. Sometimes, he had to remind himself that he'd only been here a couple of weeks, because everything about the place and the people had a habit of convincing you that you'd been here much longer, maybe even that you belonged here.

At this point, he figured he'd walked almost every inch of the beach. There were miles of it. Soft golden sand, stretching out as far as the eye could see. Dan never imagined that the coastline of the west of Ireland would be like this. Rather, in his imagination, he'd have considered the grey cliff face, choppy waves, chewing into jagged rocks; perhaps he'd expected the rattle of old pirate ships and the rush of mountain dew running through the ditches as well, but none of this could have captured the reality of staying in the little cottage.

He couldn't say it had made everything better, but it had certainly improved how he felt. There was no job to go back to in London, not that he'd actually been searching for one. The only search he'd been actively pursuing since he arrived here was over at what remained of Saint Nunciata's.

He had hit brick walls at every turn when it came to tracking down his birth mother and as each day passed his motivation to carry on searching was waning. Of course, it might be easier if he'd told people what he was about, but it turned out it was harder to break a secret the longer it had been kept. He really hadn't been hopeful coming here that he'd actually track down anything more than the little his adoptive parents had already told him. He was a mixed-race baby, brought to London from Saint Nunciata's babies' home over thirty years ago for a well-to-do Catholic couple.

He'd read too many articles online – too many children who'd met the same obstacles and too many more who'd managed eventually to penetrate the layers of bureaucracy and religious secret-keeping, only to find a frightened and bitter woman who wanted nothing to do with them. The notion that he should let sleeping dogs lie was beginning to settle on him gradually. He wasn't sure he'd ever really been that committed to finding the woman who gave birth to him anyway. What kind of woman doesn't go looking for the child she gave up all those years ago?

'We can't judge those girls by today's standards,' Elizabeth said softly. 'Ireland was a different place then. I don't expect you to understand, but the girls who ended up in the convent – well, there was no choice.' Elizabeth had tried to explain what it was like, but the sadness that passed across her face told him far more than her words. She'd been a regular visitor to the women who had lived in the convent until it was closed. Perhaps she had known his mother? They had gone to see the old building, a sprawling grey, derelict structure that had angels at the doors and serpents in the remaining stained-glass windows.

Although it was emptied over a quarter of a century ago, there was no denying its looming presence; there was an eerie feeling of ghosts who would never fully rest. 'For some, perhaps it was better than the alternative – many of the girls came from simple farming backgrounds. Back then, a *respectable* man would prefer to have a dead daughter than an illegitimate grandchild.' She shivered then, perhaps remembering things she would prefer to forget. 'Come on, let's walk around the old gardens, this place isn't going to do either of us any good.'

Dan looked once more at the building, mostly boarded up, apart from the occasional window where the storms had blown away their covers, revealing stained glass that might have been striking once. He wondered for a moment if he came back again and broke in – would there be files? 'And inside?'

'No,' Elizabeth said, almost reading his thoughts. 'This

is it. They cleared out everything. Every last bed sheet was sent off to some unfortunate Third World mission; every scrap of paper was burned on a bonfire that seemed to last for weeks before they closed the place up.'

'God.' Dan exhaled, hating the regime that had locked down answers so firmly and cruelly from so many.

'God? I think they lost sight of him long ago.' Elizabeth shook her head sadly.

'So, where has everyone ended up? I mean twenty-six years ago? They can't all be dead and buried already, can they?'

'Scattered to the four winds mostly,' Elizabeth said as they turned around the back of the building. 'In the end, the girls who were left were taken into sheltered housing. Most of them wanted to get out of Ballycove – there was nothing for them here and the notion of starting afresh seemed like the best thing for them. There was only a handful in the end, women who'd gone in years earlier and never managed to make their way out again, until it was too late.' She pointed towards a tall black railing topped off with neat white crosses and ending with a narrow gate – hardly wide enough for two people. She pushed it in and waited for him to follow. 'I've kept in touch with one or two of them, but they won't be a lot of help to you now.'

Dan realised they were standing in a graveyard – but not a graveyard like he'd ever seen before.

'It's been decommissioned, now of course; all of the nuns buried in some sister convent at the other end of the country,' Elizabeth supplied. They walked the narrow path, between two rows of identical black-painted iron crosses. Each had the name of the nun it had stood over inscribed in neat white script across its middle. The crosses dated from 1876 and bore names like Concepta, Assumpta, Benedict and Deceline – all long gone out of fashion – if they'd ever been in vogue. Each name was followed by the same epitaph – *humble servant of the daughters of hope*. It sent a chill through Dan; of course, it reflected perfectly the lives led by these women. They had been in service, their every thought and action dictated by a regime that held them in a sort of ante-room from everyday living. It didn't excuse the stories Dan had read since he began his search – terrible stories of women made to suffer for one mistake. Still, something of the loneliness of the place – there wasn't a flower in sight – diluted some of his anger towards these women who until now, he'd seen only as his mother's tormentors.

'They weren't buried in the local cemetery?' It wasn't really a question, more a confirmation. 'But what about women or children who died here? Some must have died in childbirth, back then the mortality rates were…'

'Ah, yes,' Elizabeth said sadly and she told him about the large plot for babies who died before they were baptised in the nearby cemetery. 'The grave of the angels was opened for any stillborn baby, so even my own son was interred there.' She smiled sadly. 'There were no names on the grave, no mark that he'd ever been here – but that was the way. There was no other choice.' She sniffed, perhaps keeping in the tears for the child she'd lost and who'd been cruelly rubbed away. 'The mothers, as far as I know, were buried there too, but separate to the babies. I'm not even sure if they put permanent markers on those girls' graves either.'

'So, they've been forgotten.'

'Oh, dear, Dan, they were brushed out of Ballycove as soon as they came here. Most of them were already dead as far as their families were concerned; it was only the lucky ones who managed to get away and make new lives for themselves. Not many were brave enough to come back and live in Ballycove – there was nothing for them here.'

'And the nuns?' He was looking at her now, hoping against all hope that maybe there might be one or two still living in the village.

'Ah, the nuns – now that's a different story altogether. Mostly they transferred into other convents, but they were already a dying breed. Vocations had petered off by the time they decided to close up here, so in many ways, even if the state hadn't intervened, the convent would have died a natural death anyway.'

'Would they help?'

'Help?'

'If I was trying to track down someone in particular?' He couldn't meet her eyes; instead he looked back at the narrow gate that led into that strange graveyard. This place had shaken something up in him, something that had been buried for far too long. And then suddenly he felt an unfamiliar well of emotion. He'd never actually told anyone this before. Tears began to well up in his eyes and he rubbed them fiercely.

'It's all right, Dan,' Elizabeth said softly. 'I understand. You're trying to find your mother, aren't you?' She turned over the engine and then smiled kindly. 'Maybe Sister Berthilde would remember...'

At least, since he arrived in Ireland he had settled into a routine, that didn't involve getting drunk or dawdling with his maudlin thoughts as he counted what was missing as opposed to what was not. That had been the problem with London, he thought now as he stood looking out into the Atlantic Ocean.

He'd take it as progress; anything was better than standing still. He looked back up the hill towards the village. It was the middle of the week and life was trundling on as normal for the people of Ballycove. Rising high up into the rock, he could hear the occasional car wind its way through the streets. Chimneys puffed out their blue grey smoke into the woollen grey sky and somewhere, across the way, a dog barked loudly, its demand to break free an unending chorus into the resolute sunshine. Dora was jumping energetically to catch a glimpse of life beyond the narrow boundary wall that was just a fraction too high to permit her unfettered liberty. She was ready for a walk and he was glad of the company. With everything else, he knew Lucy hardly had time to bless herself at the moment and a spaniel; well they are energetic little things, aren't they?

Dan wondered about the scruples of walking to the spot where he knew he could settle himself comfortably for an hour to listen to the voices that were swiftly filling up his manuscript. It wasn't as if he was watching them; actually, he did everything he could to make a comfortable spot with his back to the ladies so he never laid eyes on them after that first embarrassing time. But it was their voices, their stories, their gay abandon, which was what drew him here each night. Night fell quickly here, but over the last few evenings, he had seen the daylight stretch out a little longer across the uneven water.

Someone had told him that the sun set fifteen minutes later here than it did in London. He wondered what he'd do when the evenings became so bright there was no hiding in the cave. He was not a voyeur. There was nothing lurid in his desire to sit and listen to the giddy and sometimes poignant conversations of the Ladies' Midnight Swimming Club. There had been nights when he had wept, hearing of Elizabeth's life and the truth of what it was to be so naively trapped into a marriage that never had even the glimmer of a chance at fulfilment. He cried too when he heard Jo, whose only fear of dying was leaving the people she loved so much behind to fend for themselves. He'd written down her words, but on the page, they didn't carry the same poignancy – *how can a woman die, when there is so much more to be done?* she'd railed, her tears only too obvious on her cracking voice.

'They won't be alone; they'll never be alone. I know it's not the same, but I'll be here, watching out for them,' Elizabeth said with a steely determination that seemed at odds with the little woman he knew who favoured twinsets and pearls when she wasn't diving into the wild Atlantic Ocean.

'Shall I tell Eric that you've become a complete harlot,

throwing off your clothes at every opportunity?' Jo said, breaking the sadness with her own brand of humour.

'Oh God no,' Elizabeth shrieked. 'Not a word until I'm there to see his jaw drop.'

That was why Dan came here every evening, to listen to women whose friendship had sustained them through the unthinkable and was continuing to sustain them. That was what his book would be about – *the indomitable spirit of friendship*.

The following morning blushed pink across the sky, falling into a deep blue as the ocean crept up towards the horizon. Shards of tawny, rosy light cut in through the half-opened curtains on Dan's bedroom window– plenty of time for a walk and to gather his thoughts. The sea breeze seemed even fresher today, if that was possible, and Dan enjoyed its coldness pressing on his face and then on his return journey pushing him along against his back. But it wasn't the sea or the breeze, or the soft sand beneath his feet that was making him smile today. Rather, the reason he felt this unaccustomed lightness inside had nothing to do with any of those things and at the same time had everything to do with how life was unfolding.

Late the previous night, he'd taken his courage in his hands and contacted Harry. He'd sent a sample of the novel and been rewarded by an early morning return email. The writing he'd already pinged off to his agent was developing further in his mind. Harry had sat up all night reading through it and he felt exactly as Dan had. This had the potential to be a decent book – this was the idea they'd talked about so many times late into the night.

'This is a movie in the making, if the sets are half as good as you make them sound on the page,' Harry said when he rang later that day.

'Let's see if we can't make it into a book first,' Dan said softly; he'd had his fill of scripts to last him a lifetime. But he knew that was the secret to Harry's success, this notion that there were always bigger mountains to climb. Of course, for Harry, it would be the royalties too – there was no denying that there was a big difference between a decent movie royalty and a successful book.

When he'd rung earlier in the morning, Harry had been excited, taken up in the sort of enthusiasm that Dan knew could not be thwarted. He replayed their conversation over in his mind again as he walked along the beach. He was excited at the prospect of climbing back into the book again, with fresh eyes and yes, maybe with movie camera eyes this time. This was the kind of challenge he'd needed, but perhaps he just hadn't realised it until it presented itself. He was ready to grow, as a writer, ready to push into a new territory and there was no question: he'd assured Harry that the only place this book could possibly be written was right here in Ballycove.

20

Niall

They'd spent the day in Dublin, gathering up belongings, because perhaps they both knew that they would not be coming back here until his grandmother had passed away. School was out, his mother's job at the hospital had been filled by some young eager doctor and no-one was going to miss them particularly from their previous lives if they never came back again. His mother was driving but a million miles away in her thoughts, so she hardly noticed the profusion of flowers along the main road into the village, nor did she comment on the fact that the foliage was abundant with the trees constructing light green canopies across the road. As summer heightened, these would become heavier and darker until they threatened to upend and bend down so low, it felt as if you could touch them.

Niall had slept for most of the journey. He'd heard his mother mutter that it would be a blessing if he was old enough to drive and take over while she closed her tired eyes for a while. *If only*. That was something he'd love: driving on a main road. He wanted to ask if she knew at what age you could legally drive in Sydney, but he had a feeling it was better to keep his eyes closed and pretend to be asleep. He'd heard nothing back from his dad, but that didn't mean his mother hadn't. All he could do was cross his fingers and wait. Niall wouldn't admit to being glad to be in Ballycove, but certainly, it was better than school. Dan had invited him over for food and to watch his favourite show on Netflix, which was releasing its second season the following day. Tonight, his mum seemed eager to sit down and have a chat with him, he hoped it would be about going to live with his Dad in Australia.

'Your grandmother will probably have eaten by the time we get home; just you and me for dinner. What do you fancy?' his mother asked as they turned up towards the top of the village. The evening light was drawing in now, and high on the headland, Niall could just about make out a light in Dan's cottage. Off in the distance, the seagulls were pulling in over the ocean, probably headed for the pier; perhaps the last of the fishing boats had just docked for the day. 'Niall?'

'Oh, I don't mind, whatever's easiest is fine.' Anything was better than school dinners.

'It's a takeaway so. Will you pop in to the chippie for both of us?' She handed him her debit card and pulled in outside the door.

'Go on ahead, I'll walk back,' he said as he got out. They

were lucky to make it in time. It seemed almost everything in Ballycove closed early. A bell on the back of the door announced his arrival in the shop and the young guy behind the till nodded at him. Niall didn't recognise him. They were probably around the same age, but this guy looked as if he had dedicated the last year of his life to the gym. He had the shoulders and arms of a man much bigger and older, and from his neck sprouted a slightly too small, spotty face. He muttered something – perhaps a greeting. It was hard to make out. Everyone knew his name here and it used to really get up Niall's nose, but these days, he just accepted it. He'd been the talk of the town after that night when they'd all thought he'd thrown himself in the sea, but the curiosity around him had quickly died down and no-one had ever been nasty to him.

He stood looking at the menu over the high counter. His mother always ordered the same thing here: freshly battered locally caught fish and chips. Niall fancied a kebab instead; he was deep in consideration when he heard the door open again. The kid inside the counter brightened and Niall looked across to see what had pepped up his smile. There, standing near the counter was the girl from the piano shop.

'Hello, Zoe, what can I get for you?' Muscles asked. The girl had the softest, straightest, silkiest black hair Niall had ever seen. On the ends, the very tips had been dipped in a light pink dye and it perfectly matched her pink hoodie. Niall stood behind her for a minute while Muscles made a bit of a drama about dropping a basket of chips in the hot oil. 'There we go. Is your old man working late again?' he said, handing over a can of Sprite and ringing up the cash register.

'Yes, he has to finish by tomorrow because someone is coming to collect a baby grand he's been working on all week,' the girl said and her accent was clear, local, but with an inflection of something else thrown in. When she turned around, she did not expect Niall to be standing behind her. 'Oh,' she said, as if jolted a little by his proximity. 'You startled me...'

'Sorry,' Niall muttered and for a moment, they did an embarrassing sidestepping thing where each of them moved, but still stood before each other. 'Sorry,' he said again.

'So, you said.' She smiled now and her face creased into something that approached a giggle. 'You're the apple pie kid?' she was confirming more than asking. 'My dad loved it.'

'Oh yeah, that's Niall Nolan,' the guy behind the counter supplied too helpfully, as if Niall was some kind of dummy.

'Yeah,' he said, then wondered for a moment if he could drag out the conversation a little longer, but the guy behind the counter coughed and Zoe looked back and it seemed as if the moment was lost. She turned and headed for the door and off into the falling evening probably forgetting about their embarrassing two-step already.

'That's Zoe Huang.' Muscles rubbed his chin as if it was some great crossword puzzle he was figuring out. 'Now, what can I get you...' He rang up the items Niall ordered, and Niall slipped a bar of chocolate in to round it off. 'Grand.'

'Thanks,' Niall said, pocketing the chocolate, and he waited for his food, looking out onto the empty street outside.

'Her father is the piano man – they've got the shop over on Garden Square,' he called after Niall, as if it was information that vitally needed to be passed on. Still, when Niall left the takeaway, he turned right instead of left, following the path back behind the main street and into the slightly leafier Garden Square. There, at the centre of the road, he watched as the girl stuck her key in the front door of a shop called 'The Piano Man' and closed it out firmly after her. Niall had passed by here many times before, but he didn't have any interest in pianos and certainly not great big grand ones like the sort that ranged about beyond the windows of that shop.

He looked now at the shop. It was a three-storey building and upstairs he could make out a kitchen in one of the rooms with pine units and a vase of flowers just inside the window as if sitting on a dining table. In the window next to it, the curtains were pulled so it was impossible to make out what was there, but he assumed it was some kind of sitting room, with bedrooms at the top. The shop door opening again made him start and he moved back into the shadows of the road he'd just walked along. He watched Zoe Huang pull the shop door tightly behind her and push in through the door next to it, presumably into the family home upstairs.

Niall breathed out again. What would she think if she

saw him standing there watching her? That he was some kind of sad nutter? Probably. But then, after search and rescue had been called out and half the village alerted that he'd been washed out to sea, maybe that's what everyone thought anyway. Perhaps it was time to pull himself together and change that? That notion settled on him like a growing wave of earnestness – yes, it might be time to do a bit of growing up, especially if he was going to move to Sydney.

He stopped for a moment, looked back at The Piano Man, and he realised that perhaps waiting on in Ballycove for a little longer might not be such a bad thing after all.

'I thought you must have gotten lost,' his mother said as he dropped the take away on the little kitchen table. 'Was it very busy?'

'No, not really,' he said separating their food. They were both preoccupied and Niall didn't want to hazard a guess at what was going through his mother's head at this point, but he was pretty sure his grandmother was top of the list. Maybe, just behind it, was the notion of Niall heading off to Sydney. A little stab of guilt niggled at him at this thought. He pushed it from his mind as quickly as he could.

It was funny the things he missed now – not those things you'd expect, but rather small things. His dad's coat hung across the newel post, the occasional bristle of laughter from the kitchen, the smile on his mother's face, just because they were all together. They'd been happy, or at least that's what Niall had believed. His mother thought so too; perhaps that's why it had all hit her so badly. It would always feel as if they were somewhat fractured, as if they were never quite whole again and Niall just couldn't see a way to make this better. Maybe running off to Sydney was actually the coward's approach. Perhaps he should just stay here and make the most of things? Was it worth giving it a shot, here in Ballycove, a new start? Dan had said he had nothing to lose and maybe he was right.

'Will you set the table pet?' she asked and he slid place mats out for them both, popped down some cutlery and took down two glasses and a couple of cans of Coke from the fridge. 'Thanks, love,' she said as if he'd just undertaken some great feat, but then, he realised, that she looked so tired, even setting the table could be enough to finish her off. It was the silence of their meals that bothered him the most now. It was as if, over the last while, the small talk had been sucked from them, so now, there was only the sound of scraping cutlery and noisy chewing to punctuate their mealtimes. It was his fault of course; he could see that. In the beginning his mother had worked hard to try and keep the small talk going, but he'd bitten her head off at every turn, as much because he was angry with himself as he was with his father, but it didn't matter, because the only one he could take it out on was his mother. Wasn't it time to change?

'How was your week?' he mumbled.

'Eh?' she asked, a little startled. 'It was good, thanks, busy, you know, between the surgery and Mum.' She sat down then and poured water into her own glass. 'And yours?' she asked tentatively and he almost wanted to kick himself, because he could see that this is what he had made for them. He had been the architect of these uncomfortable silences that might yet have to stretch across the globe if he moved to Sydney.

'Yeah, my week was all right, I suppose, just kicking about the village. Today was a bit weird.' He bit off slightly too much kebab.

'Being back in Dublin?' She looked at him. 'I suppose it doesn't feel like home anymore, does it?'

'Did it ever?' he said and then he was sorry, because he sounded as if he was being cruel. 'You know what I mean, compared to here, with Gran and being here all the time, not having to go to boarding school. It's just... different,' he settled on.

'Yes,' she said and smiled. 'I suppose it is more like home than what we had in Dublin.'

'Any word from Dad?' he asked lightly, not really expecting there to be.

'Actually, I was speaking to him during the week,' she said and she dropped her fork as if the effort of relaying the conversation was too heavy to share her energy with eating at the same time.

'Oh?'

'Yes.' She smiled, a little too brightly. 'He'd love to have you out there, just as we thought. There are things to organise of course, but he suggested perhaps going out near the end of the summer, if that suits?'

'So, I'm going to Sydney? To live?' He couldn't quite believe it, a new life opening up before him, with his dad far away from this place.

'Yes, if it's what you really want,' his mother said. Her smile was almost wooden. 'But of course, you know that

if you want to come back, if it's not what you expected…'
She bent her head down now, played with the food on her
plate for a moment. 'I just want you to be happy, Niall.'

'Thanks, Mum,' he said and he did something he hadn't
done in a very long time; he reached across and put his
arms around her shoulders. 'I can't wait.'

PART 4

July

21

Jo

Jo always thought she was that rare breed, both lark and owl. Quite simply, she went to bed late and got up early – all her life. She smiled sadly now, thinking of one of her favourite mantras when Lucy was a teenager: *There'll be time enough for sleeping when we're dead*. Well, it looked like she'd know the truth of that either way soon enough. She wasn't being negative, but she knew, not just in the early hours of the morning, but rather with every ticking second that her time was drawing to a close much more quickly than either the doctor or Lucy would admit.

She was tired all the time. A trip down to the cove for a midnight swim now took days to recover from and a full day's bed rest to prepare for. It was worth it. Apart from when Niall came and sat on the end of her bed and tried to coax her into a game of cards, the sea was her one true joy. Swimming with Lucy and Elizabeth had become the oxygen she needed to carry on. It was cathartic and invigorating, even if it left her physically depleted for days afterwards.

Lucy understood and Jo was just grateful that her daughter had managed to discard her doctor's knowledge and allow her mother to carve out what remained of her time as she wished. There would be no operations or chemotherapy or any other kind of interventions that would lessen the quality of the time she had left. Jo had insisted there would be none of that pretending that everything was going to be all right, when it so clearly wasn't. She couldn't bear the notion that tears would be bottled up now, so that the people she loved would be flooded with sadness when she left them. She wanted them to get it over with, so when she was finally gone, they could start again.

'I want to be celebrated,' she said as they swam in temperatures that seemed to her to be icier than mid-January. Of course, she knew, the water was perfect for July, but everything about her body was letting her down at this point. 'None of this nonsense with people going about with long faces; I want people to remember me and smile.'

'We'll certainly do that,' Elizabeth said. 'Do you remember that day when I bumped into Eric leaving the Maynard house?'

'What's this?' Lucy asked.

'Oh, dear,' Elizabeth said then, realising that she would have to share the memory with Lucy also. 'Your mother was there the day I realised that Eric was...'

'He was paying out-of-hours visits to a man who lived in the square.' Jo tried to be diplomatic.

'It turned out, he'd been seeing Bobby Maynard for years,' Elizabeth added sadly. 'I only realised when I saw him leaving the house and righting his jacket on the way.'

'We were coming out of old Mr Abbott's bookshop.' Jo smiled, remembering well the day. The sun had been breaking through after days of rain and she'd felt oddly optimistic that perhaps summer might finally be about to arrive. 'He had the bloody cheek to tell you to go home and not spy on him, if I remember rightly,' Jo said.

'Thank goodness your mother was there,' Elizabeth said a little wistfully to Lucy. It had been the start of their real friendship. That day, Jo had learned the secret at the heart of Elizabeth's marriage and she'd proved herself a loyal and strong friend over the years afterwards.

'Oh God. I can imagine, poor old Eric.' Lucy laughed now, knowing only too well the tongue-lashing Jo would have given him for treating her friend so badly.

'Safe to say, he never crossed her again,' Elizabeth said softly.

'It didn't really change things for you though,' Jo said sadly. It still bothered her that Elizabeth had spent a lifetime shackled to a lie of a marriage when she might have made a life with someone who cherished her and maybe even had a family of her own.

'No. But if you hadn't stood up to him that day, we both know my life would have been a lot worse.' Stillness wafted across the water and they both remembered Eric pushing Elizabeth to the ground and with that one horrible move, Jo had known that she would end up another statistic of ongoing domestic violence if she didn't step in straight away. 'She has a deadly right hook. Did you know that?'

'Yes, well, he bloody deserved it and let me tell you, if I run into him in the next world, he's in for another bashing for leaving you up to your bloody eyes in debt at the end of it all.'

'What if we were to have a charity swim?' Elizabeth said suddenly. 'We could have it in aid of whatever you'd like, Jo, and you could be part of it...' She didn't continue, because they all knew she'd only be part of it this year and that was if they were very lucky indeed.

'We could,' Lucy said then, turning over from her back. Jo could feel her daughter's eyes on her. 'We could ask all the women in the village to join us for a midnight swim and...'

'The Ladies' Midnight Swimming Club could keep on going...' Jo said softly, but she felt an unexpected swell of emotion at the idea of it.

'We're going to keep on going – you know that already,' Elizabeth said good-naturedly. 'But this would be different. This would be every woman in the village. All of us, out here in the darkness and raising money for...'

'Breast cancer,' Lucy said firmly. 'I think it should be breast cancer. Pink ribbon – it's the best cause I know of. What do you think, Mum?'

'I love it,' Jo said softly. 'There's only one thing...' She laughed now, threw her head back on the water and strangely, the sound of her own laughter was unfamiliar. It was the cancer of course, eating through her insides. 'It should be in the nip. A dip in the nip! That's what

I'd enjoy most, thinking of all of you, down here, in the altogether and jumping into the water...' She could just imagine every woman in the village, from the most uptight to the most unlikely, coming down here and rallying for each other and every other woman who might be affected by this horrible disease. 'Think about it, Elizabeth, even old crabby boots O'Neill... herself.' And they all began to laugh at the notion of Eric's former receptionist pulling off her interlocking knickers before diving into the cold Atlantic.

22

Dan

Elizabeth was true to her word. It had taken a few weeks to organise, but she'd managed to set up a meeting with one of the old nuns who had once been in St Nunciata's. Sister Berthilde was ancient according to Elizabeth and so rather than transferring to another convent they'd shipped her into a nearby nursing home; apparently no-one had expected her to last so long after it all finished up.

The nursing home was tucked away at the end of a very well-maintained drive, with only one discreet sign pointing you in the direction of Cois Farraige – which Elizabeth translated as Riverside. A small stream ran through the grounds, but it had been fenced off, probably in the name of health and safety for residents who might end up losing their way. Inside, the unmistakable aromas of early dinners and late breakfasts mingled with a velvet underlay of cleaning products, chiefly bleach and something that probably purported to be pine. Still, he had to admit, the reception – a medley of muted greys and golds – wore the air of a health spa as much as any nursing home he'd ever have imagined. A young, ponytailed girl on reception insisted on showing them to the day room after she watched him rub disinfectant cream on his hands.

Sister Berthilde had the frame of a woman who had spent her life in combat with everyone and everything that dared to cross her path. Even now, although he presumed that age had shaken out some of her volume, her hands, ears and nose were all large enough to put on any man who had a decent frame to match. Her mouth was set in a long, downward scowl and her eyes watched him from beneath their wrinkled hoods. They were distrustful from the moment Elizabeth introduced him and part of him felt pity, that for a woman who spent her life serving others, she did not expect a visitor who might have come with good wishes.

'I was born… well I think I was born in the orphanage,' he began gingerly, once he'd settled in a chair opposite her.

'No,' she said emphatically.

'But.'

'It's quite simple Mr…' She curled her lip for a moment then carried on, as if his name would make no difference to her. 'I held every baby that was born in our care, and I can tell you without a moment's hesitation, I never held you.' She looked resolutely towards the open fields that stretched out into the distance.

'But you can't be sure…' He leant forward. It seemed convincing this woman was most important. After all, the records he'd seen so far had no trace of a birth on the date he knew to be his birthday. There was no mention of his adoptive parents on any register as having received a child from any of the institutions for miles around. 'Look, you're my last hope. I understand that you tried to keep secrets for the girls who found themselves in your care, but things have changed now. No-one really cares anymore, apart from those of us who are affected by it.'

'You have no idea, have you?' The old woman leant forward and he could smell her age, a concoction of staleness and baby powder – as if they might balance each other out. 'Those girls had sinned. What they got – a roof over their heads and someone to take on their offspring – that was more than they deserved. Most of them hightailed it off to England as quick as they could and probably covered over any mention of our convent from any man who might be fool enough to marry them. If I had a penny for every baby I put through my hands back then, well, there wouldn't be a starving population in Africa.' She looked at him now disdainfully.

'And you call yourself a Christian,' Elizabeth whispered so as not to upset the gentle balance of the day room. 'Do you have any idea of the pain that you've caused to so many? Holier than thou – the lot of you, well none of you was perfect – you gave those poor unfortunate girls a living hell and for what? So much for compassion and forgiveness and not throwing the first stone.' Elizabeth's voice wavered, as if she might cry with the injustice of what she'd witnessed; instead she gathered herself crossly. 'You were always an evil old cow, Berthilde. For once in your life, can't you do something to make life a little easier for your fellow man?'

'Well indeed, and you can afford to talk.' The old nun turned from Elizabeth towards Dan.

'I certainly can. I might have made my own mistakes, but I never set out to make other people pay for my own shortcomings.' With that Elizabeth got up from the chair and stormed out the door.

'The truth is, even if you manage to locate the wretch of a mother who gave birth to you, there's a very good chance she won't want you any more now than she did back then.' Berthilde spat at him and he knew that this was it. He'd come to the end of his search, such as it was. It hadn't been long. A couple of forms filled in and sent off to the health service and a day spent trawling through scant social work records that meant nothing to him really. He got up from the chair opposite, considered wishing the old nun good luck, but had a feeling she'd rather if he just left.

Outside, in the corridor, he stood for a moment to gather his composure. He felt winded by the nastiness of the old girl. *What kind of person turns into someone like that?* he wondered.

'Fancy seeing you here?' Lucy's warm voice dragged him back into more familiar surroundings.

'Yes, I was visiting Sister Berthilde.'

'Ooh, lucky you,' Lucy said ironically. 'Is she her usual bundle of laughs?'

'Hmm, well, it depends on what you find funny, I suppose,' he said, but he felt utterly deflated after the visit.

'Oh, she's always been a complete dragon, don't mind her,' she said and he joined her as they both made their way back towards reception. 'You were braver than most to come anywhere near her.'

'I almost wish I hadn't now.' He wasn't sure if he was more upset with her words to him or at how upset Elizabeth had become.

'Are you all right? You look as if you've seen a ghost.'

'I...' He stopped for a moment, looking out towards a small residents' patio. He was too deflated to keep this secret any longer. 'Unfortunately, Sister Berthilde was my last chance.'

'Your last chance?' Lucy stood for a moment and then her eyes widened, and he could almost see her adding up his interest in St Nunciata's and his visit to the nun. 'Oh God, I'm so sorry, I never realised. You weren't pinning your hopes on that evil old bat?' Lucy shook her head.

'I've tried everything else I can think of and Elizabeth suggested perhaps asking her for help. I'm glad it's not just me?' Dan asked hopefully.

'Definitely not. She's always been a bit barmy and nasty too. Really, when you hear horror stories about what happened in some of those places, I always think old Berthilde is the devil incarnate and it only takes one bad egg.'

'I'd say she's rotten to the core all right.' He smiled then. 'At least Elizabeth gave her what for.'

'Good for her. You're not giving up though.' They were at reception now. The ponytailed girl had left her post and Lucy dropped the medical folder she'd been carrying on the desk, pulling a pen from her jacket to fill in whatever updates it needed. 'Are you?'

'There's not much else I can do. I've filled in all the forms; Sister Berthilde was my last hope.'

'Have you tried Mother Agatha?' She looked at him then, waiting for him to say 'yes' probably.

'Mother Agatha?' he repeated as if he'd just lost the ability to reason.

'Hang on, let me fill this in and we'll have a chat outside.' Lucy flicked open the file, wrote in her notes quickly and signed with a flourish, by which time the receptionist had returned and she confirmed that all was well with the patient she'd come to see, temperature down and it looked like there was nothing to worry about.

'So, Mother Agatha?' he repeated a little stupidly as they made their way towards the car park.

'Yes. Have you met her? No. Of course you haven't, she's been living with her family over in Ballybrack for the last few years. Arthritis, really very debilitating, according to Mum; it's totally riddled her spine and spread out from there. She can hardly walk at this stage. That's the thing about these women: they suffer on in silence for years and by the time they actually go to a doctor there is so little to be done about things.' Lucy smirked. 'Well, I'm not sure Berthilde ever suffered in silence, but then, thankfully, she's a rare old kettle of piranhas.' They had reached Elizabeth who was standing next to her car.

'I'm so sorry, Dan, but that woman – honestly, she's had it coming for a long time.'

'Don't worry; she deserved every word of it,' Dan said

smiling at Elizabeth. 'Look who I met and she's just been talking about a nun called Mother Agatha.'

'Of course, Mother Agatha – I never thought of her, but I'm not sure she'd know a lot about Saint Nunciata's. She worked mostly in the local hospital, helping in the maternity ward.'

'Still, I'd love to go and see her if there's a chance she might know something...' Dan heard the words trip from his tongue, despite the fact that only a few minutes earlier he'd promised himself this would be it. No more. Let sleeping dogs lie and all that jazz.

'Unlike Berthilde—' Lucy nodded back towards the nursing home '—Mother Agatha will be thrilled to have a visitor. She was the last Reverend Mother in the convent, so she'd surely have a good idea of where you might be able to track down more records.'

'Did they send all of the babies over to English families, do you think?'

'I don't know. Nobody really knew much about what went on there. It was all kept very hush and the truth was, I'd say, the older people wanted to forget or even better pretend it wasn't happening under their noses.' Lucy shook her head sadly.

'Elizabeth was the only one to get her nose in the door of the orphanage. She raised plenty of money for them with all kinds of fundraisers and she used to drop in occasionally to help out where she could.'

'I didn't do half enough, but I did as much as they'd let me. It was a fine line, between being allowed to help and being seen as stepping over the mark.'

'The way I hear it, you helped a great many of those girls get out of there when they might have been stuck for years on end.'

'Ah well, I only wish I could have helped more,' Elizabeth said sadly, 'but it's all in the past now. You do what you can, don't you?' Elizabeth said modestly.

'I'm sure it took courage, a lot more than telling old Berthilde what you thought of her, just now,' Dan said. He could imagine Elizabeth years ago, helping as many as she could and probably more than she'd ever admit to. 'Would you come with me, to meet Mother Agatha?'

'Ah, Dan, I'd be delighted,' Elizabeth said placing her hand gently on his arm. He had a feeling it was assuaging. She did not expect the old nun to know anything more about his birth mother than Berthilde and he wondered once more, if he was on a completely wild goose chase. Still, he knew with certainty that these were the questions that had truly brought him here, more than any solitude or novel writing.

23

Elizabeth

It had been Lucy's suggestion, to go and see her husband's solicitor. Stephen Leather was as old as Eric, and yet they couldn't be more different; they'd never really been friends.

'I'm not sure I'm the right person to advise you,' he said kindly, but he pushed his glasses up over the bridge of his nose as he jotted down exactly the position that Elizabeth had found herself in financially since Eric's death. The news of the envelope outlining the damage of his gambling debts hidden in her husband's possessions had come as an uncomfortable surprise to him.

'So, you see, I'm penniless, really, by the time the gambling debts are paid off,' she said and she felt a pinprick of tears in her eyes again.

'That's a tad fatalistic, isn't it?' He smiled at her then and she wondered if he wouldn't have made a much better doctor than Eric. 'Listen to me now.' He leant forward. 'These debts, I know it feels as if they are hanging about you, but the truth is you're living in a huge house, with what has to be a thriving practice attached to it. If you sold up everything in the morning, you'd surely still have enough left over to set yourself up in a nice little flat somewhere, wouldn't you?'

'Do you think so?'

'My best advice to you, Elizabeth, is that you need to take matters in your own hands. I know that's not easy since you've let Eric take care of everything over the years.' He was speaking slowly, picking out his words, because at the end of the day, they both knew, that Eric hadn't really taken care of things at all.

'So?'

'Don't wait for the banks to turn up on your doorstep looking for their money. They will sell the lot for a song. Legally, they only want to recover what they are owed, so you could be out of there without so much as a penny over the amount if a bidder came in on the button.'

'I see. So I have some decisions to make,' she said thoughtfully.

'You need to decide what makes the most sense to hold onto and what you really just want to let go,' he said smiling at her.

'Should I go to the bank and just explain…' But there was no point, because as far as she knew, there was money owed to several banks and she was certain they would each race to foreclose before one another.

'I wouldn't, not if you could sell up quickly, which you might. The practice might be a desirable enough business. I hear you have a new doctor there who is really very popular about the village. Would she possibly think of taking it over in a more permanent capacity?'

'I don't know. The timing is terrible for her and even if it wasn't, it's going to take a lot of money...'

'Well, I'm sitting here long enough to know one thing.' He pushed his chair back from his desk.

'Oh?'

'These things always work out. Why not put out the feelers gently? Go and visit the estate agents, see which they think is more likely to sell and do up your sums. See exactly how much you need to make to pacify the banks – then at least you'll have a fair idea.'

Elizabeth thought it was strange how some things just seem to snowball. A few nights earlier they had been swimming when they agreed on the idea of the charity swim.

'The Ladies' Midnight Swimming Club – of course we'll continue it after...' she said. They needed something to focus on, well, she needed something to focus on now, otherwise she would go mad thinking of the way the world as she knew it seemed to be sliding away from her.

The following morning, Elizabeth felt that old familiar feeling of doubt. *Seriously*, that nagging voice in her head asked, *are you really thinking of asking every decent woman in the village to strip off all their clothes and go galloping into the freezing sea? For money?* No matter how Elizabeth worked it out in her head, reminding herself that it was in a very good cause, Eric's derisive laugh broke through her resolve. But then, she remembered Jo's enthusiasm. *She* wanted this to happen and, most importantly, *she* wanted to be part of it. She was aiming to be fit enough to make it down to the second cove along the beach and go skinny-dipping with everyone else by the middle of August. Elizabeth knew she couldn't let her down.

Jo slept late most days now, napped in the afternoon and took it easy after dinner – it seemed as if she saved herself to go midnight swimming with Elizabeth and Lucy whenever she could. It had become her social life, now she didn't have the energy to gad about the place at her usual speed. Last night, Elizabeth had made her a boiled fruit cake and they'd caught up on all the village gossip for the week. It caught her by surprise; now she was ensconced in an almost full-time capacity as the practice receptionist. She heard every little tittle-tattle from around the village. Not that she could discuss what went on in the practice; Mrs Kenny's gout and Mr Parkinson's lumbago were strictly off limits, but it's not as if anyone wanted to hear about them anyway.

No, instead, sitting there all day long with a stream of locals passing through, she caught up on everything from the local tidy towns operations to the most pressing deliberations of the parish council. Really, sometimes, Elizabeth felt quiet light-headed with the amount of information coming at her, but then, in the evening, she would ramble off upstairs, grab her coat and head for the cove, with Lucy and sometimes Jo, to laugh their way into the darkness. Into the sea.

She hadn't done a thing about getting something organised. In fact, for a woman who'd spent a lifetime on committees she wasn't even sure she knew where to start. Another day almost over already and now she could feel the whole idea bubbling away like a wanton pressure that was pursuing her every move.

'Are they worth making an offer on?' Lucy was smiling at her, pulling her from her thoughts.

'I'm not sure, it depends on how much you've got?' Elizabeth said.

'Go on then,' Lucy asked, leaving back the final medical file of the day. She'd just shown Miranda Corrigan to the door. There wasn't a lot you could do for old age, but Lucy's bedside manner seemed to give her a great lift.

'I... it's silly really.' Elizabeth shook her head. 'It's this charity swim; I'm not sure where to start...'

'Why?'

'I can't imagine telling old Miranda Corrigan that we're all stripping off down to our birthday suits and does she fancy sponsoring me fifty pence to freeze my bottom off in the midnight waves.'

'Why not? I can almost guarantee you Miranda will be the first one into the water if her rheumatism doesn't kick in on the day. Callie will be there for sure.' She was right of course; Callie Corrigan was a good sport. 'In fact, I'll ring Callie first thing in the morning. She'll get all the girls in the mills to sign up for us.'

'Really?' Elizabeth brightened.

'Of course, and when we get posters printed and sponsorship cards, I promise, every woman in the village will join it.'

'People *do* love Jo.'

'They do and it's a really good cause,' Lucy agreed. 'But they love you too and they'll all turn out to support this; they'll turn out to support you. It's only five weeks – not long at all.' Lucy looked up at the calendar. It wasn't that far away but by then Elizabeth knew she was calculating that Jo would be much weaker. 'Don't worry about getting people on board; our only worry is keeping Mum well enough to join us on the night.'

'I know. That's why it's good for us to have something to think about outside of...' Elizabeth let her hands fall to her sides. 'Jo is so looking forward to it. I think it could really be something to aim for. You know what she's like: she won't give in too easily.'

'You're right. Let's start focusing on this properly, instead of things we can't change.' Lucy kept her voice firm. 'We can put up posters here, talk to every woman who comes in the door...' Lucy stopped. 'I'll ask Niall to put a poster together and we can print it off...'

'Really?'

'Okay, so we'll need to get a permit from the council and then ring the local branch of the charity, tell them what we're planning. I'll mention it to every patient in the surgery and if they're not up for joining us, we'll get a contribution out of them. The charity will surely help with the admin for us and sponsorship cards. We can knock some support out of the drug suppliers and...' Lucy grabbed a pencil and paper from the desk, started a to-do list. 'Here, how's this?'

'Well, it's...' Elizabeth read through it. There was a list of things to get done for the next few days, but everything could be organised from right here in the surgery. 'It's perfect. What would I do without you?' she said softly and she realised, that if she sold the surgery and Lucy moved on, she'd be losing so much more than just a good doctor for the community and a great colleague, she'd be losing a dear friend.

True to her word, Lucy spent the next few days rallying support from every female patient who came through the door, so much so, that by the time Monday morning rolled around women were arriving at the surgery to pick up their sponsorship cards and sign up for the challenge. Young and old, it didn't seem to matter. Even the newly installed vicar, Mrs Snead, a large woman with heaving bosoms and an open face, added her name to the list. By the end of the day, Elizabeth was quite overwhelmed.

'How on earth did you get so many people interested?' she asked Lucy as they stood outside the surgery later, closing up for the evening. The street was empty now. The only noise above their heads were the church bells ringing out six o'clock.

'I didn't do a lot, apart from popping into the supermarket and mentioning it there too. It's just spread like wildfire ever since. I suppose the fact that people are so fond of Mum and then again, unfortunately, so many families here have been touched by the disease, everyone just wants to get out and do something positive about it.' Lucy shrugged as if it was nothing.

'Thank you, I'm very grateful. I couldn't imagine going in to the supermarket and telling them I was going skinny-dipping and encouraging the whole village to follow me in...'

'Oh, I didn't see it quite like that, and anyone I've spoken to thinks it's going to be great fun as well as raising lots of money for a good cause.'

'Hey,' Dan called to them as he marched along the road. 'What's this I hear about you lot going cavorting about in the altogether in a few weeks' time?' He was laughing and Elizabeth realised, that was how people would see this whole thing. It was light-hearted fun, not the same as when she went swimming with Jo and Lucy, with the sea rumbling through her thoughts and her mind blanketed from any worries she might have once felt. This was going to be quite different, more of a fun way to spend a night than a meditation.

'Ah, so the word really is out?' Elizabeth said happily. 'I'm afraid it's girls only, of course. If you boys wanted to organise something separate for another weekend, we'll all be cheering you on.'

'No, thanks, I think I'm fine. I'll just sponsor you both, if that's all right, and let you get on with it.' He turned to Elizabeth and smiled, making her heart flip in some unfamiliar way. 'Now, I was actually calling to see you too, if you have a minute.' He nodded back towards her house.

'Of course,' she said, a little intrigued, since she didn't really get the chance to entertain very often. 'I'll see you tomorrow,' she called to Lucy who was locking up the surgery door for the night.

He was, Elizabeth decided once they arrived in the dark hallway, a rather elegant young man, considering he spent his time in casual clothes. There was a subtle grace about him. Perhaps it was his hands, so long and slender and yet manly enough to reassure you that he could take care of anything that came his way. He had kind eyes too, really, the sort of eyes that if Eric had them, he'd probably have looked more like a caring sort of man. Eric's had been hooded and mostly bloodshot. They moved quickly, but at the same time, seemed to slide rather than fall upon you, which was unfortunate for a doctor. When she remembered him now, it gave him more the look of a reptile, the kind of man who had little empathy and less sympathy for the less well-off around him. Yes, Elizabeth thought, unfortunate traits in a doctor. Dan's eyes were brown and they crinkled softly out into creases put there by smiling and sunshine, but not yet really tinged by age or worry.

It was strange, Elizabeth realised, that once she wouldn't have considered letting anyone into the kitchen; well when Eric was alive certainly, it had been firmly her territory. Since he had been buried, it was where she brought everyone. Today, she pulled out a chair and pointed him towards the big carver before the window. Over the last few weeks, she'd built something of a nest around that corner, with extra cushions, an old shawl, her book and a lightly scented candle that one of the young medical reps had given her. A set of binoculars sat on the window ledge. They were probably as old as herself. She used them for keeping an eye on the various wildlife activities in her overgrown garden.

She'd spotted a fox there earlier this morning. He

had stood, as transfixed as she, staring back at her for a moment. It was impossible to tell who was trespassing and who was most surprised by the other. The sight of him had given her an odd feeling of contentment. It was as if she'd been granted a special audience just to start her day off on a rather lively footing. An exotic happy energy danced within her as she shared the apparition later with Lucy and the patients in the waiting room.

'This is cosy,' he said brightly, looking out at the long wilderness that benefited from the morning sun far more than any light from the west. He picked up the glasses for a moment, looked through, focusing first and then glancing about the long grass and finally towards the sky where a family of ducks were swiftly making their way back to their nest away from the cool waters of the river, which ran along by Corrigan Mills.

'It's probably the place I spend the most time. The rest of the house has grown far too big for me as the years have gone on… but I suppose, I'll miss it once I sell it on…' she said softly with a conviction that surprised her. She had wondered if she'd really miss much about it apart from that one corner and her little job in the surgery if she had to let that go too.

'You're selling up?' he asked turning towards her. He dropped the binoculars, suddenly interested.

'I haven't done anything about it yet, not really, because it's a big step and there's quite a bit to be sorted out, what with the surgery and everything, but yes, I'd like something a little more modest.'

'This *is* rather grand.' He smiled and made a funny face

and they both laughed. 'But it suits you. I can't imagine you living anywhere else.'

'It was my husband's family home; they rather had notions...At this stage, I'd just like somewhere cosy that felt right. A small garden would be nice too, but then, I have the full beach to call my own for most of the year, so...' She waved a hand. She'd love to move in next door to Jo's cottage, but of course, houses on the seafront didn't come up very often.

'This is a beautiful house, so much potential. I'm sure there will be lots of interest.'

'Oh, I don't know, potential is a very dangerous word these days. There's a lot to be done with it, really, if you wanted to bring it up to its former glory. I suspect if I put it on the market it's likely to be flattened, perhaps turned into a second supermarket with a car park across the back garden.' Elizabeth tried not to think of that too much. The notion of the families of birds she'd watched for years being turned out to find a new home was enough to instil the kind of doubt she couldn't afford now. 'Anyway, I haven't even put it up for sale yet...' She smiled.

'Well, you know, if you did think you wanted to sell, I'm sure there would be lots of interest...' Dan inclined his head slightly. 'It would be perfect for a big family with roots here. If it was a few years down the line, I might even have a stab at it myself.' He laughed softly at that.

'Really? You'd consider moving here permanently?' Elizabeth looked around her kitchen. She couldn't imagine anyone wanting to settle here at such a young age and alone. 'Surely, you must be getting bored by now. A single man – London must be calling out to you.'

'No, I've had my fill of bright lights for now. I'll stay here until I have my book finished and then who knows.'

'You're lucky to have secured the cottage. You couldn't help but be inspired there.'

'Yes, but it's just rented and...' he looked out at the garden again '...there's no real future there, much and all as I love it. I mean, the views are spectacular,' he said softly.

'They are pretty nice here too. From my bedroom window, I'm looking right across at the lighthouse. At night, if I leave my curtains open, you can catch the faint shadows of it against the bedroom walls.'

'That must be lovely,' he said and if he wanted to take a look, he was much too well-mannered to suggest it.

'It's soothing really, I mean, in the storms you can hear the crashing of the sea and all year round you have the bells from the church. It's perfect really.' She laughed a little. It was a tinkling sound to her ears, the kind of laugh that she remembered as hers from many years earlier. Then she cleared her throat slightly. 'Of course, if you were really serious about taking it on, there are a few things that are not quite so perfect.'

'Oh?'

'Well, yes, there's the roof for starters – I imagine it's going to need a whole new roof. The rafters are on the point of collapsing and I've lost slates over the years, so there's probably a bit of damp up there too.'

'That's to be expected. I mean, the house must be up on two hundred years old.'

'It's that, easily, and of course, that means you can't actually do anything you like with it. It's a protected building, so everything has to be run by the planners.' She shook her head sadly. 'It's one of the reasons my husband was reluctant to do much with it when he was alive.'

'I can understand that. Back home, you can be tied up for months in red tape and still not get anywhere.'

'Yes. It's all very well, but now they want everything to be fuel-efficient and A-rated this and ecologically sustainable that. To be honest, there isn't a scat of insulation in the whole house.' She shook her head sadly.

'Do me a favour?' He leant forward slightly.

'What is it?' she asked.

'Don't become an auctioneer?' He smiled and seeing the funny side of it, they both laughed. 'You're talking yourself out of selling it for all the wrong reasons.'

'It's a big house for one,' she said softly. But as she said it, she had a feeling it would suit Dan if he were to stay in Ballycove. There was that same solidity to him as there was to the house. It was substantial; the kind of property a successful writer should be living in, rather than a poky little lean-to on the side of a hill. Actually, when she thought about it now, it would suit him perfectly, if it wasn't for the fact that he was single and it was a bit of a ramble of a house if you were here alone. 'And—' she pointed towards the end of the garden '—there's all of that. Those stables and the coach house at the end, I mean. They are as big as some of the cottages on the other side of town, you know.'

'Why on earth didn't you move the doctor's surgery

down there?' He asked the same question that she'd asked herself a million times over.

'I'm afraid my husband wasn't one for change. Once he settled in, that was that.'

'Pity, because they could be just perfect, all that exposed brick? And you'd have untold privacy if you did things right. Doesn't that end face out on Garden Square?'

'Yes, I suppose it all makes sense, but it's a bit late now, isn't it?'

'Oh, Elizabeth, it's never too late to change.' He leant back on his chair and surveyed the long garden stretching away from the house. Of course, she thought, it was all pie in the sky; he wouldn't really want to settle here, would he?

'It would also make a lovely writer's shed,' she said laughing.

'That's more like it.' He smiled.

'It's a great spot when you're here in summer, although I've found it a bit rambling on my own,' she said almost under her breath.

'It is big, but maybe I'll meet some nice Irish *cailín* and I'll fill the whole house with a brood of kids and then, who knows, I might need to buy next door as well.' They chatted some more about the house and in the end, she agreed, if it was going up for sale, she'd leave it to the experts. Elizabeth felt that by the time she flicked on the kettle, another small piece of her future was in some way falling into place.

'Tea or coffee?' she asked lightly.

'Neither – I thought, you might like something a little

stronger.' He reached into the bag he'd placed on the table and took out a bottle of Hennessy.

'That's certainly going to warm us up more than my ordinary old pot of tea.' She smiled and reached up to take down two wide tumblers.

'Brace yourself,' he said lightly as he poured a generous measure of brandy for them both. 'I hope you're not planning on swimming after this. I might have to follow you down and supervise!'

Elizabeth smiled at him. 'So what exactly am I bracing myself for?' she asked, sipping her drink slowly. It was delicious, a heady mix of warm and cool with the heavy smoky aroma of a man's drink, but the delicate fruitiness of something that was expensive enough to appeal to even the lightest drinker.

'This,' he said, reaching into the bag once more. 'I'd like you to take a read and tell me what you think.' He was smiling at her now.

'Is this your new book?' she asked, wishing she could remember where she'd left her reading glasses, then realising they were hanging about her neck since she'd only just left the surgery. She fumbled with them for a moment, breathing on them and wiping off the day's wear and then she placed them delicately before her eyes, before scanning over the first A4 sheet. 'Oh, is it…' She looked at the date again, just to check. 'Oh, my goodness, it *is* the one you're working on now.'

'It's almost finished. Actually, they're waiting for it in London and I'd been about to send it over a few days ago… Then I thought that perhaps you should have a read first.'

He smiled again, but there was a hint of embarrassment about his eyes. 'I stayed up all night formatting it, so...'

'But why me?' She was a little incredulous, and frankly quite chuffed. 'I mean, I feel very honoured, but surely there are people who know far more about books than I do.' She nodded towards the book at his elbow. 'All I ever read are romances...' She laughed thinking of the little bookshop and the hours she'd spent there too many years ago now.

'There's nothing wrong with that,' he said gently. 'My mother reads exactly the same and she is my best critic. She could spot a missed emotion a mile off and thankfully she's not afraid to tell me either.' His smile remained, but his eyes saddened, and she had a feeling that occasionally, he must miss having his own family close by. 'Anyway, I don't want you to edit it, or anything like that; I just want to hear what you think of it.'

'I'd be delighted to do that...' She looked down at it again. 'Is it almost finished?'

'The first draft almost is, but this is a cleaned-up copy of the first third of the book...' he said a little casually, but then he leant forward. A playful look about his eyes made her lean in closer to hear his next words. 'Okay, well this is between us, it's slightly longer than I'd planned, but how can you contain all of this...' He waved his arms about and she assumed he was talking about the landscape and not her rather gloomy kitchen. 'I'm hoping my agent will pitch it as a movie idea.' He exhaled as if it was something he'd had to keep to himself, and then he picked up his brandy and sipped it pleasurably.

'A movie? How exciting – imagine, Ballycove on the big screen,' she said and then she thought of something: 'I wonder if they'd come and film here...'

'Oh, don't worry about that, it's a long way off. Really, I just want you to tell me what you make of the characters and the story, nothing more. If you like it.' He stopped. 'If you're okay with it, then I'll send it off.'

'If I'm *okay* with it?'

'Well yes, you see...' He looked out the window for a second and she could almost see a little emotion that might be exactly what she felt before Lucy took the idea of their fundraiser in her hands; it was apprehension. It crossed his features only fleetingly, but it was there. 'It's set here, in Ballycove.'

'Yes, don't tell me are we all in it?' She was joking now, rubbing her hands together.

'No, not all, but the main character is a lot like...'

'Seriously, who?' Elizabeth figured it had to be the new lady vicar or perhaps it was Lucy; how deliciously perfect if it was. 'Please, you just have to tell me.'

'Well, it's... you, actually,' he said, a small hint of a smile hiding at the corners of his lips confirmed that he wasn't kidding; he was actually serious.

24

Lucy

By the grace of God, or perhaps just her own conniving and surreptitious evasion, Lucy had managed to keep herself so busy that she didn't break down with the heavy sadness that weighed on her every time she thought about her mother. Still she felt as if she was teetering on the edge of having her heart broken once again – only this time, there would be no repairing the fracture losing Jo would cause.

Everything with Jack, well it was all too raw to compare, but she knew the only reason she survived it was because Jo had linked her through the worst. She was over him, well over him it turned out now that she had something so much bigger to worry about. She'd stopped crying for Jack months ago and now it felt as if she was too empty of tears to find them for her mother. Maybe, at times, when she was immersed in the surgery, surrounded by people who were beginning to mean more to her every day, she could convince herself that they would find a way forward.

She was, in spite of herself, enjoying her work. Even though most nights, she lay awake, listening to the waves crashing against the rocks, thinking about Jo, trying not to fear the worst, she still got up each morning and made the best of things. In the surgery, it was so busy, she hadn't time to turn around, never mind brood about Jo or worry about Niall. If she was ticking off her list of priorities, he'd slid quite a bit down the scale. He seemed happier in himself, since she'd told him about Sydney – that was as far as she could let herself think.

The notion of being surrounded by friends and community buoyed her up much more than she could have expected. Every so often, she remembered that Dan was walking down to her mother's cottage and taking Dora for a long walk each day when he really didn't have to. He'd struck up a friendship with Niall too and even if she still worried about her son, at least he had something to ground him here in Ballycove for now.

Her mother was being extremely chipper and while that might not come as a surprise to people like Elizabeth, Lucy knew that even the most positive people buckled at some point under a cancer diagnosis. If Jo had down days, she managed somehow to hide them from the people around her and Lucy figured that took some special kind of bravery or love for your nearest and dearest.

The fundraiser was doing a lot to keep them all positive. It was something to aim for and regardless of what Elizabeth decided to do with the surgery, Lucy had made up her mind she would be in Ballycove for as long as Jo needed her.

The surgery? That was another question that hung over her. Lucy had a feeling that if she sold up her little house in Dublin and added to the money she had left over from the sale of the rather affluent address she'd shared with Jack, she probably had enough money to buy both the house and the business. The problem was that even if she was sure it was the right thing to do, Elizabeth needed all the cash together – now. Lucy and Jo were probably the only two people in the village to know the extent of the debt hanging about Elizabeth's neck.

Eric O'Shea had been a drinker and a gambler and he was much more prolific at both of these than he had been successful as a country GP. The end result was that his wife was left with a shell of a house, the remains of a business and a string of debtors who could foreclose at the first sign of a jugular exposed. To be honest, she could see the potential in the surgery. With a little investment in the property and equipment, it could be a really good way to make a living.

She could, if she wanted to, make her permanent home here in Ballycove; she could easily settle in here for the long haul. There were worse places she thought; actually, there was probably nowhere better. The roads were free of clogged-up traffic, you were a stone's throw from an unpolluted empty beach and she knew everyone and knew they were good people. She would be welcomed here, not just because they needed a doctor, but because she was one of them.

Still, it seemed none of that mattered. The timing was terrible and she couldn't think beyond Jo's cancer – whereas

Elizabeth needed a solution sooner rather than later. Lucy had no idea what her future held and so, how on earth could she make promises of the sort that required sinking her life's savings and her whole future into a village at the far end of civilisation. Anyway, she couldn't think about that now; her only priority was Jo. Really, all she could do was keep treading water: going to work, coming home, waiting, waiting. Sometimes she wondered what exactly she was waiting for, but then she'd raise her head from her busy day and remember.

Her mother had faded away to a fraction of the woman she'd always been. She barely ate now and what she did never stayed down for very long, so her weight had plummeted and her skin held that grey colour that only smokers and the very ill wear without the knowledge that it marks them out. Her medication was so strong that although it kept her pain at bay, it also tired her out, so she spent most of her day sleeping. It was as if she used up her whole store for Niall – he was, for both of them, the highlight of each day. Lucy and Elizabeth still met each evening for the Ladies' Midnight Swimming Club. Jo managed to join them on rare nights when her body seemed intent on taunting them all with a burst of energy that vitalised her into the woman she'd always been.

Last weekend, it seemed she'd wizened even further into herself and there was the addition of a rather stubborn cough that halted somewhere in the back of her throat. Lucy had taken her temperature, filled her with as many oranges to increase her vitamin C as she could and said a silent prayer, even though she'd never been one much for God.

They were four weeks off the Dip in the Nip and really, Lucy couldn't see how Jo could possibly go into the freezing waters of the Atlantic Ocean without perishing – literally. She was adamant there was no point asking the consultant before that and even if she didn't agree, silently, Lucy knew she was right.

'Oh, Lucy, you worry far too much about me,' Jo said and put her hand up to stop her saying another word. 'It's really sweet, but you have to stop. It's going to be fine; I'm made of tougher stuff than you realise.' She shook her head.

'Will you at least mention the fundraiser to the consultant the next time he does his rounds? Let him know the lunacy you're planning...' Lucy had a feeling she might as well have been talking to the pots and pans.

'I will, if it'll make you happy,' Jo agreed in the end, but still Lucy had a feeling that if her mother had to be carried down that beach, she had every intention of showing up on the day. God knows, near enough everyone who visited the treatment ward had been signed up for a ten- or twenty-euro sponsorship donation. 'I can't let my fans down,' she'd said laughing then.

'They need never know. I'm happy to go into the water for your share as well as my own,' Lucy said.

'Oh dear and you'd let me miss out on all that fun. I don't think so. I'm really looking forward to it. Even old Mrs Wills is going and she must be ninety if she's a day.'

'Holy crap,' Niall snorted from behind his phone. 'What's she thinking? The sight of her in the buff will be enough to frighten every fish from the bay.' Jo winked at

Lucy. They still laughed because Niall pretended he didn't hear what they were saying mostly.

'I suppose we'll just have to hope for a heat wave,' Lucy said and bit down on her words as she was saying them, because really, there was no surer way to predict snow in August than pray for sunny weather in the west of Ireland.

Perhaps it was because the fog was so very heavy the following week that on Wednesday morning Lucy never noticed the For Sale sign in the garden next door to their house. The Murphy house had been owned by the same family probably since it was built. It had been empty since old John Murphy had finally agreed to move in with his daughter who lived in one of the estates on the way into the village. It was for the best, although when he'd told Jo, they'd all been sad to see him go and no-one had thought for a moment that the family would actually put the property up for sale. After all, John was hardly an old man. A recent fall had left him in plaster, but really, they'd expected him to return as soon as he was mobile again.

By lunchtime, news of the sign's arrival had made its way into the surgery. Elizabeth sat a little nervously at her kitchen table while Lucy tucked into lunch. Alice was still on her rounds and finishing early for a parent-teacher meeting. When Elizabeth broached the subject, her voice was a notch higher and it struck a nervous pitch in the otherwise quiet kitchen.

'One of the old dears mentioned this morning that

Murphy's cottage has come up for sale.'

'Well, that's unexpected, but perhaps it's the sign you've been waiting for?' Lucy smiled at her, but she could see the tell-tale quavers of apprehension in Elizabeth's eyes.

'Yes, perhaps.' She shrugged her shoulders, in a rather French way, and settled her eyes on something that was probably nothing at all, midway down the long tangle of garden outside. 'It seems like I'm not the only one thinking of putting down new roots,' she said gently.

'Oh?' Lucy folded away the magazine she'd planned to flick through to take her mind off Jo – she wasn't sure who she was trying to convince that it might work. 'Who else is on the move?'

'Dan.'

'Dan, the writer?' Lucy asked and she knew she sounded like an echo, but it felt like a bolt from the blue. Where would Dan go? But then, maybe she already knew the answer to that? Back to London.

'Yes, believe it or not—' a small smile escaped Elizabeth's lips and she leant in a little closer to Lucy '—between ourselves, I think he might be interested in buying this place.'

'What?' Lucy wasn't sure if she heard right, but then she gathered herself up, because this was good news, wasn't it?

'You look surprised,' Elizabeth said softly. 'Nothing is set in stone, not if you were thinking of…'

'No, no, nothing like that. I haven't really given it any thought at all since… not really.' She didn't need to add, the top-most consideration on her mind these days was Jo and they were busy enough with the fundraiser to keep much more from her thoughts. 'I suppose, I just wouldn't have thought he'd hang around.'

'Not enough excitement for him after the bright lights of London?'

'Something like that,' she said, but then, when she thought about it now, this place suited him. There was an earthiness about Dan that Lucy couldn't imagine in London. 'So, he'd buy the lot?'

'We haven't actually talked nuts and bolts, just that if it ever came up for sale, he might be interested in looking at it.' She smiled. 'The notion of having to repair the roof and insulate the place didn't seem to faze him either, so that's positive.'

'It certainly is,' Lucy said, but the news hit her in a way that she'd never have expected and she wasn't quite sure how she felt about it, or indeed why it affected her so acutely. She would really have to give the whole idea some thought, because now, sitting here with Elizabeth, it all seemed so much more pressing. If this house was sold, well, wasn't it once, so long ago, the house of her dreams? Of course, then she'd believed that if she lived in a big house at the top of the town, she'd be living here with her husband and a couple of kids and maybe a great big bruiser of a dog too. She could cross Jack off her wish list that was for certain now. She was pretty sure that she couldn't afford to go up against Dan if he wanted to buy the place.

'Are you okay?' Elizabeth asked kindly.

'Yes, I'm fine, just lost in my thoughts.'

'I haven't actually done anything yet, so don't worry and

even if I do sell on the surgery, no-one's going to be able to take it on immediately.' She reached out and squeezed Lucy's hand.

'You mustn't worry about me.' Lucy smiled. 'Really, I still haven't settled on a plan and much as I enjoy being here, with everything else that's come my way over the last year, I'm just reluctant to make any major decisions until I'm sure.'

'Very wise.' Elizabeth reached forward and topped up both of their cups from the coffee pot on the table. 'It's all pie in the sky anyway. I haven't even looked at Murphy's cottage.' Her expression changed. 'To be honest, I was never keen on her,' she confided. 'Eileen – she never smiled, never thought she liked me very much.'

'I don't suppose Eileen Murphy liked anyone very much; I really wouldn't take it too personally.'

'Still, to find myself living in her house after all these years?'

'You need to go and have a look first, then decide.' Lucy knew if there was much to be done here, there was every bit as much work to be carried out on the little cottage next door to her mother's. She sipped her coffee thoughtfully. 'Do you think Dan might still be interested if you were to only sell the house and garden and move the surgery to the old stables at the end of the garden and keep it all completely separate?' Lucy had a feeling she was only putting the words on what was running through Elizabeth's thoughts now. 'It's still a very impressive residence and the garden is huge. He'd have a really secure boundary at the finish if the doors and windows were blocked up from this side.'

'I think it would be well worth taking a look at it, don't you?'

'Absolutely,' Lucy said and although she wasn't really sure why, she felt a little better with the notion that the surgery would remain separate to any sale. 'Now...' She pushed Elizabeth's phone towards her. 'You'd better ring up about that cottage.'

The next three weeks flooded into each other. Jo's cough developed into something approaching a chest infection and it culminated in a trip to hospital and antibiotics so strong, Lucy wondered if they were veterinary prescriptions. The mention of hospice by one of the young doctors was enough to catapult Jo from her bed and when Lucy arrived back that evening, she was sitting in the day chair with bags packed by another patient Jo had collared from the corridor.

She spent the following week at home in bed and although Lucy was glad to have her back at the cottage, it didn't stop her worrying like crazy that with her compromised immune system, even a chest infection could become a serious health complication for her. Fortunately, with a lot of TLC, hot soups, vitamin C and plenty of gossip from the village by the end of the week, Jo looked much brighter.

'Actually, I'd say you look ten times better than you did three weeks ago,' Lucy said. It was the Saturday afternoon and she was sitting on the double bed, facing out towards the sea. She was watching one of the local fishing boats bob across frothy swells that looked like little more than ripples from here. Lucy knew well enough those pretty waves were probably eight or nine foot high, chewing viciously at the boat.

'Really, I think you're trying to make me feel better.'

'No, if I thought you looked worse, I'd have packed you off up to hospital again.' It was the truth, although from her mother's expression she wondered if it sounded like a threat to her. 'You really do. I think the week has done you good – a little holiday in the middle of it all.'

'I've been spoiled here between the lot of you. It's funny, but even the little things like my own cotton sheets and being able to toddle to the loo without having to let a nurse know where I'm going, it's been nice to have the time.' Jo sighed. 'It's been a bonus having you here; you know I do appreciate it, but all the same…'

'What are you saying? I want to be here.' Lucy laughed; she wouldn't be anywhere else now.

'Still, the time is passing and if you want to make the most of your time away from the hospital, this wasn't in the plan.'

'We both know you'd have been quite content for me to hang about here until I'm as ancient as dear old Mrs Wills. The reason you're sending me off now is because you're afraid I'm only hanging about for you.'

'Well, aren't you?'

'Maybe,' Lucy said. 'But that doesn't matter. I'm actually very happy here.' The words tripped off her tongue easily, but when she'd said them, she stopped, because somehow within them there was certain wisdom. She was *very happy here*. Actually, she was far happier here than she'd ever been in Dublin. She was much more fulfilled working as a country GP than she could remember being in a big hospital situation. The truth was, now she thought about it that had always been her ambition. The only reason she'd settled into working in a hospital for so long was because it suited them both while Jack worked towards becoming a surgeon. Why had she not seen this before?

'What is it?' Jo tried to pull herself up higher on the pillows.

'It's nothing...' Lucy sighed. 'Maybe it's not, but you know I've dithered about what to do next?'

'Lucy, it's what you needed. Time to think...' she said gently.

'Yes, I know, but that's the thing: it's been so busy here, I haven't had time to think.'

'I'm sorry, it's...'

'No, you don't understand. It's a good thing. I've been so busy, I've stopped thinking and actually, I just gave myself my answer. I'm happier here than I ever was in Dublin. I don't want to go back to work in the hospital again. I want to work as a GP and I can't think of anywhere I'd rather work than here, in Ballycove,' Lucy said and she couldn't help smiling. 'There's only one small fly in the ointment now that I've decided.'

'Elizabeth has sold on the practice?'

'No, not as far as I know.' Lucy laughed. 'The only thing wrong now is that we can't celebrate with champagne, not until you have those awful antibiotics behind you.'

'Well, I shall have something to look forward to then, won't I?' Jo laughed and she held out her arms and folded them around Lucy in the warmest hug she could manage from beneath the heavy quilt. Then she held her daughter back, for just a moment. 'You're sure, darling, that this is the right thing for you? Moving here to Ballycove and taking over the practice?'

'I don't think I've ever been more certain of anything in my life, Mum,' Lucy felt a glow of optimism for the first time since Jo's cancer had been diagnosed. 'Now, all I have to do is agree a deal with Elizabeth.'

25

Niall

It seemed to Niall that the summer had raced into itself. It was hard to believe that July was almost at an end and soon he would be packing his bags to start a new life in Sydney with his dad. He was very much looking forward to that, no matter how much his grandmother tried to convince him that far-off fields are not always greener.

'You think nowhere is as green as Ballycove,' he'd joked with her earlier as they'd played a final game of rummy before fatigue overtook her.

'I'm right. I'll bet when you arrive in Sydney, the only green fields you're likely to see will be in some posh country club where they have sprinklers going all night long.'

'Okay, well, in that way, I suppose you have a point,' he conceded. 'But there's lots of other stuff there that I'm really looking forward to.' And there was, like seeing his dad and the amazing apartment he had bought that looked out over Sydney Harbour.

'I know, I can imagine city life is a lot more appealing than being stuck in a backwater place like Ballycove, but...'

'I know. I can always come home again.' He smiled at her then, but in the air between them hung that one thing they never talked about. Coming home here, when his grandmother had died, Niall just wasn't sure it would be like home anymore. Sure his mother would be here, but she'd be immersed in the practice once the papers were signed and she owned the place properly – even more than she was already.

'This will always be your home – you know that, Niall,' she said softly now. It was funny, but it was when her voice seemed to fade to little more than a murmur that Niall knew her words were the most important. 'You won't forget that, will you? Or that your mother is going to miss you more than anything in the world. You won't forget her, in the excitement of it all...' She closed her eyes and he knew that, sometimes, it was the worry of what would become of him and his mother that emptied her out the most.

'Don't be daft, Gran. I'll never forget Mum, and I'll never forget you either.' He leant in and kissed her gently on her forehead. When he moved away, her eyes had closed and he knew she was sleeping. Her breath now was ragged and thready as if it was racing out of her to keep ahead of itself so it couldn't be called to a halt until she was ready to fully let go.

Niall sat there, for a long while, just watching her breathe, knowing that, there would come a day when he couldn't do that anymore. He hadn't said it to either his mother or his father, but he wanted to be here when she went. He wanted to be right here, sitting on the edge of her bed, telling her that he loved her until that very last moment, because he knew he hadn't said it often enough over the years. If anything, when they'd come here at the start of the summer, he had railed against the notion of having to spend time with her. Now, he knew, he didn't want to hear the news when he was thousands of miles away. It turned out, he loved her a lot more than he'd ever realised and maybe, sometimes, he thought he was lucky, because if they hadn't been here now, he'd have missed out on the stories and the sheer fun of knowing his grandmother properly at all.

Niall slipped out of the cottage just as the village seemed to be closing down for the evening and people were driving back from their jobs in Ballybrack, making their way home for dinner and calling an end to their day.

There was a rhythm to the village and over the weeks he'd been here, it seemed as if he'd managed to get a sense of it. For the next hour or so, the pier and the beach would be empty and then, once people had watched the six o'clock news, on a nice evening like this, there would be dog walkers heading out for their evening stroll.

In the beginning, everything about the place had made him feel more isolated. Everyone knew everyone and if they didn't, as in Niall's case, they knew enough about them to have made up their minds about you. But it was a funny thing, because once he met Dan and they became friends, it felt as if he had some proper connection to the place. Gradually, he got to know people. The kid in the chipper was called Damian – he was all right, not that Niall would exactly call him a friend, but it was nice to at least have someone sit next to him on the wall overlooking the beach some days.

And then, there was Zoe Huang.

They'd sat on the pier for almost an hour the previous day. She had just come along and plopped down next to him, as if it was the most natural thing in the world. They dangled their feet over the side, just tipping the cold water with their toes. Although summer had arrived, the sea was still icy, but it was such a warm day, the cool water was pleasant.

'So, what do you do when you're not sitting here on the pier?' Zoe turned to him; she was making fun of him, but in a nice way.

'There's not much *to do* around here, is there?'

'Oh, I don't know,' Zoe said and she lay back on the warm concrete, shading her eyes from the blinding sun overhead. 'My father is dropping me into town on Saturday. There's a fair on, not anything huge or as exciting as you'd have in Dublin probably, but all my friends from school will be there... if you wanted to tag along.'

'I, oh, all right, yeah, why not,' he said lying down next to her. The sun was warm on his skin, his feet still dangling over the side of the water. 'I suppose it's the one thing that this place is missing... kids our age.'

'Well there are kids,' she said and turned to look at him for a moment, because maybe they both knew the boys who normally hung around the boats were the kind who saw anyone who was an outsider or different as someone they could mark out to bully. 'No, in my school there are lots of kids, just like us, you know?'

'Yeah, I think I do.' He smiled; there was no need to say any more.

'I should be getting back to the shop. My dad will be expecting me and if I'm late he... well, he worries about me.' She stood over him for a moment, looking out across the water and back towards the beach. 'I think it's going to be a great summer,' she said softly. 'Don't forget Saturday, at two o'clock. You know where my dad's piano shop is?'

'Sure, on Garden Square?'

'Yep, don't be late,' she called as she ran back up towards the village.

Niall stayed there for a while, until the sun became a little cooler, covered over by some light passing clouds. He decided to go back to the house and make a cup of coffee for himself and listen to some music until his mother came home.

Just as he closed the front door, he heard the phone ring loudly in the kitchen.

'Dad?' His father never rang him, not unless there was something important or it was an occasion.

'Niall, I'm just trying to catch up with your mother. Is she there?'

'Um, no. It's just me, actually.'

'Ah, how are you?'

'Good, really good,' Niall managed, because he was actually; he just realised.

'And your mother, she's...' His father's words drifted off into silence. When had they forgotten what to say to each other? Niall suddenly realised that speaking with his father had somehow become an effort over the last few years. Perhaps it was the distance? Or maybe it was the fact that their worlds had spun much further than just miles apart? Time too had separated them, so the little everyday things they might have once shared now only stood between them.

'At work,' Niall said.

'Of course she is...' His father sounded as if he was distracted.

'Dad,' Niall said tentatively. 'I'm really excited about going out to Sydney to you...'

'I'll be glad to have you. Now your mother has decided to move to that backwater permanently, I could see why you'd want to get out of there.'

'She's told you about the practice, then?'

'Yep, she even suggested that you start in the school nearest to the village and give country living a go. Of course, that wouldn't do. I mean we're city boys, aren't we?'

'She never said a word about me moving schools.'

'Well, maybe she knew how you'd react; no youngster wants to leave the city and the best boarding school in the country to live among a bunch of yokels.'

'Actually, I have a friend who goes to that school.' He didn't add that Zoe Huang was one more friend than he had in his own school.

'And I suppose all they talk about is fishing and farming.'

'As it happens, they don't have a farm. Her father is a piano restorer. She has no interest in farming or fishing,' so far as Niall knew from their afternoon on the pier. All they'd talked about was books, games and films. Zoe was as big a reader as Niall was, so they'd had lots of books in common.

'Anyway, what does it matter? You're coming out to Sydney and I was going to run it by your mother first, but I've found an all-boys private boarding school here. It's pricey and a bit of a track to and from where we are, but you'll be able to come back here to the apartment in term time. I can't wait to show you Sydney; you're going to love it.' His father sounded excited at the prospect.

'Aren't there any day schools, like a college or just a regular secondary school?'

'Of course, there are, but it's not like Ireland, Niall. You know, my job means I'm working crazy hours and well, you know how it is...' His words trailed off, because they both knew his girlfriend didn't like kids.

'Sure, no problem. Can I look it up, to see what it's like?'

'Of course. I was just about to email everything to your mother, so I'll send it on to you also, okay?'

'Brilliant.' Niall tried to keep his voice enthusiastic, but there was no getting away from the fact that Sydney sounded a lot like his life was in Dublin – just more of the same with warmer weather. Whereas Ballycove, if things worked out as his mother was quietly planning, well, it could be a million times better than jetting off to the far corner of the world. 'Dad,' he said just as his father was about to hang up on the other end of the line. 'Have you enrolled me yet?'

'Niall, I value my life. Do you think I'd dare enrol you

without checking with your mother first of all?'

'Good, it's just… well, I'd like to take a look at the place first, even it is just on the web.'

'Sure, son, no problem.'

When he put the phone down, Niall felt as if the wind had been pulled from his stomach. The elation of earlier, chatting to Zoe and looking forward to the fair the following day all seemed to disappear. Sydney sounded like a prison sentence. He'd be shunted to school and his father's apartment would never feel like home. He made a cup of coffee and sloped off up to his room. His appetite had disappeared. He just wanted to lie on his bed and play video games.

26

Dan

It was the first time he'd ever imagined his birth mother actually being real, but then, these last few days, knowing that he had come as close as he'd ever been to finding her, seemed to make her more tangible to him. It was a strange but pleasant feeling, the notion that they might be breathing the same air – then he stopped himself. He knew the chances were she'd taken the boat to London, just as the batty old nun –Sister Berthilde had suggested.

Today the sea was whispering on the sand opposite, rather than crashing against the rocks. Even the gulls had become sanguine, too lazy to consider moving off the wall across from him and instead of darting over the water they sat and occasionally dived and seemed satisfied with that. He figured he could sit here for the day, just chilling out and watching the world go by. It had been a good week; there was much to savour.

He smiled now, thinking of his agent's reaction to the

new project. He'd sent it on as soon as Elizabeth had said she liked it. As he'd expected, she didn't see herself in it at all. It was funny, because generally people never do – not really. The only ones to see themselves in his work were people whose egos were far bigger than their brains – they were invariably wrong. He supposed the fact that he'd changed Elizabeth's appearance, made her a little older and her husband a little younger had made her harder to recognise. That was about all he had changed though, because the story still centred around a woman who had managed to make a new life for herself and the key to her newfound joie de vivre was swimming in the cold and dark Atlantic Ocean.

The novel, which he'd had to hastily amend, finished up with a communal skinny-dip. Already, he could visualise the final scene, a bunch of women actresses, all heading off on a grey beach, whooping with laughter and only their lined and happy faces close up to the camera. It would, he knew with little doubt, translate into a fantastic piece of cinematography. This was a story of awakening and Elizabeth had recognised that. When she'd finished reading it, even if she didn't see herself, she confided in him that it gave her courage.

He closed his eyes now against the warm rays of the sun. He liked that notion; the idea that maybe, if it was developed into a film project, it just might give someone else courage too. He tried to tell her then that a film was a million miles off. He had to find a publisher first.

'Leave it with me,' Harry said and Dan could hear the familiar tinge of stress to his voice. It hadn't taken long for the call back. Harry had read it in two sittings. 'Bloody brilliant, mate – easily, your best work ever.'

'I'm not sure about that, but...'

'No.' Harry cut him off. 'Absolutely no false modesty – it's bloody brilliant and if anyone asks, that's what you're to tell them, okay?'

'I can't see anyone asking, unless you mean the curlews?'

'You're not still over there, are you?' It sounded as if he was stretching out his arms, trying to straighten up his back after hours curled around the manuscript.

'Where else do you think I'd be?'

'Oh, I don't know, maybe London?'

'What on earth would I be doing in London?' But of course, Dan knew: London was meant to be home. For someone like Harry, it was the centre of the universe.

'And when are you moving back?' That was Harry, always cutting to the quick.

'I'm not. I'm thinking of making an offer to buy a house here,' Dan said, his voice controlled, but firm.

'You're not serious?' Dan started to laugh.

'Actually I am.'

'Well, make sure it's a good investment property, because you don't want to lose an arm and a leg when you have to sell it on.'

'I'll do my best to get something suitable,' Dan said softly, thinking of the house he had set his heart on a few days earlier. He'd have to talk to the bank, organise a bridging loan, just until he could offload his own apartment in London and tell his mum and dad that he wasn't planning on living there anymore.

He sat for a while longer, enjoying the peace. He deserved a break. He'd worked hard to get the novel down in just a few weeks and now, he was going to enjoy a few days with absolutely no writing or thinking, plotting or planning.

27

Elizabeth

Elizabeth couldn't help being just a little disappointed when the auctioneer rang to say that a generous offer had been made on the house next door to Jo's.

It was hit-and-miss timing. That offer had come in a week ago and now, there were two buyers interested in it, and Elizabeth knew, even if she had freed up the cash from the sale of the surgery, it would be madness to get into a bidding war on the little cottage.

Still, she knew there was a lot to be thankful for. Lucy was buying the surgery and that alone meant that she could easily clear the debts and if a cottage on one of the little side streets should come up that she liked, she could buy it without having to wait for her own house to sell. The best part of it all, apart from the news that Lucy would be staying on in the village was that she'd offered Elizabeth a full-time job.

She, Elizabeth O'Shea would be a full-time receptionist

in the practice. Lucy had gone out and purchased a brand-new computer and a very comfortable chair that was practically designed to make Elizabeth feel as if she was made for the job. With Niall at her elbow for the first few days showing her how to navigate around the new desktop, she was soon feeling as if she'd been doing it forever.

'I don't know what to say.' She had started to cry that evening, when Lucy told her she absolutely wanted her to stay on.

'You're going to say, yes, of course,' Lucy said. 'Don't we make a great team: you, Alice and me? I have no intention of changing that; in fact, it's the best part of coming to work here every day.'

'Oh, Lucy, I'd love to continue working here. You have no idea what it means to me.' She couldn't begin to put it into words. It was more than just giving a mental two fingers to Eric who never believed she could do anything more than keep house and play bridge. Although, she knew that thinking of him looking down on the surgery now, well, it tickled her to know how much her working here would probably really annoy him. No, rather it was the fact that they wanted her. She'd done a good job, sorting out a proper filing system, looking after patients while they waited to see either Lucy or Alice, making sure that everything ran smoothly. From the first few days, Elizabeth had organised everything from lunch to cashing up the night's takings.

'I'm just so glad you decided to stay,' Elizabeth said to Lucy after they told Alice about the plans for the surgery.

'I would have decided much sooner, if it wasn't for...'

Jo's cancer hung on those unsaid words. 'Really, when I look back, I'd have been eaten up with regret if someone else had come in and taken over.' She smiled then. 'I couldn't imagine going back to Dublin now.'

'You've come home,' Alice said simply.

'Yes, I suppose I have,' Lucy said.

'There's a lot to do, to bring it up to the kind of standards you've been used to in the hospital,' Elizabeth reminded her.

'We don't have to do anything immediately; we have time to think,' Lucy said, looking about the waiting room fondly. 'And anyway, it's a profitable practice. It won't be long until I can start ploughing some of the takings back in again.'

'I can't wait to see it transform,' Elizabeth said. She had no doubt that Lucy would make it into the best surgery for miles around and she was right, of course. Since Elizabeth had started to receipt every patient who came through the door, it was obvious that Eric was making a lot more money than she ever realised. Of course, now there were more overheads, three decent wages to pay to Lucy, Alice and Elizabeth, but still she shuddered as she imagined how much Eric had frittered away in the pub and the bookies.

'To Ballycove medical practice.' Alice raised her coffee cup. 'And many more years for all of us working here together.'

'To us,' Lucy said and they clinked glasses happily. 'We'll have to organise some champagne and toast it properly when all the papers are signed off,' she said laughing then and Elizabeth had a feeling it would be only the first of many celebrations to come.

It was her new thing, checking the calendar each morning and counting down the days until their midnight charity swim. It was hard to believe it was only a week away. She reminded Jo of it when she went to visit her dear friend later that morning.

'You'd better be behaving yourself,' she said mock crossly.

'Never,' Jo whispered. She was tired today. On days like this, she was almost unrecognisable from the woman she'd known for so long. And yet, Elizabeth had seen her like this before and then, a few days later, she'd rally round enough to turn up for their midnight swim. Of course, Lucy would be giving out and telling her that it was unadulterated madness for a woman who'd been so unwell only days earlier to be stripping down and getting into the sea in the middle of the night. But Jo was still Jo. Her friend had never allowed anyone's opinion to sway her from her chosen path.

'We have only days to go, so no funny business now.'

'Don't you worry; I have every intention of being there. I'll be expecting a round of applause at the very least.' She laughed.

'You'll be lucky. I'd say half the women of the village will be far too busy covering over their peculiar bits to dare put their hands together.'

'You'll be surprised.' Jo smiled and Elizabeth thought

her heart would break because there was so much spirit left in her friend's eyes even if the life was being drained from her body.

'So, you must be over the moon about Lucy staying on.'

'As are you, I'm sure.' Jo cocked an eye on her. Then she looked out towards the window. 'It's the right thing,' she breathed. 'It's the right thing for both of you.' She closed her eyes. 'I want you to look out for each other… when I'm gone.'

'Stop it. Don't talk about that now.'

'No.' Jo raised a hand that was almost skeletal. The skin hanging from her bones made Elizabeth want to wrap up her friend so nothing further could happen to her. 'I have to say this to you. You're going to need each other. The Ladies' Midnight Swimming Club, you need to keep it going; *you* need to make sure that you're both…'

'We're going to see each other every single day.' Elizabeth tried to laugh.

'You know what I mean. You need to talk to each other. She has an unhappy marriage behind her; she needs to meet someone new. It's not too late for her to have a larger family. It's what she always wanted.'

'And you want me to find her a good husband? I'm hardly qualified to advise on that front.'

'No, but you're well placed to make sure she doesn't marry another one like the one she married before.' Jo shook her head. Elizabeth knew she'd never liked Jack Nolan no matter how much she tried to pretend that she did. 'It's not just that though, you'll both need a good friend. I'll do what I can from…' She raised her eyes towards the ceiling.

'Will you stop it? You know I'm going to look out for her...' Elizabeth said and now the tears were much too close to say much more. Instead she looked out at the sea opposite. She loved it here.

'Good. That's as much as I'm going to ask you to do for me.' She smiled then and there was no hiding that devilish sense of humour. 'For now.'

'Yes, all you have to do for me is turn up on the fifteenth when we're all out there swimming in your honour.'

'I'll be there,' Jo said softly and Elizabeth just prayed she would.

PART 5

August

28

Jo

It seemed to Jo that she woke before anyone else on the morning before they were due to launch into the water as the Ladies' Midnight Swimming Club. There was no point being awake now though; it would be the other side of the day before she'd even think of getting out of the bed. She'd learned, over the last few weeks, that getting the most out of the time she had left was all about pacing herself.

She felt badly, because she could see in Lucy's eyes the worry that some days she didn't get up much further than raising herself onto an extra pillow at her shoulders. It was enough to watch the world unfold outside her bedroom window and anything more she needed to know was supplied by Niall and Elizabeth when they came to sit on her bed each day and fill her in on all that was happening in the village. Dan had taken to visiting her too, now that he had finished writing his book, during the day when

Lucy was at the surgery. He would let himself in the side door and make them both a cup of tea, before depositing it on her bedside table. He'd sit and listen while she told him all she knew about village life when St Nunciata's was up and running. Sometimes, if she hadn't the energy to talk, he'd tell her about his life in London and how he'd found out about where he'd originally come from.

Jo wasn't sure if he'd told anyone else in the village, and somehow, that made these visits from someone who'd been a stranger only weeks earlier when he'd brought Niall back that night, all the more special. Then, when he'd finished his tea and rinsed out both of their cups, he'd offer to take Dora for a walk along the beach. Later, Jo would hear the gate creak and know that the little dog had returned weary and happy after her excursion.

Like saving herself for the occasional swim at the cove, Jo had been shoring up her energy for this day. Honestly, sometimes when she lay here alone, she knew that if she could make it out into the water with the other ladies, she'd happily come back here and close her eyes and let that be the end of it all.

What more could she really ask of life? She'd had a great run of it, enjoyed every single moment, if she was honest, and that hadn't stopped just because she was told that she was dying. She was still enjoying every day as much as she possibly could. She had a beautiful daughter, a grandson she loved the bones of and a friend who'd remained as loyal over the years as any husband could be expected to be. She was leaving behind a village that would miss her. From the very top of it to the bottom, she knew every single person and she also knew that in some way, she'd touched every single life here in her time.

She'd had her rows, of course. She'd had a real scuffle with old Eric O'Shea, but he deserved everything he got. The village might remember her as outspoken, but mostly they would remember her as pioneering one good cause after another – or at least, that was as much as she could hope for now.

The carriage clock, a wedding present that lasted longer than her marriage, chimed out to tell her that it was too early to rise just yet. She turned over and closed her eyes again, lingering on the edge of sleep and dreams of throwing herself into the velvety Atlantic waters – it was only nine hours away. All she had to do now was rest and then with a little luck she'd go for what she knew was probably going to be her final midnight swim.

29

Lucy

They were lucky it had been the hottest August day on record in fifty years. It was one of those days when even resting your foot on the sun-burned path left you feeling as if you were risking scorch marks to the soles of your feet. Lucy had looked out at the shimmering tarmac on the road outside the surgery at lunchtime and it felt as if the whole village had retreated from the overwhelming heat. Even so, Lucy worried that it would be too cold for Jo, but at the same time, she knew she couldn't stop her mother. Honestly, she suspected a team of charging rhinoceroses couldn't keep her off that beach if they tried. Just after she finished lunch, she heard a light tap on the door and when she went to check she found Dan standing there with a silly grin on his face and parked outside a cross-country scrambler thing, which was somewhere between being a motorbike and a tractor.

'I thought this might come in handy,' he said and then

angled his head to see past Lucy. 'Is Jo still intent on going down to the shore?'

'What do you think?'

'I'd be surprised if she wasn't.' He laughed. 'So, I thought, maybe you could bring her down on this. I borrowed it for the afternoon,' he supplied helpfully.

'Me, drive that? I don't know if I can.'

'Sure, you can,' he said, grabbing her arm and pulling her along the garden path behind him. 'Come on, I only learned myself earlier. I can teach you though, nothing to it.' His enthusiasm was infectious.

'I really don't know about this.' She halted at the gate.

'What's to know? She can't walk all the way down there and I'm certainly not going down in the middle of a couple of dozen naked women – the whole village would have me down as a peeping Tom for the rest of my days.'

'I suppose, there is that.' She tried to sound serious, but then they both started to laugh. 'Okay, let's see if I can get the hang of it.'

'The trick is, to go slow…' he said starting the ignition.

'Like everything in life,' she murmured, and then he looked at her, caught her eye for a moment too long. She hadn't meant anything by it, but oh God, suddenly, she realised he probably thought she was flirting with him. 'Come on, let's get this show on the road.' She laughed, but it was a nervous sound and she wasn't fooling anyone.

'Right.' He smiled and started the engine. He drove them along the beach, shouting and pointing towards the controls as they went. When he cooled down the engine he was still shouting, until he realised that they were almost in silence. 'So, it's just like driving a car, only a lot more basic. You can do that, can't you?'

'I suppose so,' she said although she'd never admit to anyone that even driving her own modest Mini made her feel a little nervous. She hopped across into the driver's seat gamely and had a go. And it was not too bad at all. So, she started and stopped a few times, but Dan was kind enough to put her conking out down to an airlock in the diesel pipes – or something along those lines.

'So, what do you think?' he asked as she parked it outside the cottage again.

'Thank you,' she said simply, because it was probably the most thoughtful thing anyone could have organised for Jo.

'Stop it. I just thought, she might not be fit to walk all the way down to the cove and I spotted this rambling about the hills one day. The farmer was happy enough to lend it to me for a few hours; people are lovely here like that, aren't they?'

'They are,' she said smiling and then, she dropped her voice a little. 'It's one of the reasons I've decided to stay on…'

'You're staying?' he asked and then she saw something else: he blushed. 'I'm so glad… for you and for Elizabeth.'

'If you're planning on staying too, that'll be two new faces at the Christmas fair,' she joked.

'My family in London think I'm mad to want to stay here.' He smiled now. 'We'll have to see what Tuesday brings,' he said a little nervously. She had almost forgotten about his arrangement to meet the old nun the following week.

'It's going to be fine; Mother Agatha is nothing like Sister Berthilde,' Lucy said as reassuringly as she could manage.

As night drew in the village had an almost carnival feel to it, as though something exciting was about to take place. It was almost as if the whole sea was holding its breath. The waves, instead of crashing tonight, slipped in gently, icing the sand with a damp velvety coating. The local men's group had dotted lanterns along the sand and they burned a bright and almost hedonistic path to the cove. Jo loved it all and Lucy caught a tear falling from her eyes when they stood looking at it from their front door.

There was no telling how much money had been raised for the hospice, but on the night of the swim, women turned up not only from Ballycove, but also from several of the neighbouring towns too. Lucy saw a few of the female medical reps and even Thea Gilchrist – the locum who'd covered in the surgery before she'd arrived – turned up with a sponsorship card and a fat envelope filled with twenty-euro notes. They had organised for the swim to take place at exactly midnight. Most of the women would just about dip in and quickly out of the water. Lucy knew it was much too cold for many of them to hang about and the fun would be in that first icy blast and then running up and quickly drying off again.

The charity had been good enough to organise a photographer, who was going to take some shots, but promised that, somehow, they'd manage to keep it all very modest.

'I'll strategically add in a pink ribbon to cover everyone's jiggly bits at the end,' she intoned to the startled Elizabeth as she began to unpack a fairly complex-looking camera. 'These shots, well, you can see them for yourself when they are done and if everyone is happy, the charity will use them to promote and thank you all.'

'We'll see,' Elizabeth said tightly. Lucy knew that she wouldn't fancy having her bottom on display for the laughing country man to ogle before his breakfast.

'Now, will someone say a few words?' They were standing; almost two hundred women in the sheltered cove, wearing a selection of heavy coats and bathrobes, waiting for the moment when they'd drop cover and make a run for it.

'Go on.' Lucy gave Elizabeth a little shove.

'It was really Jo too.' Elizabeth held out her hand and brought Jo with her to the centre of the gathered circle. 'Ladies.' She cleared her throat, while the chatter died down for a moment. 'We just wanted to say a quick word of thanks. Thanks to everyone who has made the effort to collect sponsorship and support this worthy cause, but thanks even more so for turning up here and being such good sports. Today's swim is our way of telling cancer to...' She paused, seemed to think for a moment, and then looked across at Jo. 'Well, to bugger off; it's not going to get the better of us.'

There was rapturous applause and maybe it was as much because of the way the words were delivered as it was the sentiment behind them. It was very obvious from Elizabeth's tone that words like bugger were not often, if ever, uttered.

'Jo, Lucy and I swim here every night. Or at least every

night for as long as Jo could – so today, on the finest August night in my memory, we're delighted to invite you all to join the Ladies' Midnight Swimming Club.'

There was wild applause at this so when Jo cleared her throat, they had to wait for it to die down before she spoke in her soft and delicate voice.

'I won't say much… because I can't.' She laughed. 'But as you hit the water, maybe together we'll all shout it out…' There was a round of applause from the gathered women.

Bugger off, cancer; you're not going to get the better of us.

And with that, there was a mass shuffling out of coats and bathrobes, a wild almost riotous roar and nearly two hundred women went scarpering off into the freezing Atlantic waves, with Elizabeth, Jo and Lucy leading them all.

30

Jo

Jo couldn't quite believe she'd made it. Of course she knew she wouldn't have, not without Lucy and Elizabeth and even Dan who'd rallied round with that off-roader ride to take her down the beach.

It had been magical; travelling along with Lucy, waving to the many women who'd turned up for what she knew for certain was her final midnight swim. The beach was glorious, lit up with a trail of tall burning lanterns that the men had set up earlier all along their path to the cove. Even the sea, gently murmured its story to her. She loved this place, and no matter what fear woke her in the middle of too many nights to count since she'd learned her prognosis, she always knew that this was where her spirit would remain. She convinced herself the sea knew that too and it whispered its welcome as if she was already part of it.

The cove was resplendent in light. The women who came

from far and near were all ages and it seemed to Jo they had only one thing in mind and that was doing something for each other and every woman who came after them.

As she hit the water, she knew that this was the night of her life. It felt as if this is what it was all leading up to. She embraced the water like the old friend it was. Soon, she felt it envelop her with its invisible cold embrace and she was swimming out, far beyond her depths, the waves carrying her further and further into the silky darkness.

'Mum,' Lucy called from far behind and something in her voice made Jo stop and turn to see the outline of her daughter in the moonlight. 'Wait for me,' she said and Jo was reminded of when she was a little girl and she couldn't bear her mother to go out of sight for any length of time at all.

'I'm here, don't worry,' Jo whispered and she turned over onto her back to gaze up at the stars overhead. She lay there for some time with Lucy at her side and when she felt tears run down her cheeks she knew that it was the sweetest sadness she could have ever wished for.

'Oh, Mum,' Lucy said beside her and then Elizabeth was at their side.

'It's time to go back in. Are you ready, Jo?' Elizabeth asked gently.

'Yes. I'm ready,' Jo said finally and she looked across at Lucy and Elizabeth. Their faces were full of love and apprehension and Jo wondered if she could find the words she needed to say to them. She felt as if her whole body was brimful of emotion, a toxic mixture of the inevitability that lay ahead, the love that she knew would never die for these two extraordinary women and the gratitude for a life that could lead to this utterly sublime sense of peace and appreciation. 'I really am ready now,' she whispered and with that she started the long swim back to the shore.

31

Dan

D an figured there wasn't much point returning to the
cottage while the swim was taking place. He'd only
just have walked back when he'd have to turn around and
walk down again. The community centre committee had
organised a welcome home celebration for the swimmers
when they returned from the beach. Already the whole
village had turned out to applaud the women. At this hour
of the night, the pubs and hotel were closing up, but they'd
all been canvassed for donations and between Lucy and
Elizabeth, they had managed to garner enough sparkling
wine and hot punch to ensure that the welcome would
be warm.

The beach was striking, with lit lanterns marking
out the route down to the swimmers in the distance. He
threw his jacket over the wall and sat next to Niall and
Zoe, enjoying the atmosphere. The women really were
very lucky. To be fair, he'd arrived here in the stormiest

weather. Warm days like they'd had for the last few weeks seemed to transform the village to a whole new realm of beauty.

It reminded him of being a kid – long summer days spent hanging out with nothing much to do but feel the sun on his face. He thought of the women at the far end of the beach and wondered, for a moment, if perhaps his mother might be one of them. He could see the group of women making their way back across the sand. They were a raggle-taggle bunch and he imagined Elizabeth at the front of them leading them along with Jo being chauffeur driven by Lucy in the off-roader. He was glad he'd been able to make some small contribution.

His mobile knocked him from his thoughts. He looked at his watch. It was almost one o'clock in the morning. The number buzzing insistently on his mobile wasn't instantly recognisable, but he answered it anyway, his voice wary of bad news at such a late hour.

'Hey, writer guy.' It was Harry, his agent from London and it sounded as if he was in full-blown party mode. Dan imagined him, stationed in some trendy club, surrounded by the most beautiful people and making this final work call out of hours amidst the movers and shakers on their wind-down at the weekend. 'Sorry about the time. I'm in New York at a trade fair so everything is a bit all over the place.'

'Hey, yourself. Shouldn't you be cutting deals and making us both some money?' he asked.

'I think I've done my bit for the week actually.' He sounded happy. 'I just wanted to tell you that your book is creating such a buzz that already it's being fought over by some of the biggest editors around.'

'And of course, you told them?'

'I told them put something in a proposal for us. It's out on submission and I'll be letting everyone else know on Monday that we're officially going into talks on it.'

'That's good. What are they like?'

'Honestly, top and bottom of our wish list, but they don't know that, so it's good. We're going to be looking at top dollar, but I have a feeling knowing you, you'll go for one over the other because they'll treat this with the kind of loving care it deserves.'

'So, we're on the way to having a book deal.' A ripple of excitement was beginning to bubble up in Dan.

'Yep, it looks like it and not just one if we can agree on the details.'

'That's great news. I think it deserves a bit of celebrating,' he said and then he realised, that was exactly what Harry was going to set about doing.

'I would say big, big celebrations. They want it badly and I think this could really be a whole new vista opening up for your work. And you know, now that the publishing industry has made such a big thing of it, there's a good chance we'll have the movie companies hammering down our doors by the middle of next week.'

'Harry, you're the best. Have I told you that lately?' He was making fun of his friend, but they both knew, so far, they'd been a winning combination. It looked as if their luck was holding still. Dan hung up the phone and thought about going back to the cottage. He had a couple of cans of beer in the fridge and the remains of a bottle of red wine in the cupboard. He was glad he was here, that he'd gotten this news tonight; it wouldn't be much of a celebration there on his own. He jumped from the wall and headed across to the hotel before closing time. There was no reason he couldn't bring along a couple of bottles of decent champagne and see if he could talk Elizabeth, Jo and Lucy into sharing a drink with him to celebrate. In fact, this was such good news; he would buy a glass for everyone in the village.

'Dan.' Jo welcomed him with as much warmth as ever when he arrived at the reception the village had set up for the swimmers. 'I'm so glad you came. I wanted to thank you for that fancy car you organised for me today.' She was beaming, smaller and more fragile than before, but there was an unmistakable light shining from within her, so it was impossible to imagine it being extinguished.

'Oh, it was nothing; really Lucy did all the hard work.' He looked around the hall. It was packed. 'You've managed to pull a crowd.'

'Yes, haven't we just.' She laughed. 'Ah, look here's Lucy now.'

'You made it.' She handed him a glass of wine. 'I thought you were going to hang around the village and then we'd bring the buggy back and…'

'Never mind that.' He put down the glass, and pointed back at the crate of champagne he'd carried over from the hotel. 'This is a celebration.'

'Ooh, lovely,' Elizabeth said arriving at his elbow. 'What are we celebrating?'

'Apart from the fact that I made it into the water today and I'm still here enjoying the party?' Jo joked.

'True.' Lucy smiled across at her mother, who even if she looked frail, seemed happier than Dan had seen her since he'd met her.

'Also, it looks like my book is going to be signed in a major publishing deal…'

'What?' Lucy screamed. 'I can't believe you didn't say that the moment you came through the door. Oh my God, Dan, that's the best news ever…'

'Not quite, but it's definitely up there with the fact that I've just seen the Sale Agreed sign going up on the house next door to your mother's. Now, that's worth celebrating.'

'*You* bought Murphy's cottage?' Lucy said a little incredulously. 'I can't believe it. I thought you had your eye on Elizabeth's house?'

'Well, I might have had, but when I heard you bought the surgery, I figured either Elizabeth would hold onto it, or you might want to buy it yourself…'

'I didn't put in an offer because I thought you wanted to buy it!'

'That's the most wonderful news,' Elizabeth said clapping her hands and Dan watched as a glance passed between Elizabeth and Jo and he wondered if he'd missed a step. Somehow it didn't matter. It felt as if everything was unfolding exactly as it should.

32

Niall

At just after two o'clock the following day, his mother opened the door to his room. He had slept solidly after their late night celebrating the charity swim and this morning seemed to come much too quickly.

'Niall,' she said softly. 'Are you awake? It's just that Zoe is here...'

'Here?' Niall poked his head above the quilt and sure as wheels were round, there was Zoe Huang standing in the narrow doorway next to his mother.

'Come on, sleepyhead, my father is almost ready to go.' She smiled and closed the door gently; he could hear them both pad towards the living room. He sprung from the bed, sprayed some deodorant vaguely in the direction of his upper body and flung on a clean T-shirt, before ruffling up his hair and rinsing his mouth out. There wasn't time for much more getting ready, and then he bounded downstairs without looking back.

'What time will you be home?' his mother called behind them, forcing an apple into his hand as he went.

'By six, Mrs Nolan,' Zoe shouted as they raced out the door.

Soon they were jogging back into the belly of the village and up towards the piano shop. They stopped next to a dusty old Ford that didn't look as if it ever went much further than the end of the road and back.

'Ah, Zoe, you found your friend?' Mr Huang pulled the shop door firmly behind him.

'Sorry, I was late, Mr Huang, I slept in. It was a late night.' That at least was true and now he was so hungry, he almost felt weak.

'Yes, but your grandmother must be very proud,' Mr Huang said kindly and he sat in the car.

'Yes, I think she had a wonderful time, thank you.'

It turned out Niall's first impression of Mr Huang's car was probably right. He was a very nervous driver and he never passed thirty miles an hour for the whole journey. Through the village and on bends he lowered down to no more than ten miles per hour. The journey to the next village would take an age, Niall thought, but strangely enough, because they chatted happily on the way, it seemed that they arrived much too quickly.

'I have some business to catch up on, Zoe. I'll meet you both back here at five, okay?'

'Sure.' She reached up and kissed her father on the cheek and then they were racing to the furthest end of town and the Ferris wheel that Niall had spotted as they'd approached. 'All of the kids from school will be here. You'll like them,' she said as they neared the fair.

Zoe was right. The other kids, about a dozen of them in all, were just like Niall. Regular normal kids, who played video games, listened to the same music and watched reruns of television shows over and over again, so they knew the lines off by heart. These kids were not broken into camps of either rugby or maths geniuses – they were just ordinary. And he had a blast. Three hours disappeared into fish and chips, dodgem rides and sitting on grass in a circle talking about nothing and maybe, just a bit of everything. By the time he got home that evening, it felt as if he was becoming a different person.

'You had a nice time?' His mother looked tired.

'Yeah, it was all right,' Niall said, but he couldn't help but smile. 'Will I make you a cup of tea, Mum?' he asked as he put on the kettle to boil and it struck him, he wasn't sure how his mother drank her tea. After all, she made him coffee all the time, but when was the last time he'd offered to make her a cuppa? He couldn't remember; probably some Mother's Day long ago, when he'd slopped tea and orange juice on a tray alongside badly buttered toast and a dandelion from the garden in a vase.

'Lovely,' his mother said lightly. 'Just the one sugar, I'm trying to cut back.' Niall placed the cups on the kitchen table.

'So, any more news from Dad?' Niall began. They were still waiting for the promised prospectus to arrive for this fancy school Niall would be attending when he got to

Sydney. For some reason, his dad still hadn't gotten round to sending it on.

'Yes, I got him last night. He's sent on some brochures...' She sipped her tea. 'It looks nice, lots of sunshine and it's even got a pool and a fairly decent-looking library.'

'Yeah?' He sounded less enthusiastic than his mother.

'He's really looking forward to you going out there,' she said warmly.

'So am I.' But Niall wasn't sure that he *was* looking forward to it anymore. After all, it sounded as if it wouldn't be very different to being in boarding school in Dublin; instead of freezing in the winter, now he'd be boiling in the summer.

'We'll have to get you a whole new Aussie wardrobe...' She was flicking through her phone, looking at khakis and loafers.

'Mum...' he said tentatively, 'Dad said you were thinking of enrolling me in the local school if Australia hadn't been a runner.'

'It seemed like the obvious choice. After all, it's different being a GP to doing night shifts, and I know that even if you don't complain, you're not happy at St Brendan's.'

'You never said...'

'Well, there was hardly any point, not once your father agreed and, anyway, I didn't think you'd want to move back here. You've always seemed so set against it. Who knows, if it wasn't for—' she nodded towards his grandmother's bedroom '—maybe I wouldn't even have considered it. But, with you in Australia, it seems silly to go back to a job I hate in a city where really I don't feel I fit in anymore.' Her face clouded over, just a little and he recognised immediately that the emotion was hurt. His attitude, everything about the way he'd been these last few months had been cruel and he knew now he had to do something to make it up to her.

'I'm sorry, Mum, for the way I've behaved, you know. I must have been unbearable most of the time.' He mumbled his apology. He was too embarrassed to look her in the eye, so instead he inspected his mug as if it held the divine answers to unlock the top levels of *Mastermind*. 'I'm glad you're getting the chance to start a new life somewhere you'll be happy.'

'Honestly, Niall.' She reached out and squeezed his hand. 'You have nothing to say sorry for. It's been a tough few years for both of us, but we've come through it. We're fine and now, look at you, my big man, off to Australia.' She smiled bravely.

'Still, I'm sorry, Mum, for... you know, everything – the way I've been to you and to Gran.' He felt hot tears rise up in his eyes, but he was not sad. It felt as if they were caused by some other overflowing emotion, like the release of a dam he'd been holding onto since the divorce.

'Oh, Niall.' His mother's eyes were filled with tears too. She pulled herself up from her chair and moved to his side of the table, wrapping her arms around him tightly. 'I love you so much, you know. I only want you to be happy.'

'I know. I've been such a brat though; I don't know how you've put up with me.' They both laughed at that. Niall rubbed his hand roughly across his face.

'Don't say that. You were entitled to feel a bit lost for a while. The divorce wasn't easy on either of us. I'm so proud of you.' She was hugging him so close, he thought he'd suffocate, but this once, he would not complain.

'Ah, Mum, come off it, now; get a grip on yourself.' He shoved her away and ran his fingers through his hair, spiking it up so it looked as cool as he could manage to make it.

That night, Niall Nolan lay in bed for a long time, his eyes counting out the stars through the open skylight above his head. He remembered what Dan said to him, about families and time passing. At the time, he didn't believe it could pass half fast enough to the end of the summer but now, with his trip to Sydney impending, he felt a sense of what that meant. He would be leaving at the end of August. According to his father's email, that meant there was less than two weeks here in Ballycove and he planned to make the most of every single minute of that time.

33

Elizabeth

It seemed to Elizabeth that the weekend sunshine had taken its parasol and decided to hightail it as far away from Ballycove as it possibly could on the Tuesday evening when Dan was due to pick her up for their drive to meet Mother Agatha.

Elizabeth emerged from the surgery, with her large pink umbrella shading her from the considerable downpour that threatened to wash them all away if it continued. She smiled eagerly, as if she expected something positive from this trip. The truth was she knew that dear old Mother Agatha had nothing to do with the placing of babies from St Nunciata's. All the same, she'd been a kind woman and a good Christian and Elizabeth hoped it would be enough to open some chink in the mystery of finding Dan's mother.

'If I was superstitious, I might think this weather wasn't boding well for us,' he said as she sat into his car.

'Oh, don't be worrying about this. This is the west of

Ireland – we're going to get forty days of rain either way. The only question is which season it'll turn up in. Better to get it over with now when there's some chance that September will dry things up again.'

'I know I've said it already, Elizabeth, but I really appreciate you doing this with me,' he said as he pulled out into the road.

'Oh, for goodness' sake, I'm looking forward to catching up with Agatha. I was very fond of her when she lived here in Ballycove. It's just a pity that she's… well, you'll see what I mean when you meet her; she's almost completely housebound these days.' They passed the journey chatting about everything from the mundane weather to the latest update on his book. Dan was easy to spend time with and interesting too. She directed him to a small housing estate in the next town. The houses here were built eighty years ago at least, mostly with single glazing in their windows and old-fashioned railings around handkerchief-sized gardens.

'This is where Agatha grew up, before she joined the convent. Her sister never left here, never married either, so I'd say she's just glad to have her back.' The rain had eased off enough to encourage Elizabeth to leave her umbrella in the car. She'd brought a round biscuit tin, which contained her own home-made apple cake. 'Agatha always had a sweet tooth,' she confided, 'not like Berthilde. That old witch is sour to the core.'

The door was opened before Dan had a chance to ring the ancient bell and Agatha's sister Delores ushered them into the front room. There was no getting away from the smell of boiled cabbage, but the house was cosy, with photos and postcards from all over the world pinned on the back of the sitting room door. 'Mother Agatha has friends in just about every mission you can mention,' Delores said proudly.

Delores, thin and brown-eyed, was the complete and utter opposite in every way to her sister. Mother Agatha was the fattest woman Elizabeth knew, decked out in black from head to toe with a sheath of white at her neck and a small veil sitting askew on her thin grey hair. The old woman held Dan's hand for a fraction longer than usual, but her light blue eyes twinkled with something close to satisfaction. 'Oh my...' she said softly, looking from one to the other. 'Oh, my, my, my.' She was smiling broadly now.

'We've come about...' Dan started, but she held up a hand.

'Of course, you have, dear, but you've already figured it out, haven't you?' She looked towards Elizabeth, but it wasn't a question, it was a statement of fact.

'No. That's why we came here. Dan is trying to trace his mother and you're his last chance. There doesn't seem to be any record of him in St Nunciata's.'

'Dear me.' Agatha shook her head sadly. 'No, there wouldn't be... He was born in the hospital.'

'I don't understand.' Elizabeth looked at the old nun now.

'It's very simple. This child didn't come to us because his mother wasn't married; I remember him very clearly because his circumstances were so very unique. I placed Dan with his adoptive family in London,' she said simply.

'I did. I can remember that journey very clearly,' Agatha said softly. 'You were a beautiful baby.' Her voice sounded very far away, as if her memories were dragging her back. 'But of course, that was a long time ago.' She looked from one to the other as if waiting for them to place the final pieces of the puzzle before her. She pulled herself up in her chair. 'I felt the people who took you were good people. Was I right?'

'Yes, they are very good people, the best parents I could have asked for really.'

'And yet, here you are,' the old lady said sadly. 'It's never the same though, is it? You must have always wondered. I mean there was never going to be any hiding the fact that you weren't their child, was there?'

'No I suppose not. If anything, the way they told it, they made me feel even more wanted than if I'd been their own flesh and blood.'

'That's good; there was no missing the kindness in your mother or indeed how much they both wanted you.' She laughed then, a gentle, hollow sound. 'You know I did think of holding onto you myself. On the journey over, I dreamt about not letting you go, maybe running off to London, but it was all just fantasy. I couldn't have kept you anymore than... well...'

'You remember my mother?'

'Oh, my dear, dear man.' She shook her head. An expression of something that was more than just sadness crossed her eyes. 'I knew her well, in fact...' A small tear ran down her cheek. 'You really have no idea, do you?' she asked then.

'No. That's why I came here.'

'You came to the very best place…' Mother Agatha said kindly.

'But you said he wasn't born in St Nunciata's?' Elizabeth said and suddenly when she looked at Dan she began to wonder if perhaps…

'You already know, don't you?' The nun smiled at Elizabeth, a playful movement of her lips.

'No, as Elizabeth said, I've just met brick walls everywhere I've turned. It's as if I never existed.' Actually, after seeing the convent and meeting Sister Berthilde, he had told Elizabeth he might have to accept that he would never know who had given birth to him; perhaps he would have to make peace with that. At least Elizabeth felt that she'd tried to make him understand now why he was given up and maybe he could feel more compassion for the woman who gave birth to him than he did any kind of bitterness.

'Indeed, it probably is that.' She looked towards her sister. 'Delores dear, will you bring in tea and if you don't mind, Dan, I'd like to tell you all a story when we've had a slice of that lovely cake Elizabeth has baked for me.'

It seemed to Elizabeth as if the room, old-fashioned and all as it was, was the perfect place to drink tea and listen to stories, so they sat back and waited until she'd had a large slice of cake and brushed the crumbs from her robes; then she was ready.

'The story I'm going to tell you now, is of a young girl who found herself in trouble at a time when there was nothing else for it but to give up your baby or forever bring shame upon your family. However, this young girl did what she thought was best for her baby and she married a respectable, older man who promised to give both her and her child a good life. Perhaps it would have all worked out well, in the end...'

Elizabeth felt her chest constrict, the most terrible opening up of pain somewhere deep within her, as if a vast chasm of grief was about to engulf her. She felt the tears trickle down her cheek, but there was no stopping them. Dan reached out and took her hand and she held onto it tightly, as if her very life depended on it.

Mother Agatha looked across at Elizabeth now, who had started to cry, a soft keening sound that might have come from a heartbroken child but she nodded at the nun to continue.

'Except the man she married was not what he seemed to be and unfortunately the child she was carrying turned out to be more like his biological father than she ever realised...'

'Oh, God. Vano?' Elizabeth whispered. 'He was Roma, but I never thought...'

'No, of course you didn't, dear, how could you? You were hardly more than a child yourself. Anyway, when the baby arrived – coloured and obviously not the child of Dr O'Shea, the midwife panicked. Sister Bernadette took the child out for the doctor to decide what the best thing to do was.'

'After all this time...' Elizabeth shook her head. There was no wrapping her understanding around the words that were upending the sadness she'd carried for so many years.

'You see, a man like that—' Mother Agatha leant towards Dan now '—so very respectable, front seat of the church every Sunday, well he couldn't possibly bring home a coloured baby, could he?'

'They told me you died, that your heart was too weak.' Elizabeth was crying now, the tears racing down her cheeks, her shoulders shuddering, her expression a mixture of relief, sadness and sheer joy. 'Oh, my darling boy…' She reached out and placed her hand on his face, still taking in the truth of it all. 'My, darling, darling child, I can't believe it's you after all this time.'

'So, I'm…' Dan couldn't find the words. It was all too much to take in, but he was crying, tears of happiness. His eyes were filled with the same joy that Elizabeth knew was marking out her own.

'Anyway, I was given the charge of placing this coloured baby with an English family. To be honest, I hadn't a clue where the baby had come from, only that it had arrived in the orphanage in the middle of the night and there was no mother to show for it. But then, at the time, it wasn't unusual for a baby to be left off, the mother probably hoping that a good home would be found and she could get on with what was left of her own life.'

'So, how did you…' Elizabeth wasn't sure what she wanted to ask first, but she knew Mother Agatha had to get her story finished before she could begin to pick apart the million questions, they both had for her.

'The problem was, I didn't realise for many, many years exactly who you were. It was not until old Sister Bernadette was dying that she told me where the baby had come from.

You know, by then, Ireland had changed and for some of us, brave enough to go out into the world, we realised that not every orphan was well placed; indeed very many were sent to places you wouldn't put a dog.' She shook her head sadly. 'By then you would have been a young man. I could only pray that I'd done the right thing in leaving you with the family we'd found in England.'

'Oh, yes, my mum and dad, they really are salt of the earth,' he said and a feeling of gratefulness welled up in Elizabeth.

'Sister Bernadette was racked with guilt over her part in it all.' She looked now at Elizabeth. 'Of course, she'd panicked and then once she'd brought the child out, there was no changing Dr O'Shea's mind. He... well, we both know the sort of man he was and there was no going back, was there? I mean you believed your child was buried in the grave of the angels. God knows, you spent enough time up there cleaning it up and putting flowers on it every week.' She shook her head sadly.

'It wasn't wasted time. Those little babies deserved that at the very least,' Elizabeth whispered.

'Yes, they did indeed.' She stopped for a moment. 'Oh, Elizabeth, I'm so sorry, but by the time I realised, it was too late. I agonised over telling you the truth, but then I felt that there was no telling what knowing after all that time might do to you. It could send a woman mad – I think, if it was me, it might have tipped me over completely.'

'It's a lot to take in,' Elizabeth said, but she reached out to the old nun. 'But I understand, things were so different then. Everyone was doing what they believed was right.

You, Agatha, above any of the nuns in the convent, I know you would have paid a heavy price worrying about the rights and wrongs of it. But it was beyond our reach, back then, we were all so powerless.' They both began to cry now, but it was as if they were both somehow released – these were not tears of bitterness or sadness, but rather joy beyond which Elizabeth had ever known.

Eventually, rubbing her eyes, the nun turned to Dan. 'The truth is… if it's not too politically incorrect to say it, I'd remember you if I was without a single other memory. You see, Dan, you were the only baby we'd ever had at the orphanage who wasn't as white as new boiled potatoes. Your beautiful golden skin set you apart, so there's only one person who could be your mother – and that's Elizabeth O'Shea.'

34

Lucy

The weeks that followed rolled into each other much too quickly. Summer holidays had never slipped so deliciously or slyly by. Lucy snatched hours away from the surgery when she could in July and August, ostensibly so they could spend time together before Niall headed off for Australia, but mostly they just sat at the end of her mother's bed, talking of things that happened over the years, mainly because they all knew that those hours would never be played over again. Since the charity swim her mother seemed to have lost all of her vitality. Now, she stayed in bed all the time and even drinking the energy smoothies Niall made took so much out of her that they took turns holding the straw to her lips.

The past couple of years, which should have been happy for all of them, had worn them down and now, in the time that was left, it seemed that their relationship had taken on fresh new warmth as if to crash together as much as they could before Lucy was left alone in Ballycove.

'How will it work? When I go... you're moving back here full-time, will you...?' Niall asked one afternoon.

'I'll sell the house in Dublin. I have no interest in keeping it on. It'll be money in the bank now that I've bought the practice with my savings, and I'll be a confirmed country GP.' Lucy smiled.

'You... you should buy Elizabeth's house,' her mother whispered softly. 'Let her have this place. It would set you both free to start afresh.'

'Oh, Mum, I don't know...'

'It sounds perfect to me,' Niall said. 'You'd be living right next to the practice and it'd be a great project to take on. You'd love it, Mum.'

'Think about it,' her mother whispered before closing her eyes. 'I'd like to know that everything is settled, before I...'

'I promise, I will.' Lucy bent forward and kissed her gently. 'I'll have a chat with Elizabeth, see what she thinks.'

'Good.' Her mother sighed with a satisfied quiver of her lips –the merest of smiles.

'You know I kind of envy you all, here,' Niall said softly.

'No, you don't.' Lucy smiled. 'We'll be facing force-nine winds in winter while you're basking in the hot sun.'

'With my red hair and white skin?'

'Okay, wear plenty of sun cream.' Lucy laughed and then she looked at him. 'You're going to love it. I only hope you'll want to come back for holidays and all that.'

'Sure, if you'll have me.' That was it, really – Niall clearly wasn't so sure that there would be a place for him. Perhaps he was already sensing that his move to Australia would put more than miles between them. Lucy's life would take on a new unfamiliar shape of which he would no longer be a part. When Lucy thought about it, her biggest fear was that he might feel he didn't fit properly anywhere anymore.

'Of course we'll have you,' Lucy whispered, then she picked an imaginary piece of fluff from his grandmother's cardigan. 'Well, as often as you'll come home and of course, your father will probably have plans for most holidays so…'

'Probably. I'm sure he will,' Niall said softly.

And that's what it would be, one long trip, of staying in places that were not home. Niall looked out the window in silence, lost in thoughts that seemed to pull him in two. Six months ago, he'd have been packing his bags the minute his father agreed to have him. But now, over the last few weeks, his mother could see a new life was beginning to open up for him here in Ballycove. He had friends and a place he was beginning to call home. Was he already seeing the green of those far-off fields was not all emeralds? Perhaps. Lucy hoped he'd realise what he was leaving before it was too late.

She had a feeling he'd miss more than just the countryside and Ballycove. He'd miss his family, his mother and, yes, he'd miss his grandmother, but then, he'd miss her anyway, although perhaps he'd miss her even more on the other side of the world. He'd miss Dan who had taken Niall under his wing in a way that had meant so much to Lucy. Then there was Zoe too and the large group of friends he was so recently beginning to make. The truth was, he had gotten to know more people over the last few weeks than he had in all the time he'd been coming here and he liked them, Lucy knew. He was finally fitting in.

'Mum, say if I didn't go...'

'If you didn't go?' Lucy turned to look at him now.

'Yes, say I decided to stay here, in Ballycove, with you and go to the local school and we lived in the house on the hill – our house, a new start for both of us...'

'I suppose... your father would be very upset.' She looked out into the garden for a second. 'Are you saying you'd like to stay here after all?'

'I think so, yeah, if it would mean living here with you, being a proper family, going to a regular school and...'

'Leaving Dublin, boarding school and settling for the local college?' She looked at him and it felt like some of the stress and fatigue that had filled her head for months was slowly falling away from her eyes. 'Oh, Niall, if that was what you wanted, I'd be over the moon, and nothing would make me happier, but are you sure you'd be happy here? It is a bit of a backwater...'

'I'd like things back to how they were, before, you know, me and you and well, if you met someone new, I'd say we could all be happy together, right here in Ballycove.'

'Niall, you've made my day.' Tears were streaming down her eyes now and she pulled him close, hugging him until his embarrassment made him shrug her off.

'That's all I needed to hear. Take care of each other for me,' Jo said softly, and then she took a long ragged breath and closed her eyes. That was it. She had just left them as easily as walking out to the next room with only a parting smile on her lips to let them know she was happy to go.

'Oh, Mum,' Lucy said, sadly, tears falling from her eyes as she leant over and kissed her mother's forehead for the final time. Next to her, she heard Niall begin to cry, a soft murmuring sound that he couldn't quite disguise. 'She's gone,' Lucy whispered, but she had a feeling that her mother had been happy knowing that things were settled enough for her to leave them so peacefully.

35

Elizabeth

Elizabeth couldn't remember the last time she'd seen such a sunrise – maybe never, she realised as she lay back on the calm water. She had come down to the cove because she couldn't stay at home when it looked so beautiful. It seemed to her that everything around her was whispering her name. Today was the day. It had taken almost six weeks to finalise everything, but it had been remarkably uncomplicated in the end. The sale of her grand old Georgian had slipped through easily. Lucy and she had agreed terms between them and only then had she gone and spoken with her solicitor. It might have been a clear swap – God knows there was plenty to be done with the old house – but Lucy insisted on paying market value. With Eric's debts cleared and taking out the price of Jo's cottage, Elizabeth found herself with a very comfortable cushion on which to balance her future. And of course, she still had her job at the surgery – somehow, against all the odds that Eric had stacked against her, things had turned out well.

Dan had been more than generous in his offer for old John Murphy's cottage and she was delighted for him. It turned out they would be neighbours. Mother and son, in adjacent cottages facing out onto the seafront – it was perfect really. Of course, she told him, he was paying way over the odds, but the truth was, once she had agreed to buy Jo's cottage, she knew that there wasn't another corner of the village that could ever feel more like home to her. If she'd had to pay four times the amount, she'd still have considered it a bargain!

It was a funny thing, but Lucy couldn't stay there, not without Jo, and she loved the great big Georgian, well she loved the idea of it at least, or what she'd thought it was or perhaps could be, one day.

The house, when they walked through it was three times larger than Lucy had expected and for a few worrying moments Elizabeth was afraid it was too large. 'I love it,' Lucy had said and Niall had already bagged a large room at the top of the house as his own.

And now, this morning, here in the gathering light, Elizabeth could think of only one thing. Today was the day. The day when she would move into the little cottage, so work could begin in earnest on the big Georgian. She felt a giddy rattle surge through her on the water and she turned over to swim towards the shore. Along the water, she watched as a family of starlings took off into a beating vibrating murmuration, heading inland towards the nearby lake. She tried to quell her anticipation, but really, in her mind, she'd already left the big lonely house on the hill. Oh, yes, try as she might, she could not knock out the sense of optimism at this wonderful new start in life. The changing tide eventually sent her scurrying back to dry and dress herself.

She was looking forward to hot tea and a large bowl of porridge when she reached the house. She knew, she should be sad, leaving a place that might have been her home for over thirty years, but the truth was, she was shedding it like an unwanted coat. It had been a house, not a home, but she had a feeling it would welcome Lucy, Niall and whatever other lives filled it from now on with open arms.

Elizabeth tried not to check her watch too often once she opened up the surgery. She couldn't wait to get back to the cottage and settle in for the evening. It was a very big day; Dan was going to collect his parents from the airport and she was finally going to meet the people he called Mum and Dad.

'I'm really nervous,' she confided to Lucy when they stopped for a quick cup of coffee after eleven o'clock in a rare but welcome window between patients.

'You have nothing to worry about; they are going to love you and knowing Dan – they are going to be lovely people. It's going to be fine.' Lucy squeezed her hand reassuringly. Then she reached forward and topped up their cups of coffee before settling back to relax for a few minutes more. 'Are you sure you won't miss this place?'

'What's to miss? I'll be just down the road, and I have a feeling I'll still be popping in here occasionally.'

'It's going to be great, isn't it?' Lucy nodded towards the end of the garden.

'I think so.' Elizabeth looked down to the row of coach houses and old stables. The wilderness had been tamed along one side, where the builders had already brought down a cement mixer and other equipment to block out the two large doorways that opened up on the garden. It would take another week or two before it was completely sealed and the roof secured. They were hoping that by the end of autumn, it would be ready to move the surgery in there. It really was a wonderful start to Lucy's new career as the owner of the practice.

'Shall we go down for a quick peek before we go back to work?' Lucy asked jumping up from her chair suddenly.

'You're the boss now,' Elizabeth said and they both laughed at that, because it seemed strange having only sold the practice on to her so recently to think that the future of the village's health now lay in Lucy's hands.

'I am, amn't I?' Lucy said, her eyes dancing with the pleasure of it all. 'In fact, when you think of it, we have more than just your cottage to celebrate.'

'We certainly have,' Elizabeth said linking her arm as they headed out through the kitchen door to inspect how the building was coming along.

Over a week later and still, Elizabeth couldn't believe her luck at securing Jo's cottage and saving the practice. Dan's parents had returned to London, promising they'd be back for Christmas. Elizabeth liked them even more than she had expected to. Already, they were sharing recipes in a WhatsApp group that included Dan's extended family and Elizabeth felt as if she was being welcomed to its very heart. She was walking down towards the end of town on a sunny Saturday morning when her phone rang again.

'Hello,' she answered carefully, falling back on that default doctor's wife setting when she wasn't quite sure who was calling.

'Elizabeth?'

'Yes.'

'Hi, it's Clara, we met that night on the beach. Do you remember?'

'Ah, yes, Clara.' Vaguely, Elizabeth recalled a short dumpy woman who had taken to the water like a woman possessed and had been one of the last to leave. Of course, she had more reason than any to enjoy the freedom of the midnight waters. She'd survived breast cancer twice and although her body was a map of scars and crevices, her spirit was large and Elizabeth had warmed to her immediately.

'Well, I came back to my workshop – I told you that I do a little engraving and...'

'Yes, you're the artist?'

'Sculptor, mainly, but yes, I draw too. Anyway, I had a piece of marble here. It was gifted to me, really, a leftover piece that no-one seemed to want.'

'Oh?' What was the woman talking about? Elizabeth wondered. But she was too polite to interrupt.

'It's white marble, really pristine, and it's very large; well over eight foot. I thought, wouldn't it be perfect, if we could commemorate your friend Jo and everyone else who's had the big C? I have some great ideas for a really nice sculpture – if you wanted to take a look – and maybe we could place it there, beside the cave so all of that loss could be in the shadow of something positive that we all did together?'

'You want to dedicate it to Jo?' Elizabeth felt her eyes begin to well up with tears. She had just arrived at the cottage, was standing at the wall, overlooking the sea opposite. 'That's so nice; I don't know what to say...'

'Do you think it's a good idea?'

'I think it's a wonderful idea. I think she'd have loved it and yes, she loved what we did that night. She giggled her socks off and probably would have stayed in the water even longer than you, if we didn't drag her out!' Elizabeth laughed, remembering her friend.

'Right, well, if you call up to my cottage, we can agree what should go on it first, and then we'll see about moving it into place and checking if the council are all right with us erecting it.'

'Oh, that sounds just perfect.' Elizabeth closed off her phone and stood for a moment with her hand on the gate. 'Did you hear all that, Jo?' she whispered to her friend. Elizabeth had a feeling she'd always be close by, so long as she was near the cottage and the sea. 'Isn't that something to make you smile?' Wasn't it funny, she thought, after all Eric's years as a respectable GP and no-one had offered to mark his time serving the community? And yet, here she was remembering Jo as if she'd never left. It was funny all right and she smiled sadly.

She pushed in the gate and made her way up along the path. Across the road, she looked far out, beyond the pier, to where the breakers were white and pristine in the dark blue sea. It felt, for a moment, as if they were washing away the years that she'd somehow let slip by and in that clearing, Elizabeth recognised that the woman she'd become today was not so far removed from the one she might have been, had life thrown a different hand her way. She caught her breath, as somewhere on the breeze, she heard Jo whisper…*Welcome, Elizabeth, you are home at last.*

Acknowledgements

So here we are at the end of book number six and again, there are so many people to thank.

First off, thank you to everyone at Aria for making this a very special journey – particularly to Hannah Smith, my brilliant editor and her team, Vicky Joss, Nikky Ward, Lauren Tavella, Geo Willis, Helena Newton, Annabel Walker, Sue Lamprell, Leah Jacobs-Gordon, Lizz Burrell and David Boxell. To Laura Palmer who took on this project as it was about to be born – I am very glad to have you on board!

To all at Gill Hess who have opened the gate – it's very much appreciated.

A huge thank you to Judith Murdoch – this brilliant title is down to you, but also the ongoing editorial advice and unstinting optimism, you are a tonic!

To the bloggers, the librarians, the booksellers and anyone who has helped on the journey of this book into your hands – thank you.

I have the most fantastic support network of friends and colleagues locally – thank you.

To my wonderful family, Seán, Roisín, Tomás, Cristín,

James – Mr H, Bernadine and Christine Cafferkey – thank you.

And finally, to my readers – I have undoubtedly, the loveliest readers in the world – the ones who've been around from day one and those who are new to the books – thank you!

Read on for a sneak peek of

The Gin Sisters' Promise...

**Three estranged sisters.
Six months to come back together.**

When Georgie, Iris and Nola's mother died
and their father disappeared into his grief, the sisters
made a pact: they would always be there for
one another, no matter what.

Now, decades later, they haven't spoken
for years and can barely stand to be in the same
room. As his health declines, their father comes up
with a plan to bring them back to one another. In his
will, he states that before they can claim their
inheritance, they must spend six months living
together in their childhood home in the village
of Ballycove, Ireland, and try to repair
their broken relationships.

As the months progress, old resentments boil
over, new secrets threaten to come out and each
sister must decide what matters more:
their pride, or their family.

Can they overcome their past and find a
way to love each other once more?

Prologue

Ballycove, Ireland, Twenty-Eight Years Ago

The saddest funeral I was ever at. That's what the mourners had whispered as they'd left the remaining Delahayes standing by Iseult's grave. And now, perched at opposite ends of the living room, Iris and Georgie were drowning in their own grief, but it was little Nola – just seven years old – who needed her father the most and there was no way round it; there was nothing left of him to give. He was suffocating when he knew he should be comforting his children.

The cry that emitted from Nola came as gasping gulps, as if she was going under, smothering in the cold waters of despair. She was far too small for her feet to touch the bottom of her grief, far too young to navigate these treacherous waters.

Iris heard her first. The choking sobs startled her from her own wretched melancholy. 'Nola,' she cried, fearing the worst. Panic gripped her; she couldn't remember seeing Nola since they set off for the funeral earlier. But that wasn't right. Of course she'd seen her. Nola must have sat in the church pew at the end of their row, stood next to her and Georgie by their mother's grave. She must have been there in the car when their father had driven them back to Soldier Hill House.

Sheer horror propelled Iris from the window seat. How could she have forgotten about little Nola? In the hall, Georgie too was racing to find their youngest sister, panic etched across her features, only just edging past the devastating grief overhanging each of them. They crashed into each other at the foot of the stairs.

'Where is she?'

'Oh, God.' Georgie was frantic, her eyes wide, a slight odour of sweat emanating from her clothes, a mixture of the painful day and the near-consuming fear reflected in Iris's eyes. Another gulp came from the alcove, just outside their father's study, and their eyes dropped to the pathetic bundle of dark clothes lying on the floor. Nola. In her best dress, the one their mother picked out for Christmas Day. Maroon velvet, too heavy for a July afternoon, too festive to mourn your mother in.

'He just left me here.' Nola wheezed between disconsolate sobs. 'First Mammy and now Daddy. All I wanted was for him to put his arms around me, like Mammy did, and tell me everything would be all right, but it won't be all right now, will it? It'll never be all right again.'

'Come here.' Iris pulled Nola into her chest roughly. Georgie too fell on top of them, bundling Nola in their weeping cocoon so she could hardly breathe. But somehow, the familiar scents of her sisters – washing powder, the faintest remains of their mother's perfume, which they'd all applied that morning, and that slightly tangy end-of-day smell that you only got in the summertime – were strangely comforting. 'We're all here together. That's the main thing, Nola. That's all that matters now. We'll be okay. Everything will be fine – you'll see.'

'But you're going to leave. You'll go off and forget about me and then I'll be here alone, with Daddy, and I can't stand it.' She was gulping down the words now, almost hysterical with grief and pain and maybe fear too.

'We're never going to leave you, Nola,' Iris said, 'I promise. How could we possibly ever leave you?'

'We couldn't,' Georgie said solidly in that way she had of saying things that let Nola know she'd never let her down. 'We'll always be the Gin Sisters, remember?' Georgie said using the abbreviation of the initial letters of their names that their father had coined.

'Oh my God, yes! We can make our own little club, just us, with a promise that means we're always going to be together. Nothing will ever come between us.' Iris was flushed, trying hard to make things better for her younger sister. There had been too much sadness already today. She found herself smiling at her own silly idea.

'Really, our own club? The G-I-N Sisters – get it, gin sisters?' Nola scraped her hair from her eyes, drying off some of the tears that stained her cheeks. 'I love that idea.' She breathed out slowly.

'We'll need a constitution.' Georgie pulled a mock-serious face to make more fun of it. She could always be

3

depended on to be the strong one.

'Yes, Georgie, you can write it up. Now, quick, go and get some paper and a pen, Nola.' Iris fell back on her heels; she'd do anything to make Nola feel better. The poor kid, they were all too young to lose their mother. But Iris felt she had some additional gravity because she had just become a teenager, even if Georgie always tried to rub it in that she was one year older, but Georgie would never be the maternal one among them – they both knew that. Whereas everyone said Iris was cut out to be a wonderful mother someday, and in truth it was the only ambition she had in life.

Beyond the door, she heard the muted sounds of her father shuffling about, and Iris imagined him filling up a tumbler of whiskey and slouching in the large armchair with that photograph of their mother that he'd taken long before they'd ever had children or, it seemed, worries. Still, it was better that he was here and not down in the distillery where it seemed he could lose track of time entirely. Delahaye Distillery, his life's work, was becoming an all-consuming distraction, maybe his only way to cling on at this stage.

'And no boys.' Georgie was scribbling down the club rules to Nola's subdued delight. Georgie already knew that Iris was in love with a boy called Myles who didn't even know she existed and probably never would.

'Eugh, of course no boys.' Nola scrunched up her face.

'And ice-cream every Friday.' Iris tried to make her voice sound as if she really could be happy again one day.

'Just for us,' Nola said on a breath that was still ragged,

but at least her little body had stopped shaking. 'And you'll never leave me?'

'We promise we'll never leave you,' Georgie and Iris chorused together. Anything else was unthinkable.

I

London, November, Present

Iris closed her front door behind her with a kick that felt like a final exclamation mark on a very long day. It had been that way for a while. Her sister Georgie would probably say that work should fulfil you but, Iris thought irritably, not everyone could be as lucky as Georgie when it came to finding a career that could jam up all the other cracks in her life. She pushed the notion of her sister from her mind as quickly as it had arrived. It was automatic now. She didn't waste time thinking of either of them anymore. What was the point when there was no forgiving or forgetting the hurt they'd caused her all those years ago? It was much better not to think of them at all.

Iris groaned. Her head was throbbing. She wasn't tired, just irritated with another day like every other. She was sick to the back teeth of reminding people to turn up to dental appointments they didn't want to keep. She was bored of having the same conversations about the cost of root canals and crowns and children's braces. Becoming a receptionist at a busy London dental practice probably wasn't anyone's burning ambition. It was a job, a way to make a living – nothing more, and if she could afford to throw in the towel she would have left years ago. But someone needed to earn a steady wage in the house. In fairness, her employers were generous with her wages and a hefty Christmas bonus was always thrown in to keep her there for another year. Maybe she was expecting too much from life.

She was early. She'd meant to stop off at the fish market – they were having homemade fish and chips for dinner. Myles's favourite. She hoped it would pull him out of the distanced silence he'd put between them over the last few weeks. But in the rush to catch her morning train, she had forgotten her purse and so she'd come directly home.

Though she didn't think so at the time, later, she wondered if maybe she knew that this was it. The day she'd dreaded since the very first day of her marriage to him.

His bag stood ready at the foot of the stairs. Myles was a cameraman, freelance for a news channel. It paid a pittance but gave him access to all the big news stories and held a certain glamour he'd leaned on more these last few years, now that his looks were beginning to fade.

'Iris.' He stopped, dead still in the hallway, as if he'd been confronted by a raging lion on the savannah instead of his wife home from work on a wet and miserable Wednesday afternoon. 'I…' he started. 'You're early. I wasn't expecting you yet. I'm…'

'Yes?' Iris waited, working to keep her face blank while

the words *please, please, please don't do this* exploded in her mind. Iris folded her arms about herself. Perhaps it would stop her trembling when she heard the worst. Of course, she knew what it was. It was a woman – younger, prettier and probably with enough money to make up for the loss of the house and their savings that leaving her would cause him.

'I'm leaving you. I've met someone else.' His words were faltering, but she hardly noticed because it felt as if the world had already started to spin away from her. 'She's called Amanda... She's—'

'Please, Myles, please don't do this. Don't leave me for some bit of skirt that's going to be by the wayside in a matter of weeks. Come on, we can work through this...' She was pleading, but she might as well have been reciting a shopping list, because he just went on gathering up his belongings. His keys. His watch. And then in the kitchen, he hovered for a minute before picking up four of the fresh scones she'd baked that morning. She watched him, wordlessly now, because she'd run out of things to say, or was it that she didn't know where to start or where to end?

'It's not like *that*... This is different.' He dragged a hand through his hair. For a moment, his expression seemed to dip into something like anguish and Iris experienced a dart of panic. Could he really be in love with someone else?

'I'm begging you, Myles, please, don't do this. What do you want me to do? I'll do anything, anything for you to stay.' She was shrieking, unable to control either the words or the desperation. Hysteria pummelled against her ribcage where her heart should have been.

His restraint silenced her, suddenly, as if a plug had been pulled from the very heart of her. And for a moment, the only sound in her world was the low buzz of the refrigerator.

'You need me, Myles, don't you see?' She took a step closer to him, and tried not to notice that he took a step back from her. 'This is us, Myles.' She waved her hand around their little semi. 'Twenty-three years of us! We're meant to be together. Think of everything I've given up for you, everything—'

'Oh, please, Iris, I'm sick and tired of hearing the same old saga. No-one asked you to follow me to London or to cut your family out of our lives.' He spun around with a look of pure disgust as his eyes travelled over her. She felt the power going from her legs, could hardly stand straight beneath his loathing stare. 'That was all you, all your doing. We might have been millionaires if your old man included us in his will, but that's never likely to happen now, is it?' He shook his head, as if it had been that simple, when they both knew there was so much more to it all than that. There was so much more to them. 'And as for those crazy sisters of yours – you can't blame me for falling out with them.'

'All right, all right, let's forget Georgie and Nola. This isn't about them; it's about us. Look at how far we've come. Most couples don't make it past...' She stopped, because suddenly, she knew there was something else. Something she hadn't figured into this scenario in all the times she'd played it out in her worst nightmares. If it was possible to imagine anything worse than Myles leaving her, she had a

9

feeling that there was even worse to come.

'No. I can't do this anymore. Iris, there's something you should know...' His voice became almost a whisper and she had to lean forward to hear him properly. 'Amanda is pregnant.'

It felt as if she'd been slapped across her face. She reeled backwards and fell against the wall, felt herself drift slowly towards the ground. Could you actually die of shock? Or of a truly, truly breaking heart? 'Pregnant? How on earth could that be?' Myles wasn't ready to be a father. He'd told her that so often, it was like a mantra. It was always next year, or the year after, or after I get this job finished or when we have more money. Of course, there were times when she had pined for a child, but she told herself nothing was more important to her than Myles.

'We are having a baby.' He said it so simply, he might as well have been talking about the football results.

'But...' She felt the words that she had intended to say trickle away from her. Myles was going to be a father. It had all been for nothing. It was the annihilation of her very soul. She let her body go, floated up above it and watched as it fell about her like a puddle to the floor. Pathetic. He bent and picked up his bag, stepped over her, like someone else's rubbish on the pavement. He stood for a second that could have lasted a lifetime or might not have happened at all. And then he was gone.

The house was desolately quiet. The hours somehow drew themselves out into days and then one week fell into a second and there was still no contact from him. The stillness clawed at her imagination. Here, in the pristine tidiness of a life spent ignoring the ever-widening gap between hope and acceptance, it seemed as if the silence was taunting her. Could she really go on like this forever? She was still a young woman, just forty. Forty, had seemed to be ancient to her when her own mother died of septicaemia all those years ago, but now, women her age were starting companies, starting families, starting over. Women her age were looking forward, but all Iris could do was look back.

She played her relationship with Myles over in her mind from that very first day. She'd had a crush on him long before he ever noticed her, but then at the village fete, it seemed the sun shone extra bright and he'd ambled up to the Delahaye Distillery table. Iris still felt butterflies in her stomach when she thought about that first time he'd walked her home and kissed her at the gate. Long and lingering, much too grown up for her age. She'd been a kid, just sixteen and never been kissed. God, how had they ended up here?

He'd been gone a month and still wretchedness flooded her; it felt as if she was drowning most days. And strangely, she knew, the worst part wasn't losing Myles, rather it was the fact that he'd betrayed her so badly. A baby. She had always wanted a family but somehow, for Myles, there had never been a *right* time. Today she rolled out of bed after midday and staggered towards the hall mirror. She examined her reflection: prematurely grey hair, pallid complexion – the most fresh air she got these days was rushing for the London Underground. She tried smiling, but it didn't seem to fit her anymore, rather it was an unnatural use of her muscles, which had gotten out of the habit of joyfulness. She'd even lost weight, not that she needed to, but her wedding ring slid up and down her finger now as if it too wanted to get away from her. What did it matter if she faded away, miserable and alone, really? She should reach out; she should have people to reach out to. Wasn't that what you did in times of crisis: find a shoulder to lean on, share your misery and halve it in the process? Friends and family. Hah!

She hadn't really made any close female friends over the years, or none that had actually stuck. Her own fault. She'd become jealous and distrustful of any woman coming too close to Myles. As for family, Georgie and Nola were the last people she'd call; she wouldn't give them the satisfaction of turning their backs on her as she had so willingly done to them all those years ago. They hadn't spoken in ten years, not since that disastrous party at the family distillery when they'd had the mother of all fallings-out. Perhaps, she should have reached out to them, just as her father had reached out to her a few months earlier. They were *In Touch*. Something she'd never expected would happen again, but the letters he'd started to send her months earlier had found a chink in the armour she'd worn against her family for the last two decades. They had graduated to phone calls. God, who'd have thought these would become the highlight of her otherwise empty life?

Outside, a tapping noise broke into her miserable thoughts. She looked out the window to see a crow, digging in the eaves opposite, as if he might eventually come across nuggets of gold. Iris found herself wishing he might find something worthwhile. His beak went up and down, *tap, tap, tap, tap,* and all the while dark, voluminous clouds loomed heavier over the rooftops with each passing minute. That meant only one thing. London weather was nothing like in Ballycove, Ireland; everything – even the storms – were far more civilised here. Why was it that after so many years, she still compared the two places and always Ballycove came out the best? She sighed, flicking across the lock on the window – not that it was likely to so much as rattle. This little semi hadn't enough personality to make a sound she couldn't identify.

It would have to be sold, of course. Wasn't that what happened when people got divorced? It had been her home for the past twenty-plus years and despite its lack of character, the thought of losing it made her heart ache.

Or maybe Myles would want to buy her out of it somehow. Suddenly, she wasn't sure that she wanted to hand it over to Myles and the new family he was embarking on – not that he'd suggested it yet. As far as Iris had managed to glean from his Facebook page, he was living with this woman, Amanda Prescott.

Sometimes she saw her whole situation with terrible clarity. What if her sisters had been right all along? All those years, when she'd believed they were jealous, maybe Nola hadn't wanted to take him for herself and maybe Georgie really had seen him steal from the distillery? Perversely, that only made her hate them all the more. Well, at least it was unlikely she'd be running into Georgie or Nola anytime soon.

About the Author

FAITH HOGAN is an Irish award-winning and bestselling author of six contemporary fiction novels. Her books have featured as Book Club Favourites, NetGalley Hot Reads and Summer Must Reads. She writes women's fiction which is unashamedly uplifting, feel-good and inspiring. Faith has an Honours Degree in English Literature and Psychology from Dublin City University and a Postgraduate Degree from University College, Galway. She is currently working on her next novel. She lives in the west of Ireland with her husband, four children and a very busy Labrador named Penny. She's a writer, reader, enthusiastic dog walker and reluctant jogger – except of course when it is raining!

To keep up with the latest news from Faith you can sign up to her newsletter here:
faithhogan.com/sign-up/

You can find out more about Faith on her website:
faithhogan.com

facebook.com/faith.hogan/
Twitter: @GerHogan